GHOSTS IN THE GLADES

STACI ANDREA

KINGSLEY
PUBLISHERS

To Landon and Axton…

Strength is not based in stature but is developed through time by repeatedly falling down and clawing your way back to the top. Your worth is not determined by physicality, but by what your heart brings to the table. Bravery doesn't always come with a battle sword, but it's sometimes just a determined voice that says, "I will try it again." You two are absolute forces of beautiful souls who I am blessed to call my nephews, and I thank you both once again for reminding me what courage can look like. Oh, and you're pretty cool to hang out with.

Also by Staci Andrea

Beneath Her Lies
Lake Laps
Fraidy Hole

Awards for Staci Andrea

2024 ScreenCraft Cinematic
Book Competition Quarterfinalist

2024 Maxy Award – Ghosts in the Glades

2024 Killer Nashville Claymore Awards Winner –
Ghosts in the Glades

2023 Killer Nashville Finalist- Claymore Award,
Best Southern Gothic

2023 Longlist London's Page Turner Awards,
Screen Adaptation Needed

2023 Literary Titan Five Star Gold Award Winner

2023 Literary Global Finalist

"To curl up in fear, like a cat trying only to protect the organs in its belly, does you no good, Boy. To make yourself small in these parts is just asking for the predators to pick away, slowly and meticulously at your bones, gnawin' on your marrow until you are nothing left but a specter of what you once had been. You want to win this? You want to claw your way out of the underbelly of the gator, ripping its head off for the win, wearing its teeth around your neck on one of those fancy little pieces of leather that all the surfers are wearin'? Then you gotta get you a hog in the fight boy. You gotta force the thrive."
-*The Pencil Man*

Prologue

I never feared him. I never knew enough to understand that I was supposed to fear him, although maybe that was just the naivete of adolescence. Maybe it was just my loneliness desperately wanting to connect with a kindred spirit, a fellow outcast.

I had heard the rumors, of course, what he had been accused of doing to those kids after his wife had passed away, the odd hours that he would spend out in the Everglades, and the peculiar ways that he presented himself about the town. But I had never given those whispers of dark apprehension any weight within my soul. Mama had always taught me that people like me, people who were beckoned to overcome their own whispers in the darkness, the ones who were forced to thrive just on the outer edge of normalcy, share a bond. We are more alike than we are different.

That was how I always saw the quirky Mr. Scroggs—as my friend, my guide, my fellow oddball. Being set apart from the rest of the world, singled out when walking into a room full of "normal" humans, having whispers relentlessly echo behind you through every hall that you bravely scurried down… these are the things that we bonded over.

There is a kindred pact among the strange, the ones who are left out, the ones who are bullied, threatened, and abused. We search each other out. We gravitate towards each other, simply wanting to feel less alone, less fearful, less fragile. He taught me that my only vulnerability was being weak. That if I learned to wear a more structured, more confident persona, that aura would affect the way other people perceived me as well, leading them to look right past my blatantly obvious physical deviations.

To think of the terrible things that people have assumed of him… the way he had been left alone to wallow in his own grief through the years in his cozy little trailer without so much as a friendly wave, a neighborly, "How ya doing?" or really, any other human contact for so long. It pisses me off and leaves a dark stain on my view of humanity. Well, that and what I have already been put through myself. Crudely put, people are assholes.

I tried to remain calm while sitting on the floor of his cozy little trailer, the clean, yet worn, avocado green shag carpeting rubbing against my bare legs, stinging them just a bit from the nasty sunburn that still blistered my thighs from a long afternoon of chasing boars out in the Florida sun. I hadn't been successful in catching anything, so I went on out to one of the public docks and threw a line in for a few hours, hoping to snag a snook or a fat ol' sea trout, but my line had gotten snarled and my patience had worn thin. So instead, I spent some time helping a little old man whom we called "Pencil Man" get his nets and lines ready to drop off the pier for shrimping later that evening.

Pencil Man was almost a sage in those parts. He was the

type of darker, albeit kind soul who was so unremarkable that he all but faded into the background fabric of day-to-day life, yet he was also prominently always around. I never knew what his life had been like in his younger years, nor did I ever ask. It would be a few more years yet before his world would be revealed to me.

Physically, he wasn't much of a threat, but mentally, he was a hurricane who could rip you apart limb by limb. Wise didn't even begin to describe him. It was more than that.

The first time I had ever run into Pencil Man was right after we moved over to this end of town. He was standing on the corner of where our trailer court lined up with the little dime store across the way. Frazzled, his leathery skin darkly tanned from the years of hanging out in the sun, and his graying hair matted into long locks by the salty air, he sat on a cracked five-gallon bucket with a handful of sharpened pencils and a change jar. He whistled something that was familiar, but I couldn't quite make it out. I stood there, fascinated by the spectacle that had unfolded.

Little kids would excitedly wave and come running up to him asking him to do "the trick." The kids would hand him money, sometimes dollar bills, sometimes change, and they would ask to buy a pencil. His pencils were always ten cents. As he kept on whistling, he would then take their money, hand them their pencil, count out their change, and the kids would go wild. I didn't get what was going on, so I shyly walked on over to see what the old man was up to.

He sat there, staring straight ahead as the salty breeze kicked up, startling me as he spoke. "Well, boy, you just gonna stand there starin' at me like a possum eatin' grits or you gonna say somethin'?"

"No sir, I'm not staring. I just saw all those youngin's over here laughing and carrying on and thought I would come on over and sit a spell, see what all the carrying on was all about," I sheepishly said to the ground as I reached into my pocket fishing around for some change, finding a dollar and offering it to the old sage.

"How many ya want? Ten cents apiece," he said, holding up a pencil in his arthritic, blistered fingers, then dropping his voice to a near whisper he asked, "Or are you wantin' a little somethin' else?"

Confused and panicked, I stammered back, "No, just two please. I'll take two, thank you, sir." I watched as the fragile little man ran his fingers over the bill that I had given him, pausing momentarily before folding it and dropping it into his jar. He then reached into his other jar of change and grabbed a handful, counting out exactly my eighty cents. I noticed that he never looked anywhere besides straight ahead.

As he put his gnarly, yet gentle hand out to hand me the change and two pencils, I leaned in closer and saw that his eyes had no color. They were a dark and cloudy gray. He spoke before I could move away, startling the bejesus out of me, the scent of sweet butterscotch dancing off his breath.

"Nope, I can't see boy. Ain't been able to see nothin' but shadows for years now."

Ah! So that was the trick the kids were carrying on about! He was somehow able to know exactly what amount of money they handed him and gave them the correct change, all without being able to see! Grinning to myself, I thought I was pretty smart at the time, having figured out that he knew the coins by feel. But I wondered how he knew the difference between bills.

I jumped damn near out of my skin when he apparently read my mind and stopped his whistling long enough to blurt out, "The five-dollar bills have a thicker ink, and I don't give change for bigger bills than that." Then he went back to whistling his tune, contently staring straight ahead. It would be a few years before I would truly appreciate the wisdom and talents that the Pencil Man held.

Anyway, that was how I got the sunburn on this day, staying out in the sun too long, killing time with the Pencil Man. I had thought about heading back out after the sunset to see if he was catching any shrimp with the other shrimpers, because although I had never really acquired a taste for the little critters, I was always in awe of the color that emitted off of them beneath the water at night, darting around like little bright blue fireflies right beneath the surface. Some nights, the whole marina would be alive, glowing with them. Other nights, the shrimpers would sit and wait for hours with not as much as a single flicker beneath the surface. The thought amused me that these tiny little creatures were so revered, so wanted and coveted.

Instead, I made my way back home and down here, to his trailer, my body screaming at me for being late for what it was violently wanting. I hated doing this, yet I had to do it. My body craved it, yet I still hated the pain.

Carefully, I rolled up the sleeve of my left arm, exposing pinkish colored skin, only slightly burned from the long afternoon of hanging out on the docks, the scarred marks from previous injections lining my arm. My body was now covered with little bumps as a rush of cool air flowed mercifully over my sun-drenched skin, blown there by the oscillating fan that was directly across from me on the floor, making clicking noises with each change of direction that it made.

For one sad reason or another, staring at that old fan brought back a calming memory, a simple flash from the past of my younger brothers and me many years ago, innocently sitting in front of a rusty box fan in Pop's garage at the old house while he was working on his old Camaro. They were a couple of years younger than me, my brothers, Mac and Jax, and we were sitting there leaning in towards the fan, making noises and yelling just to hear how it would change the sounds of our voices. I will never know why, but it was clearly right then that I had a sharp realization that something was wrong with me. As we sat in front of the fan on our knees, I became acutely aware of just how much the boys had grown over that summer… and how little I had. Seemingly overnight, they were almost as tall as I was.

Pulling myself back from the darkness of my past, I reached into my bag that I had flung to the ground next to me, clumsily fishing around for my lifeline, the syringe that was supposed to elevate me to a new world, a world without pain, without fear, without being permanently marked as odd. I had been on a lifelong quest to outrun the sadness, to trick the depression, and to outmaneuver the obsessive-compulsive disorder that had attacked me in this life of mine with such venom. Sitting in that little trailer on the floor, holding my syringe in a shaky hand, I paused once again, as I normally do, just before forcing that bitter needle into my already abused and swollen veins. Staring around the living room, I tried to pick something to focus on, something to avert my attention from what I was about to do, because it just never gets easier.

To a kid who has always been deathly afraid of needles, just the thought of jamming one of those damn things into my arm takes a lot of psyching myself out, focusing on something—anything else, in order to do it, no matter how much I wanted to. No matter how much my small and failing body craved it.

Gazing around, I began assessing the room, trying to trick my mind into forgetting about what my trembling hand was about to do. There were piles upon piles of books, though neatly arranged, lining the walls of the living room. They lined shelves and laid in neat piles on the desk that sat in the corner. Although I wasn't a fan of the big philosophers at the age of seventeen, I did enjoy reading about technology, inventions, and things that were up and coming in the world of science. I could get lost for hours reading about new medical advances, theories of evolution, or the possibility that there was life on planets beyond our own. Cocking my head to the side and squinting heavily through salt water impinged vision in the dimly lit room, I found my focus.

There, resting on top of an old typewriter, was a familiar and well-worn dog-eared version of Shakespeare's *Macbeth*, the copy that I had borrowed the previous year when we were studying the play in school. A grin crept across my lips as her face immediately popped into my mind. Beautiful. The girl was just beautiful. And a goofball. Mags was definitely that, too.

Back in the sixth grade when I first showed up to school

here, Mags was the first girl to talk to me, and that was after a few classes where absolutely no one would talk to me at all. They just whispered and stared, in awe of the new kid, the different kid, the weird kid. But not her.

Mags never batted an eye, never really even said anything about how I stood out. Instead, she dropped her tray next to me at lunch and asked me where I came from, what music I liked, and if I was into gaming at all. That was after I had already met her best friend, Jojo, as he rolled up in his stylish wheelchair, a device he'd been forced into by way of a killer wave and a nasty surfing accident. They were inseparable, and soon, all three of us were.

Jojo wasn't in our English class last year, but Mags and I had spent hours reading and laughing, trying to make sense of the play so that when we were called on in class, we would have some idea of what we were talking about. We both feared being called on to read aloud in class, both of us terrified of public speaking and of all eyes being on us. At least if we had to do it, we wanted to be ready.

Focusing on those memories, I sat on the floor of the little living room holding the needle, my heart deliciously savoring the hours that we would roar with laughter reading, her laying on the floor, feet up on the couch, her wild, curly auburn hair sprawled out on the floor, crowning her like an angel while I sat in the La-Z-Boy, glancing at her over my book from high above. What we did understand about *Macbeth* was that it was actually a story about a man who wanted to be great. He wanted to claw his way to the top, killing whomever he had to in order to get there so he would appear strong and powerful as his wife was taking it all in stride, urging him to keep going even though the road to the top was long and hard fought, even when the kingdom wanted the both of them dead. You can imagine the horror, then, when one stifling hot afternoon I was chosen to read the lines of Macbeth's character and Mags was chosen to read aloud the lines of his Lady.

That afternoon, the curious faces of the rest of the class fell away. For about ten minutes, it was just goofy old Mags and me, sitting there in one of the hot little accessory trailers that the school had set up outside of the main building because of overpopulation and no money to build, reciting to each other the lines that we had rehearsed over and over again in the little living room, her giggling every time I goofed up a line and me focusing on the sound of her calm voice keeping me in place and grounded as I read.

For what had been the first time in a very long time, I hadn't felt like an outsider, hadn't felt weird or out of place. I didn't feel like people were paying attention to me because of what was odd or wrong with me, but simply because I was just a kid who had been chosen to read in class. They were classically bored and barely paying attention. I loved it. I craved it. I just wanted so badly to be an everyday kid in an ordinary classroom that no one really noticed, just going on about another boring school day. And I was, for about ten minutes. Then the bell rang.

Just thinking back on it as I sat on the old green shag carpet of the little living room in the trailer, my stomach lurched at the next memory that was forming, the darkness that was once again smothering yet another tiny slice of hope, snuffing out any comfort that thinking of Mags had brought me.

The all-too-familiar ache of loneliness, the shameful embarrassment of being singled out crawled up my spine as waves of nausea stirred in my gut. I felt like I was there again, rushing out into the hallway when the bell rang, excited about the absolute normalcy of the whole day, proud that for once, I was prepared and that for a tiny bit of time, I was simply… normal.

Mags had followed me out of the little accessory learning trailer, talking to me about *Macbeth* all the way to the entrance of the school and right into the main hallway. We were on our way to meet Jojo and get to math class in time before the next bell. She knew of my constant struggle with anxiety and my newly-found battle that I had waged with my OCD, and she was determined not to slow me down. I held my head high, backpack slung over one shoulder and felt good for once as we started to walk away.

Time slows down now. Panic chokes my throat with one pissed off gnarly hand as I fight the tears that are welling up in my eyes, trying not to feel the instant pain, trying to hide the formidable shame and embarrassment.

I willed myself not to cry as I watched Mags get shoved against a locker, a wretched arm pinning her there so she couldn't come to my rescue, instead being made to watch. I willed myself not to cry as my face burned fiery red and became hot with rage when someone shoved me so hard from behind that I fell forward to the ground, hitting my face against the floor, the blood oozing slowly down over my chin and dripping onto the brand-new school sweatshirt that I had to have just to try and blend in. I willed myself not to cry as I got back up into standing position, only to see that small clusters of kids had then lined the walls to watch the shitshow that had just unveiled itself in the halls.

I remember feeling as though I was about to hyperventilate as that bastard, Turk, smirked and swung a leg beneath me, swiping my legs once again causing me to crash down onto the floor, my already bad hip painfully cracking when it hit the tile. In searing pain, I laid on that cold gray tiled floor while insult after insult was hurled at me. "You freak!" came the shouting, "What a spaz!" and, "What are you, like a short Michelin Man? Damn, you're chubby, son!"

Their voices began to fade, and I once again retreated into myself, feeling unworthy of my place in this world, a world where no matter how hard I tried, I couldn't make it fit me.

Still, I did not cry. It felt like hours but was probably just a few minutes before one of the teachers actually made it out into the hall to see what was going on. Unfortunately, when he saw who was doing the tormenting, all he did was send everyone back to class.

I understood. There is a fear of people like Turk, people who run wild and have shady and dark connections. I suppose when your mom is whoring around with elite members of the Cuban cartel, you are afforded the luxury of being an asshole. There are too many assholes in this world.

A kid shouldn't be made to feel like they are less than. Less than normal, less than equal, less than loved. A kid shouldn't be made to feel lonely, depressed or, hell, even suicidal, because their body, their brain or their abilities don't fit the standard mold. I was tired of trying, tired of holding on, trying to wait it out. I didn't want to put on a brave face any longer, didn't want to force myself to be happy day after day, clinging to the hope that the next day wouldn't be as shitty as the last.

Maybe this would be the day that they see me as equal. Maybe this would be the day that they don't notice me at all. Maybe this would be the day that I would finally fit into their mold. "Fuck the mold!" I shouted out to the stale air that smelled of an old cigar as I sat in that little trailer on the green shag carpet, my hand forcing the blissful toxin into my veins, praying for a way out of it all while cursing a God whose existence I doubted for putting me into this pit of torment, a pit that I was exhausted from trying to claw my way out of. I collapsed backwards onto the rug, slumped over to one side, noticing that my hip was still tender from the last round of surgery. I closed my exhausted eyes, once again trying to will my mind to go back to her, my Mags, one of my main reasons for holding on.

I had gotten myself so worked up about shooting up, that I had begun to hyperventilate and was about to pass out once again. It never gets easier. Nothing about this ever gets easier. From where I lay on the floor, I could see his freshly shined brown wingtips with the crisp tassels appearing prominently from down the hallway. I could hear his soft, gravelly voice before I could see his aged face with the old wire-rimmed glasses come into my line of vision.

"You are at it again, boy? Is that it? One would think that you would develop a system for yourself that was a little easier, something that got you the end results without knocking your wobbly butt out on the floor every time." He spoke softly, as he always had, stifling a small giggle that had begun to emanate from somewhere deep beneath his freshly pressed dress shirt that peaked out from under his brown twill suit jacket.

"And must you holler our every time that you feed your veins that hopeful concoction? I have told you before, I don't want the dang neighbors thinking that I am killing you in here. They don't need any more fodder to back up their putrid accusations." He made his way towards me, then gently lifted his pant-legs so he could squat next to where my head now rested upon the green shag carpet as he leaned in closely with a humble grin.

"Boy, what is it in this world that you are chasing? What is it that you want more than anything?" he asked, the smell of his heavy aftershave billowing through the air and mixing with the stale smell of old cigars that already hung heavily in the room.

I lay there momentarily, trying to slow my breathing while waiting for the stinging sensation to subside and let my veins gently lay back down again, thinking about what this misunderstood hermit, this questionable old soul was asking of me. I looked up towards the beige particle-board ceiling of the comforting old trailer as it began to spin effortlessly around, dizzying my brain yet welcoming me home at the same time. Flashes of the years were rolling by, suspended in the cigar smoke-filled air, effortlessly gliding by my eyes like I had conjured them up, like I had released the heaviness and heartache into the dark abyss that had become my world.

I saw them. I saw Jojo grinning from his chair as we worked on building a new gaming system in his room. I saw Mags laughing as we were trying, although unsuccessfully, to surf at the beach as Jojo sat howling about what idiots we were and pointing out what it was that we were doing wrong. I watched my brothers float by through the air, begging me to come out of my room and play ball, pleading with me to rise from the darkness that was suffocating me and holding me down.

I saw my mama's face fall as I screamed in frustration that I wanted to die and my pops sitting at my bedside after the fifth surgery on my hip, trying to trick my growth plates into thinking they were really going somewhere. I saw all of their faces the day that my medical treatments had swallowed all of their savings and we had to sell the house that Mama and Pops had bought before I was born and moved all of what we had left into a small, yet nice two-bedroom modular home in a trailer court on the other side of town.

I saw a myriad of doctors' and nurses' faces flashing by at lightning speed, just as quickly as they had appeared and moved on from my life, continuously rolling me over to become someone else's problem, some else's peculiar riddle to solve. They smiled, nodded like they had answers to questions that they had never even been asked, and, after unfruitful attempts, walked away and passed me on to the next guy.

A thin veil of rage then began to encase my heart as the next darker images slowly started to interrupt my thoughts, painfully making known their place in my world, leaving me with a dampened spirit and reduced will to survive. I saw Turk and all the faces of the Turks that had come before him, chanting, taunting a younger me in the hallways, in the school lunchroom, on the playground. "Hey midget, you are so small! Hey marshmallow man, you got fat over the summer! Freak, you have no friends, go home. Loser, why bother even coming to school when you got no friends! Just die why don't you, big baby…" Their voices are an internal, embedded reminder that I don't belong, that I don't fit the damn mold, and that I am consistently fighting to be perceived as something more than damaged goods, something more than a lesser value.

"Hey boy," Mr. Scroggs interrupted my seventeen-year-old meltdown and pity party as the memories continued to hang in the air, trying to lull me back towards that darkness that weighs me down and clouds my self-worth and sense of purpose. "Boy…. I asked you what you want? Just what is it that you intend to do about it?"

With a heavy sigh and the haunting, fractured snapshots of my past still defiantly lingering, trying to corrupt my already precarious and fractured ego, I closed my eyes in an attempt to block out the madness. I focused on my own breathing, the chaotic rhythm of my own heart beating forcefully against my rib cage. I was still there. I was still fighting, urging myself to hang on for another day.

Mama always says that someday things will get better. Someday my body will lead me to my place in this world and I will accomplish great things. My mama never doubted my courage, my drive, or my capacity for creating a wonderful life. That was something that only I had doubted. Lying there in Mr. Scroggs' little trailer on his living room floor, sprawled out on the old green shag carpeting, I only envisioned one face, one focus on which I was placing all of my pain, all of my anger, and all of my adolescent rage. I glanced up into the eyes of a gentle soul, a kindred old spirit who had walked gracefully through his own nightmares and emerged unscathed, seemingly unbothered by the static that haunted his every move.

Staring up into his aged grayish-blue, yet stern retired headmaster eyes, I mumbled the only thing that my soul was pushing my heart to answer. "I'm not looking for greatness. I just want to be enough. I just want to fucking thrive."

Pausing for just a half of a heartbeat, I then blurted out, "And I want Turk to get what he has coming to him!"

"Well then boy," Mr. Scroggs hesitantly spoke as he rose, smoothing down his now creased brown suit pants with his slender, arthritic long fingers, "first thing you have to do is get your butt up off that floor. Then, we need to pay a visit to the Pencil Man."

Chapter 1:
Do You Know Humility?

My fingers were flying across the keyboard, frantically trying to make the final adjustments to the spreadsheet before I had to make the biggest plea of my life. This project mattered. The people whom it affected mattered. Hell, it was no secret to anyone why I was spearheading this dream-child project that I had been working on since early in my college days, when my love of technology collided with my infatuation with science.

I nervously began to fiddle with my tie, attempting to straighten it while scanning the columns of numbers that were scrolling along on the screens before me. If there was one thing that I had learned from Mr. Scroggs, it was, oddly enough, the importance in the way a person presents himself to the world. He used to tell me that I was making myself a bit of a target when I wouldn't stand my ground and meagerly backed away from the bullies that I had become so accustomed to running from in my early years. He would argue with me when I would try to dress in baggy clothes to hide my weight or disguise every other aspect of my body, subconsciously hoping that the clothes would just make me invisible for once and allow me a reprieve.

"We live in Florida, boy! It's hot enough to scald a lizard out there, and here you are walking around in baggy sweats and board shorts long enough to trip over. Kid, you are trying to hide, but it's like wearing a sweater to a swimming pool! You are bringing all the attention right to you, and not the good kind!" I grinned, thinking about all of the old man's southern sayings and bits of wisdom he had bestowed upon me through the years.

Although Mr. Scroggs had been a schoolteacher for all of his adult working life, reveling in proper English, philosophy, and science, he had a wickedly sinister alter ego as well, a side that very few were allowed to see, and most had even feared. Although he adhered to a certain level of tidiness and stringent order in his life, he also tended to like chaotic things as well. For him, it seemed to be a perfect balance of madness and order.

While he would spend his days reading about quantum physics and studying the great philosophers, he would spend evenings reading about depraved serial killers and learning about the latest technology in the gaming world.

While he spoke eloquently and very matter-of-factly most of the time, and depending on whose attention he was holding, he would let his guard down around me and throw around some of the funniest slang terms that would make me bust a gut in laughter.

How was I to keep a straight face when a distinguished elderly gentleman dressed in his brown tweed suit, little bow tie, and silver, wire-rimmed glasses would haphazardly throw around some of his favorite terms such as, "That dog won't hunt," when he thought I had a bad idea or, " I am just worn slap out," as he collapsed onto the old orange and green plaid couch after a day of doing whatever the hell it was he did all day when I was at school.

One night when I had brought the lot lease money over to him (which is how I first met him after all, as he was the acting manager of the trailer court and had been since he had retired many years before), I also brought over some of my mama's spaghetti, which was one of only five things that she was good at making, cause my mama always hated to cook.

Excited that he was having something other than the mundane for dinner that night, he hurried over to the little chrome and Formica dinette set with the faded dark green vinyl seats to set it down and have a hungry taste. It actually stunned me when this proper gentleman shouted out, "Woo-wee! That there makes me wanna slap my mama, it's so good!"

It was through watching the two sides of Mr. Scroggs that I realized everyone had two selves: the person they actually are, and the self they wish the world to perceive. People will treat you accordingly, depending on which persona you allow them to witness.

For example, when Mr. Scroggs left his trailer, he always, and I do mean one hundred percent of the time pressed his clothes, combed his hair, slapped on a little aftershave, and held his head high as he slowly crept down the street. He commanded a certain attention, a respect, if you will. I think all the years of the town folklore that seemed to ensconce him, and the suspicions and accusations that had been hurled towards him for years, had only deepened his character, even refining his persona, perhaps. Yet, back at the trailer, he would relax, though never completely, and somewhat let his guard down.

In the privacy of his own space, he would fall apart some nights when the pain of missing his wife, his beloved Emily, would weigh down too heavily on his soul. As he hunched over into a broken pile of fragility on the Formica dinette table after his typical meager dinner of tuna on bread and a couple of red seeded grapes, he would just sob.

Once, when I had been having a particularly rough time while trying to wade through the abysmal undercurrents of depression in my mid-teens, I had asked him if he honestly had ever thought about just ending it all, to make it all stop… the hurt, the pain, the noise. He said something to me that night that has stayed with me all of these years, carrying me right into my forties and ushering me back down from many ledges on which I have found myself teetering.

With sad, graying blue eyes that saw right through my soul, he put a hand on my shoulder and said, "Boy, life will hurt. Life will damn near run you right over sometimes. But it's all part of the ride. You are going to laugh. You are going to scream. You are going to be terrified. We don't get to choose when we get off. Our job is to enjoy it, and eventually, to be brave enough to lean back in the seat, throw our arms up to the sky, and taste that thrill, allowing the car to roll on down the tracks, carrying us to exactly where it is that we are supposed to be."

I now stood in my den, absentmindedly lost in thought while the computer screen blipped and went dark. With my fingers resting on the little lop-sided bow tie, I averted my gaze from the computer screens and stood there in the center of the den, just staring out of the window at water. As I faintly heard my boys, Nicky and Vinny, chasing each other around the living room beneath me, their damp feet slapping hard upon the tiled floors of my 1940's Spanish villa that overlooks the lovely little Lake Dora, it is not lost on me how far I have come and what had to be done in order to get to where I am currently standing. The responsibility that I was left with to carry on in this world weighed heavily on my now broad shoulders.

Although this sprawling estate of a home that sits on the shores of Lake Dora that my dear wife and I picked out years before the boys were born is an absolute blessing for which I am humbly grateful, my soul doesn't need it. I was happy to buy it for her, blessed to be able to afford it. But it's just a showpiece, something that aides in the facade of self that I am presenting to the world. Something that establishes me within the community that says, I am of importance, I am worth listening to.

If you knew me at all, you would know that I would much rather be living a few towns over, back in the trailer court, safely hanging out in the little living room, playing cards with my boys and having my folks over for a Sunday dinner of fried chicken and mashed potatoes, polishing it off with a dish of ice cream, then flip-flopping through the sand on down to the marina to lazily hang out on the docks to watch the old timers shrimp. But in that world, I wouldn't be able to save them. In this world, I can. And I will.

"Hey, Jett! Babe, you almost ready? We are going to be late!" My wife's voice floated up the stairs where I was still stuck in a haunted gaze, staring out towards the glittering lake as a couple of kids ran by carrying sand pails and shovels, chattering about hunting for crawdads. Still suspended in time, if only for a moment longer, I shouted back, "Just finishing up! Be down in a flash!" The words had barely escaped my lips when some part of a deep, painful memory was triggered. My heart revved up and an unwelcomed panic was now attacking my senses.

"Down in a flash." I heard the voice of a younger me, a college-aged me, shouting into the phone the day I got the call about Mr. Scroggs. I didn't think. I didn't pack. I had no idea how long I would be away from school, no clue what I was going to do next. When I got the call, I just jumped in the car and hit the road to make the short hour-and-a-half journey back home.

When I finally made it to the hospital that day, I couldn't find the courage to get out of the car. For a good fifteen minutes or so, I just sat there, hands resting in my lap, trying to find the strength to go in. He had no one. When he was brought in by ambulance, as the paramedics were going through his precisely ordered billfold, they found his contact card that only listed one name and one number, painstakingly printed in his steady and precise handwriting. Mine.

The walk from the parking lot to the doors of the hospital had been excruciating as well. The Florida heat was unbearable, and you could feel the damp warmth emanating up from the dark asphalt with each step. I was uncomfortable, out of my element even. Hell, I was just a kid. I didn't know what to do in a situation like this. Mr. Scroggs had always been the one that I had run to, the one who'd helped me balance the scales and avenge my demons. I didn't know what the hell I had in me to offer him in return.

Walking in through the emergency doors, I tried to recall exactly what the nurse had been saying when she called. I wanted to prepare myself for what I may find when I saw him.

Although he had been in his late eighties by that time, in my mind he still held the perception of one of the greats, a legend of his own making. He had still been sharp as a tack and quick witted, still pressed his dress shirts and shined his leather wingtips. Just the previous week, I had been home and stopped in to see him, catching him on his walk back from the local corner store, his wicker basket draped over his arm, filled to the brim with purchases of his weekly ration of tuna, bread, red seeded grapes, and a few bananas. Time hadn't changed him. Time also hadn't changed what he had done, and unfortunately, it had finally caught up to him.

Slowly, I made my way to the nurse's station and then on to where his room was. Confused, I noticed an armed-officer sitting post right outside of his room in the hallway. I stopped to ask the officer if it was alright if I went into his room. I was told that I could, that the officer was just there as a precaution, more so to protect Mr. Scroggs than anything else after what had happened. I can still smell the room if I focus hard enough. I had spent enough of my life in hospitals growing up that you would think there would be nothing in them that would cause me anxiety anymore, nothing there that would make me lose my carefully structured false sense of stability. You would think that the mere smell of antiseptic wash and bleach would be of no significance to someone like me, the outcast who grew up chasing diagnoses from hospital rooms to surgical floors, therapists' offices to fancy little labs. You would be grievously wrong.

My eyes didn't even get the chance to see the carnage of what had been spared of his poor body. As I flung the door open and inhaled one big breath of the lovely hospital smell, my instinct had me running to the trashcan that sat in the corner of his little room to violently hurl everything I had eaten in the previous twelve hours.

It was then, when my head was dangling over my own puke in the trashcan and my eyes were pinched tightly and fiercely burning, that I heard a slight cackle drifting over my shoulder from somewhere behind me. It was weak, but it was there.

"Boy, calm down there. No reason for you to get your undies in a bunch. Just take a minute and breathe. Calm down for Christ sakes!" His voice cackled and cracked as a low giggle tried to stifle itself from somewhere beneath the pain he was obviously in.

I didn't want to look at him. I was terrified to see the persona that I was about to witness. I didn't know how to help him, what to say, or what I was supposed to do in this situation. For a brief second, I even thought about bailing on the whole thing. I just wanted to call my mama. But I didn't. For Mr. Scroggs, I stayed on the damn ride.

When I finally calmed down enough, I stood up and washed my hands and face in the sink that sat next to the trashcan on the opposite side of the room from his bed. I peered into the little mirror that sat above the sink, trying to get a quick glance to prepare myself. The angle wasn't great and all I could see was a bandaged arm moving around in the bed, so I had to just swallow my fear, stuff it down really deep, turn, and present the persona I was trying to be that day for Mr. Scroggs. Trying to just be brave.

Seeing him, though, did stun me, and it quickly felt as if the room was being robbed of all oxygen. My chest tightened and I found myself breathing shallow breaths while frantically assessing his damage.

There he lay, a frail and willowy almost eighty-five-year-old man, an esteemed schoolteacher whose mind was brilliant yet, and whose wit was still sharp. Even now, with wrapped and bloodied arms, a bandaged eye, and a very badly bruised, possibly broken cheekbone right below the eye socket, he still commanded a certain respect. Even beaten, he seemed esteemed.

"Well, boy, is it not as bad as you had expected?" he questioned, noticing that I hadn't run away yet and that my initial reaction wasn't to violently lurch over a trashcan again when I assessed the damage that had been done.

"Oh, it's bad sir, definitely bad," I sheepishly spoke while staring at the grubby gray-tiled floor that hadn't been waxed properly in some time. The sunlight was pouring in from the window across the room, making it feel too warm in there, making the hospital smells all too prominent. I hurried over to snap the blinds shut, and as I did, a friendly little nurse made her way in.

"Well how are y'all doing in here?" she blurted out while frantically scribbling down numbers and readings from the machines that were feeding the tubing into his arms. She had him lean forward and cough as she held the stethoscope to his chest. Upon doing so, blood spurted out of his mouth as he coughed. In an instant, the usually insanely proud Mr. Scroggs looked absolutely mortified by the entire situation. Not missing a beat, the cute little nurse with the long black hair that had been piled neatly into a bun on the top of her head simply grabbed a towel from the side table and lovingly cradled his face in her hands as she wiped the blood away.

"There you are sir, nothing to worry about. When blood mixes with saliva it always appears to be more than there really is. Your lungs sound good, x-rays were clear. The blood is probably just left over in there from your nose bleeding when they brought you in. Those bastards really did a number on you, if you don't mind me saying so. You are lucky that they stopped when they did!"

"Wait, can someone please tell me what the hell happened?" I blurted out, still confused as to what had actually happened for him to end up in this painful state.

Only half paying attention to what I was asking as she was filling out more forms on her little clip board and smacking her gum, the nurse retorted, "You family, sweetie?"

Stunned at the question, I just stood there. I mean, I sure as hell felt like family after all that we had been through together. Shouldn't that count? He had no one else. What the hell did she want me to say?

Luckily, I didn't have to come up with an answer because Mr. Scroggs did it for me. Although I was floored with what came out of his trembling lips.

"Yes ma'am, this here is the only family that I have left. Now, not by blood, you see, but I do have the paperwork on file with the hospital already that was sent over by my attorney. This boy here, he is my medical power of attorney and also my durable statutory power of attorney, so he has every right to all of my medical information." Mr. Scroggs said all of this with such an air of grace that I assumed he must have been telling the truth. What a bizarre and stunning, yet beautiful truth.

The impressed little nurse with the black hair spun around towards me with a piercing gaze and sweetly smiled before pausing to address me. "Well, this man was very lucky today, and I do mean very lucky," she began as she started to get a new IV drip ready while speaking with me. "If it hadn't been for the police that had happened to be passing by, those guys would have surely killed him as he was walking home from the dime store. He has a couple of broken ribs, cracked nose, cracked orbital socket, lacerations to the back of his head that have led to a nasty concussion, as well as multiple scrapes and bruises on various other parts of his body. It was much worse than the last time." She stopped fiddling with the IV long enough to look up and raise her eyebrows at me with wide eyes, as if questioning just how much I really knew about the demons that Mr. Scroggs had been battling.

On queue I exploded, "Last time? What do you mean, *last* time? People have come after you like this before?" I shouted, perhaps a little more harshly than I had truly meant to.

Just like the mysterious entity whose role he had always assumed, Mr. Scroggs lowered his scowl in my direction and his voice then took on a menacing reverberation, one that I had never recalled emanating from the hollows of his dark, yet gentle soul in all the years I had known him.

"Listen to me boy," he began, glancing quickly over at the nurse who had hurriedly gone back to setting the new IV drip in place on the stand. Shooting me a quick wink, she lowered her head and scurried out of the room, the way young mice scurry away when the slick tomcat enters. "There are things in this world that are so dark, so awful, that eventually a man has to take a stand. Eventually, a man has to move about the world in disguise, showing the world the persona, the character that the world wants to see, expects to see. But, what if beneath that persona that the man has carefully crafted, there was a sinister part of his soul that bubbled just beneath the skin's surface, and to feed that urge, he is daunted with doing truly horrible things? Maybe he has reasoning for what he has done. Maybe there is a simple justification for the depravities that he has committed." He stopped, a cough had begun to rumble in his chest, wrestling its way up through his bruised lungs and interrupting his elaborate, almost confession-like explanation.

I was anxious, I was nervous, and I was stunned. This man, the man whom the world had pigeonholed as a monster that I had defended for years, the man who had talked me off of more cliffs than I could count, my kindred broken soul… what was he saying? Had I been that far off in believing that the world had him all wrong? What the hell was Mr. Scroggs capable of?

"So, who did you piss off then? Who are these people that have almost killed you, not just once, but twice? Jesus, man! What have you done?" I demanded, this time yelling within inches of his face with a trembling voice, trying to hold back the tears and swallowing the lump of disbelief that had formed in the back of my throat.

I remember wanting so badly to cry, to run out of there and never look back. I had had the rug pulled from beneath me and wasn't sure that my spine was strong enough to withstand the blows that were about to be hurled in my direction.

"Jett, seriously, we have to go!" I was still standing in the den, staring out the window, mesmerized by the sun's rays hitting the water out on the lake after I had unwittingly tumbled back into the darkness of my past. Beads of sweat were now running down from my temples as she entered the room.

"Jett, you, okay? You don't look so hot." That wonderful wife of mine came rushing in, dressed in her beaded dark blue gown that made her wild auburn hair stand out, making her truly look like a siren of the sea.

Nervously I let out a laugh, "What are you talking about? I'm fine. I was just going over some things in my head. You know me, ever the anxious perfectionist."

She quickly walked over to where I was standing and reached out to straighten my tie, pausing with her hands on my chest just long enough for me to give her a quick squeeze. I glanced up at our reflection in the old window panel and was in awe at what I saw.

Here stood the most gracious and beautiful woman on the planet who had walked with me head on through the pits of hell, defending me, supporting me, and pushing me towards greatness. She had seen me at points in my life where I felt worthless, where I contemplated death and pushed her away. She had watched me grow from a young kid who had no confidence, to a proud family man who had figured out how to wear the strong persona that the world didn't expect but seemed to be mesmerized by. I proudly stood between her legs with the doctors the day that our sons were born, promising them a life that would be better, different than what mine had been. There we stood, her just a few inches taller than me, locked in an embrace and ready to go do battle again on our quest for greatness.

Chapter 2:
Do You Know Chance?

I was nine when my pediatrician finally gave in to the theory that there was something not quite right with me. At birth, Mama said that I was just fine, right around the same birthweight and length that my younger brothers would someday be. Average, Nothing exciting. My mental capacity was sharp, and I always hit the normal benchmarks for growth at my checkups. Around that ninth year, however, my growth stopped, and other parts and systems of my small body began to turn on me as well.

When I would get sick, it was as if my body was suddenly tired of trying to fight it off, and more often than not, I would end up hooked up to machines in the hospital. Common colds would quickly turn into pneumonia. A simple stomach bug would knock me out for weeks. I had suffered from meningitis, multiple ear infections, a slight hearing loss, and perceived thyroid problems. My joints would ache and burn, and my hips would go through bouts of searing pain. Thus, the testing began, and years of trauma ensued.

Some of the tests weren't too bad. My aim had become

spot on when peeing into a cup. Many days I had spent in hospital rooms being x-rayed, and I suppose for a while I had become used to the lab draws, although I had to look away and found that I did better with those if I were lying down with my feet up in the air. Otherwise, I tended to puke or pass out, even as I got older.

Other rounds of testing weren't as pleasant. I have been held down by my poor mama more times than I can count. I can easily remember the burning that felt like a hot poker as the marrow was extracted from my hip for testing, and I can still feel the precise popping feeling that the needle made as the surgeon fed it up through the sections of my spine while extracting fluid to test. Mama was there for all of it, and I had always tried my best to be brave for her because I could clearly see the pain and fear in her eyes. Pops didn't do as well in hospitals. Plus, as the testing dragged on for years and then the treatments began, he was forced to keep working. Even though we had insurance, it didn't nearly cover it all, and the bills quickly began to pile up.

I was nine the day the answers finally came, as Mama and Pops and I sat in a room with all kinds of specialists flocked around us with multiple charts and graphs and answers they had tried to string together as best they could in a way that somehow made sense to us.

We sat there as they threw around fancy words, ideas of experimental treatments, and tried to assure us that I would still be able to live a full and normal life. I didn't have cancer. I wasn't dying. There was no real reason why this had happened. There was nothing that Mama did wrong. What they did know was that I had developed some form of growth hormone deficiency, an idiopathic form, as they called it. I liked that word. It sounded gritty and full of substance. Even at nine years old, I held onto that one in my little memory bank for a long time, first looking it up in the Webster's Dictionary that sat on Mama's desk that I liked to use when I was reading hard words, then having it tattooed onto my right pectoral muscle when I was being rebellious in the back of some guy's garage at the confused age of sixteen, trying to build a tough guy persona to defy the body that didn't project the image.

The loose meaning of the term "idiopathic" is that there's no known cause. When I was young, I clung to that, reminding myself that my failing and stunted body wasn't my fault. That it was just a gamble really, just by chance that it happened to me.

As I got older, however, and the years of being harassed and picked on in school had begun to weigh heavily on my psyche, idiopathic took on a whole new way of thinking and meaning in my darkened world. I then thought of it as meaning that I had no cause, was of no great use, was a waste of a life. It took many therapists and years of hard work and successes for me to see myself as anything other than "idiopathic."

The truth was that this growth hormone deficiency that I had was so rare, that only about one in every ten thousand kids or so has it. That wasn't good for seeking treatments or having other case studies for comparison. It meant that more often than not, I would need to be the laboratory hamster running on the wheel, trying whatever treatment was suggested, then jumping into a new experimental treatment when that one didn't work. It also meant that we never really knew what side effects may come from medications or how my body would react to the drugs.

A big part of my treatments were growth hormone therapy injections. When I started out on this journey in the beginning, a group of doctors had hoped that I would only need them to get me through puberty, since my pituitary gland wasn't working as it should. Unfortunately, my pituitary gland never did get the message that it was supposed to kick in and start working. As a result, I have to inject myself daily for the rest of my life just so my body will function like it should. Without those shots, my thyroid would go haywire, my pancreas would stop functioning, and I would become an insulin-dependent diabetic.

While dealing with the drugs and injections and treatments, my body also went through growth stalls and growth spurts. I could go months without growing at all, and suddenly gain a couple of inches, along with a massive amount of weight as well. It was like an evil Catch-22, as if the universe was teasing me by saying, "Buddy, we can make you grow, but we will also turn on all of your other systems at the same time, causing you to gain weight faster than height, halt some of your growth plates, while painfully pushing the others out of joint with a rapid growth spurt."

As if going through puberty and dealing with the normal stuff like zits and freaky pubic hair (or lack of) wasn't bad enough, I also had the added bonus of weight gain, massive migraines from time to time, and some hearing loss in my right ear. Fluid would routinely build up in my face and hands and ankles, depending on what my medicine was doing. I also had to start wearing glasses after they discovered that one of the medications was causing excess fluid to build pressure behind one of my eyes. The treatment for that, of course, was more steroids to bring the swelling back down, which, in turn, caused my face to get puffy for a while.

To say that I was picked on in school was an understatement. It wasn't so bad when we were really young, because at that age, everyone was still pretty small in stature. By fifth grade though, it had become pretty apparent that something was "wrong" with me. I was almost a whole foot shorter than most of the kids in my class. Still, other kids really hadn't learned about the pecking order in life yet and hadn't begun to take their frustrations out on me. Then middle school happened.

Sixth grade was an awful year for so many reasons. First, after racking up a couple of years of massive medical debt, my family simply couldn't afford to pay the bills anymore on our big, upper-middle-class home with a pool and Pop's big old garage that held all the fun stuff like the boat, the four-wheelers, and his old Camaro. We sold the house with a pool, the four-wheelers, the boat, and his Camaro, and moved across town into a nice little two-bedroom modular home in a friendly little trailer park.

I would feel guilty about that move for years because I had always believed that I was the reason my brothers had to give up their toys. I was the reason we lost the house, the pool and Pop's old car. It wouldn't be until years later, when I finally became a dad myself, that I would understand how as a parent, you are fully prepared to give up anything for your kids, whether it's a car, a house, or your very soul if it would help them in some way. I just wish someone would have helped me see that back then.

I had hoped that when we moved and I started a new school, it wouldn't matter that I had gained weight over the summer without gaining many inches in height because no one had seen me before. No one knew what I had looked like, so why would I stand out or be noticed?

Unfortunately, I couldn't have been more wrong.

I suppose that I had grievously underestimated the amount of growth that an average sixth grader would gain over just one summer. It had become glaringly apparent that first day. The most haunting part of my memories was that, for a few reasons, this was a transition I had actually been looking forward to.

First, I was hopeful that there would be some new kids that I would click with, maybe some people who would be interested in things that I liked, too. Mama had heard that this school district, although not funded as well as my previous school district, was constantly pushing for more grant money because the principal loved science and technology. The year before I got there, they were one of the first schools in the area to install a little computer lab. I was excited about that.

The other thing that I was looking forward to was working on changing my style up a bit, trying to blend in. Mama had reminded me that this was a chance to start over, be whoever I wanted to be, since no one at this school knew me. We didn't have much money to spare, but Mama took me shopping. We picked out a handful of new outfits, nothing too flashy, but things I felt comfortable in… things I felt would keep me from standing out in a crowd. I remember carefully observing other kids around town to see what they were wearing and made sure to pick out a couple of T-shirts and a new sweatshirt with the school's logo, a manatee, of all things.

Putting on my brave face that very first day, I climbed

onto the bus down at the end of the lane with my brothers, after waiting with a couple of older kids in the hot sun in front of the mailbox island that sat at the entrance of the trailer park. The school system was pretty small, so the buses just picked up everybody in all of the grades, then stopped at the elementary school first, then went on to the middle school before finally dropping off high school kids. I held the bravery on my face until we pulled away from dropping my little brothers off, and the reality of what I was about to face began to set in.

Sitting in the back of the bus, clutching my plain black backpack against my chest, my anxiety began to attack my system and I could feel the world starting to get very small as my breathing was being rapidly cut off by the shorter and shorter gasps of air that I was barely getting in. My cheeks were getting warm, and my ears began to scream with a high-pitched ringing noise that usually accompanied my panic attacks. Back then though, no one knew how to classify a panic attack, so they just called you weird.

Pulling into the long driveway at the school, I noticed the sides of my vision had started to go dark and I realized that I was starting to get the tunnel vision that happened right before I passed out. My stomach was also a ball of nerves, and I was now terrified that if I did panic and pass out, I was surely going to crap my pants as well, and wouldn't that just be the icing on the cake of a first day at a new school?

Deciding that I would rather die a thousand deaths than be mortified by an embarrassing situation like that, I clenched my butt cheeks together and started to take deep breaths. I was a sweaty mess by the time I actually got off the bus, but I was proud that I had made it that far, and on to class I went.

The first few classes of the day were nothing remarkable, which I was thrilled about. No one really talked to me, but no one had singled me out yet either, so that was a plus. I would rather be invisible than be singled out.

All too soon, it was lunchtime, which was one of the things that I had been stressing about for days. Back in elementary school, when you went to lunch, you filed down to the cafeteria and stood in a big line, then walked in another big line to go sit at the tables. There was no picking and choosing. You just sat next to whomever was standing by you in the lunch line. Middle school was a different animal, though, a free for all. You went down to the little cafeteria window to buy your lunch and then had to search for a place to sit.

This would be no problem if you grew up in the town and knew everyone, or if you had a large crew of friends that you hung around with. But what's that mean for the new kid? Sitting alone at a table? Hanging out in the hall and not bothering going to lunch? I knew that wasn't an option because I had medication I had to take. And because of my low sugar levels and high blood pressure, I had to eat a certain number of hours after taking my morning medication.

Brazenly, or sheepishly, however you wanted to look at it, I made the decision that I would go grab my lunch and if it didn't look like anyone was going to let me sit by them, I would head off into the bathroom and eat in there instead. I just didn't want to draw attention to myself. I wanted to fly under all of their radars for a while.

The lunchroom was a sea of faces, most of which paid

me little to no attention at all. I hated being the new kid, but even worse, I hated knowing that it didn't matter what jeans I wore or what shoes I'd bought. For me, based on my physical features alone, I would never fit in. I would never be popular. I would never just be left alone, no matter how badly I wanted that to be the case. At best, my wounded twelve-year-old heart just wanted to make a couple of good buddies, people who liked the same things that I did so we could hang out together. I was just so tired of being alone.

Walking away from the lunch line, staring at the sea of unknown faces with my lunch tray in my hands, Panic had once again begun to rear her ugly head. As I made a quick scan, I realized there really weren't any empty tables to sit at. Crestfallen, my body decided to try and move on with plan B, walking towards the trashcan so I could dump the food I couldn't hold in my hands and quickly head towards the closest restroom to sit and eat alone in a stall, where I would be spared the embarrassment of being stared at and ridiculed. Somehow, I figured that being alone in a bathroom stall would make me feel less of an outcast compared to the hell that was waiting for me in the lunchroom.

Right as I was about to toss my beans and sliced pears into the trash, and then carefully wrap the greasy piece of pizza with the orange slimy cheese into a paper towel, grab my milk and run, a voice wafted in my direction from somewhere over my shoulder.

"Hey, you're new here, right?" came a guy's voice, non-threatening and dare I say without getting my hopes up too high, even possibly friendly? I hesitated before spinning around to see the face that the voice belonged to.

There he sat, even shorter than I was. He was a classic Floridian, golden tanned skin and sandy colored bleached-out blonde hair that was longer, but tucked beneath his old, ratty Florida Marlins ball cap. He had multiple braided leather bands on both wrists and some type of smooth old stone hung from a leather band around his neck. His neon sunglasses sat seemingly permanently affixed to the top of his ball cap. He had a classic surfer look about him, right down to the wicked grin and the eyes that, even at that young age, had crease lines forming at their edges from staring into sun for hours while trying to pick out the next great wave to ride. He fit the mold of a classic young surfer perfectly. Except he was seated in a wheelchair.

"Hey bro, I'm Jojo!" the kid said, grinning and extending his fist towards me. It took me a millisecond to figure out how I was supposed to respond. I wasn't exactly socially graceful at the time since I hadn't really had extensive social interactions with many people my own age.

Courageously, and only after deciding that this kid was the real deal and didn't appear to be the type of guy who was setting me up for some embarrassment or joke, I balled up my shaking yet sweaty fist and extended it back towards him, knocking our knuckles together in a fist bump. Human connection had felt so good. I was lost momentarily, swimming in a sea of disbelief, ecstatic that someone talked to me and that just maybe, I wouldn't have to be the kid eating lunch in the bathroom stall. Clearing my throat and not wanting to seem weird, I quickly blurted back, "Hey! I'm Jett!"

And that was it. It would be a while before Jojo and I ever even broached on the subject of my issues and I didn't ask about the wheelchair. Beginning at lunch that day, when he led me over to the table where he liked to sit (which was off to the corner near a window that had a nice wide area behind it so he could easily wheel himself up to the table and back out again without knocking into anyone), that boy and I started talking and giving each other shit, and we haven't stopped since.

Sure, it could have been our camaraderie of being the oddballs that had drawn us together, but it was our fascination for all things tech geared and our mutual love of comics that cemented our bond. His dad was an engineer for NASA out at the Kennedy Space Center in Cape Canaveral, and the stories he had about that alone would lead to hours of us just rambling back and forth.

Sitting at his table that day, just settling into this newfound magic called friendship that had so graciously fallen into my lap, I was getting ready to dive into that greasy slice of pizza while Jojo laughed loudly, his mouth full of food, telling me a story about his latest find, a couple of cans of beer at the marina. Just then, I froze when another voice entered our discussion.

"Hey Jo-bean, who's this?" said the soft voice of a girl right next to me. I had been so focused on what Jojo was saying and so happily reveling in the awesomeness that had unfolded that lunch hour, that I hadn't even seen her sit down right next to me at the table in my peripheral vision.

"New dude!" Jojo shouted towards her. "Jett, this is Mags."

Her name was actually Magdeline D'Andrea, as in the D'Andrea's who ran the fishing charter boats out of the marina. It was her grandpa's business, on her ma's side. I never bothered to ask why she didn't have her dad's last name. Maybe as a kid that young, I didn't even notice, nor did I care. The girl came from a line of money, big money, but you would never know it. She was calm, quiet and had a simplicity about her that was almost peculiar. She sat right down next to me and very shyly and quietly said, "Hey, Jett!" before going on about eating her salad and listening to what Jojo was rambling on about, jumping in every now and then with her two cents, asking me where I grew up and what music I liked. That was when the little chance pairing of two became the tight little group of three. We would stay that way for the rest of our school years.

I had figured out that afternoon that one or both of them were in a couple of my afternoon classes too, so that made school life a little more bearable. I actually relaxed on the bus ride home that first afternoon, thrilled with how this new school year was starting out for me. I didn't know yet what fresh hell would be waiting for me just around the corner. I only knew that I had made a couple of friends, and that had to be worth something. That had to be what normal kids did, right?

My poor Mama must have been a worried mess all day because when I got off the bus and walked my way back to the trailer with my little brothers, she dang near plowed them over to get to me, wrapping her arms around me in a big hug (which I was terrified the whole neighborhood would see at the time), and immediately wanted to know how my day went. That woman's eyes filled with tears, and I am sure her body relaxed with relief when I told her that I hadn't gotten picked on yet, no one threw me into a locker or shoved me around and, get this, I actually had made a couple of new friends. Only then was she able to relax and go on about her afternoon, getting a snack of store-brand Hydrox cookies for my brothers and filling out the lot lease check for me to run down to the manager of the court. I had walked down once with Pops to Mr. Scroggs' place and figured I would be fine running the check down for Mama while she got supper going before Pops got home.

I had debated riding my bike, but it wasn't too far to the other side of the park so I decided to walk over instead. I really didn't want the hassle of getting the key to the bike from the storage locker anyway. Plus, I still hadn't changed into my after-school clothes and Mama would be madder than a wet hen if I were to fall off that old bike and get my new clothes mussed up. So, I walked.

It was a sticky, hot day that fall, much like most fall days in the south. The hot breeze had picked up at least, and the heat from the asphalt was rising up from below me as I made my way along. As the gritty dust from the partially grassed lots swirled around in the air, making my lips salty and my teeth crunch when I ground them together, I just kept walking and thinking about my day, how fortunate I had been to have met Jojo and Mags. What a freeing feeling it was to not have to feel like an outsider, to have someone reach out and give a shit about you. It was while recognizing these feelings, the feelings of self-worth and peace, that I noticed something I hadn't paid attention to the last time I had swung over by Mr. Scroggs' trailer.

Maybe Pops and I had gone the long way from the other direction because I didn't remember seeing this before. Surely if I had seen it, it would have made an impression. About three trailers down from Mr. Scroggs' manager's trailer sat a sad, abandoned trailer that had old caution tape surrounding it. The tape was weathered and shredded, still wrapped around the porch posts, and billowing from a branch of an old Cypress tree that reached overhead atop the roof of the trailer.

I wondered what had happened there, my twelve-year-old curious mind launching into overdrive, contemplating a fire (although there was no obvious damage of the home from the outside), a break-in (possible, I had concluded, though the windows looked intact from where I was standing in the road and the door hadn't been kicked in), or more deliciously in my adolescent mind, a possible murder?

Standing there staring at the sadly unkempt and seemingly abandoned trailer-house that had overturned flowerpots on its porch and an old swing-set off to its side, I shuddered at the thought of something sinister that may have happened right down the road from where I slept every night. Not wanting to spoil the greatness of my day, I decided to tuck this one away and circle back to it later, maybe ask Jojo and Mags if they remembered any news about what had happened there.

Onward I went to Mr. Scroggs' place, the lot rent check grasped tightly in my now clammy hands. I hadn't noticed that I had begun to sweat pretty hard on that short walk and actually had begun to feel a little lightheaded. I figured it was just another side effect from one of the damn new medications that my medical team had started me on now that I was being chemically forced through puberty, trying to manipulate my body into growing some more and shocking my growth plates along the way.

I walked up to the steps of his little beige trailer, which

had been kept tidy and colorful out on the porch. He had a couple of whiskey barrel planters filled with different species of cacti that had begun to bloom, as well as a little table set up that had some type of switchboard sprawled out on it. It appeared he had been either taking it apart or putting it back together.

To the left corner of the door on the porch sat a big old trunk, an odd thing to have sitting on a porch, but hey, what did I know? Without any apprehension, I pulled open the old screen door and gave the faded wood door behind it a good knock. Beyond it, I could hear the rustling around coming from within.

Glancing back over my shoulder as I was waiting, I saw a younger guy slowly riding by on his bike, just staring at where I stood, no acknowledgment, no friendly "hello" wave. He rode back and forth a couple of times before the door finally opened.

Chapter 3:
Do You Know the Outcast?

It didn't take him long to answer. I could hear the boards creak beyond the old faded wooden door with the diamond window cutout at the top as he made his way across the living room area and into the small entrance that housed the front door. Within seconds, it opened and there I stood, face to face with the formidable Mr. Scroggs.

He stood there in the threshold of his home, all five foot ten of him and maybe one hundred and sixty pounds of carefully protected lean muscle. His clothes were what they always seemed to be, dress pants with freshly-pressed front creases and a pin-striped dress shirt that had never seen a wrinkle either. As always, his small bow tie had been intricately secured into place and his old wire-rimmed glasses sat low upon his nose. He was thin, yet didn't give off the essence of frailty. Instead, his presence commanded respect, with his business dealings carried out in a very matter-of-fact tone.

"Yes, boy, what do you need?" he questioned as he answered the door, seeing me standing there in awe of his appearance at the threshold of his home, his safe space.

Still not feeling too well from the heat that I had encountered, coupled with the effects of the new medicine that I was on, I began to feel faint. I could only reach out my hand with the check that Mama had given me before feeling my heart beating rapidly in my chest and my eyesight suffering from the tunnel vision that occurs right before I pass out.

"Mama told me to bring this on over to you, sir. It's our lot rent. We live at…" was the last thing I remember saying.

The sound of a needle scratching on a record was the first thing I heard when I started to come to. Then a pause, and static before the room was once again filled with the sounds of instruments and melodies I had never heard before. There was a soft drum intro right before a light guitar rift kicked in, and a simple voice started telling the story about sitting on the dock of the bay. It was a serene song, one that really put your soul in a calm mood. Over the years, I would find an appreciation for the genre of blues music, thanks to Mr. Scroggs. But on this particular day, all it reminded me of was being in Pop's garage as he was working on cars and realizing that, although the sound fit, I was definitely not in Pop's garage.

With my eyes still pinched shut, I raised my right hand to feel what was making my forehead and eyes so damp and cool, only to find a dampened washrag sitting there, keeping the light of day at bay. Apprehensively, I slid the damp washrag down my face, letting my eyes dart open to see just where the hell I was.

There was no one in the little living room, I took account of that as soon as my eyes popped open. "Oh, Mama ain't gonna like this one bit…" I whispered to myself, thinking that she would have my head for inconveniencing a stranger and being in someone else's private home. This was something that she had always felt wasn't proper, to put out a neighbor or to intrude on their space. Besides, this was essentially a stranger, which crossed all kinds of Mama's rules. I was gonna be in big trouble, damn it, and I knew it.

I began to panic, but then my tensions were forced into the backburner of my subconscious as I began looking around the space that I was lying in. Although orderly, the little living room that I had been mercifully sprawled out in was like a treasure trove of defined history, each tiny memento fiercely holding its own space, adorning the walls and bookshelves around the room.

I could see a myriad of diplomas and awards that lined the area on the wall right above the side table to my left, seemingly teaching licenses and honors. The old record player and walnut-encased standing stereo system where the soft tunes had been billowing from were sitting directly beneath the bayed window across from where I was lying on the sofa. Glancing down, I noticed that the carpet was an old green shag, although not matted and worn, having been exquisitely taken care of for years. Curious, I sat up on the sofa, which was an old green and orange plaid print that was so worn and comfortable, you would swear the pillows could just swallow you whole. I began to peer around the room, looking for answers as to what it was that made this spectacular, yet peculiar human tick.

Staring at the bookcase that was straight ahead of me, I cocked my head trying to decipher titles, carefully placed on the shelves according to their authors and not by the titles themselves. Aside from some classics such as Poe and Shakespeare, I also saw a few of my favorites on the shelves as well, such as Ernie Pyle, a war reporter famous for putting a realistic face on World War II. I saw that Mr. Scroggs liked books by George Orwell and Mark Twain as well. What really surprised me, though, was that he was a comic book fanatic, much like myself. Excited to see some of the harder-to-find titles laying out on one of the shelves, I hopped up, albeit a little too quickly to run over and investigate.

Just as I had my hands on the cover of a very hard-to-find comic, a *Teenage Mutant Ninja Turtles* #1 first printing that was encased in plastic, his voice gently billowed from behind me.

"Careful there, boy. You took quite a tumble. Don't be moving so fast or you'll go all cattywampus on me again," came his voice, not threatening, only genuinely concerned.

Aside from being in basically a stranger's home, I hadn't any other reason at that point to feel ill at ease about being there. Running my fingers over the comic, I asked him without turning around, "You like comics, too?" I heard him chuckle at the question at hand, and then he disappeared into one of the back rooms of the trailer. I thought it was odd, but figured that he had gone to grab something. I stepped back a bit to look around at what else was gracing the bookshelves since we seemed to have so close to the same tastes, which says a lot about a twelve-year-old who spends most of his time at home reading if he has that much in common with a what… seventy-some-year-old man?

There were short stories by authors that I hadn't heard of, but was curious about, science-based magazines, and volume after volume of *Popular Mechanics* magazine. It occurred to me just by glancing over his reading material that this wasn't your typical old man. Then again, I wasn't your typical kid either, so what the hell did I know?

I glanced upward towards a few of the higher shelves where I could see what I assumed to be a photo of a younger Mr. Scroggs and possibly his wife at what appeared to be an awards ceremony. In the photo, they were standing at the podium, she by his side, holding an award and throwing her head back as if in mid laugh. She looked happy. They looked happy.

Next to that photo was a framed award for bravery in the act of humanitarianism, also known as a Civil Courage prize, presented to Mr. Scroggs by the JFK Library. I thought that was pretty damn cool, whatever it had been for. There were also other stacks of books and small trinkets that lined the shelves as well, small figures of Buddhas, prayer beads draped across different religious books of faith, and I even swear to this day that he had a small pygmy shrunken head that had dried like leather sitting on top of an old tobacco can. Years later when I would question him about it, he would only grin and say that his old medicine man friend in Africa had given it to him years ago, but then he would wink at me, and I was never able to tell where the truth actually lay.

Right as he was coming back down the hall, my eyes glimpsed something different, something that didn't seem like it belonged there. On the shelf right beneath the one that had the photo of his wife was a black and white photo of Mr. Scroggs and a boy, the boy grinning a toothy grin and all of maybe fourteen or fifteen years old. Next to the photo on the shelf was an old ball cap with the Minnesota Twins emblem on the front.

Mr. Scroggs didn't strike me as the type of gentleman to wear a ball cap, so I could only assume that the hat may have belonged to the kid. But next to that, lying on the shelf, was a small stack of newspaper clippings. I had just begun glancing over the top one that had a headline about a missing local boy when Mr. Scroggs appeared back in the living room.

"You doing okay there now, boy? You wasn't lookin' too good when you stopped by," he began as he moved towards me, extending his hand with an icy cold can of Huggins Hefe, a local beer they made over in Melbourne, a few towns over. My eyebrows must have raised in shock because he quickly thrust it into my hand and said, "Oh geez, boy, no one has to know. It's hotter than a witch's tit out there! Ya gotta drink something. Live a little, would ya? For a beer, it ain't half bad."

Feeling both terrified of him and entranced at the same time, I took the beer from his gnarled long fingers and took a long slurp. It was pretty dark for a beer, none like I had seen my pops drink, but he was right, it was icy cold and was a hungry welcome to my parched system. After I took a couple more swallows, he grinned, reaching out to take it back from me as I stood there in silence, my senses now fuzzily calm.

"Alright then, boy. That will be just about enough of that for you today. I think you best be scootching your butt on outta here before your mama wonders what happened to ya, don't you think? Besides, all I need is for your mama to call the other mamas around here and start the rumors flyin' again. You best be getting on home, boy. Let me get you the receipt to give your mama for the lot rent. Hang on..."

Walking over to the little dining area in his trailer, he leaned over to where he had a receipt book laid out on the pristine Formica dining table, and slowly filled in the lines with his precise penmanship that I would eventually be able to recognize anywhere. He turned and walked back over to me, extending his hand once again to give me the receipt for my mama.

As we walked back towards the door, he cleared his throat to ask, "Boy, now I know it ain't none of my business, and you can say so, but you passed out awful easy for someone who lives in a hot place like this. Do you have something going on with ya? Are you going to be okay to walk back home, boy?"

"Yes sir, I'll be okay. I think it really was just the heat that did me in. I had better get going though, or Mama will be lookin' for me," I answered, sheepishly, pausing to stare down at the floor.

Who was I kidding? I had never been a good liar and Mr. Scroggs seemed to be intelligent enough to see right through my line of bullshit. He didn't push though. With eyes of concern, he simply bowed his head in agreement and walked me out the front door. Right as I had hit the bottom step though, right as I had almost been in the clear to escape his grasp, he lured me back in by saying, "Hang on a minute boy, I have something you can borrow," before he disappeared right back into the trailer.

I took a few steps back up the stairs of the front porch and sat a spell, waiting for him to reappear. I could hear him shuffling some things around in the living room as I sat out there in the shade, watching a few of the local neighbors walking by.

I noticed though, while I was sitting there waiting,

that a few of the younger women who had been out on walks would slow way down when they passed Scroggs' place, staring at me and whispering to each other instead of waving a hello. I thought it was odd but didn't put too much thought into it.

Within just a few minutes, Mr. Scroggs reappeared on the front porch, beads of sweat trickling down his forehead. "Here, I found it. I saw you marveling at my comics in there, and I knew that I had a few back copies of some older ones that you may be really interested in. Go ahead and take them with you, boy," he said, extending a small pile of comic books to me that had been held together with a couple of shoestrings, though not tied tight enough to do any damage to the bindings or the pages.

"Wow, sir! Thank you very much!" I nervously blurted, too excited about the windfall of good luck that I was having that day to even be concerned about any repercussions for accepting this man's good deed. I reached for the small stack of comics, hopped down the stairs, and turned back towards him to wave goodbye. But he was already gone… already had retreated back into his trailer. And that was my first real run-in with the elusive, yet mesmerizing Mr. Scroggs.

Back at school the next afternoon, I was hanging out at lunch with Jojo and Mags again and decided to show them my recently acquired secret stash of comic books that I had been gifted the previous afternoon. Since both of them appreciated a good comic book, they eagerly dove into the pile that I had pulled out of my backpack during lunch.

"Dude, no way! You have some real old ones here! Pretty dope, yo!" was the response that I got from Jojo as he sat flipping through a copy of an old *He Man* comic.

"Wait, where did you find these?" a curious-as-always Mags questioned, flipping through a few photos that had fallen out of one of them in the stack.

"Well, I have this neighbor. Actually, he doesn't live right next door. He lives on the other side of the park and manages the place. I stopped in yesterday for my mama to pay the lot rent and he gave them to me."

"Wait, he just gave them to you?" asked a bewildered Jojo, still flipping through the comics, "Cool. Very cool."

Mags, however, just sat in silence, staring at the small handful of photos that had fallen out of one of the comics. She held one up to eye level for me to see.

With a calmness about her, yet a distinct fear in her eyes, she asked, "Do you know who this boy is?"

I stared at the photo, not recognizing who it was that she was referring to. The picture was of a boy about our age who was fishing from a pier. The kid looked happy but didn't look like he was anyone famous or someone that I should know.

I just shrugged my shoulders and shook my head before asking her, "Am I missing something? Should I know who he is?" Right then, Jojo looked over to see what Mags was talking about. "Oh damn..." was his only response before flipping the comic book onto the table and staring at it in shock.

The lunch bell began to wail, and we had to quickly start shuffling the comics and photos back into my backpack.

"Wait, you guys gotta tell me what's going on. Who is this kid and why is it a big deal that these are in the comic books?"

Mags grabbed her lunch tray and turned to look at me

with a stern and worried expression on her face. "Jett, who did you say gave these comics to you?"

"I told you, a neighbor on the other side of the trailer court. He's the manager, actually. I went over yesterday to give him the lot rent from my mama. I wasn't feeling too good when I got there, so he brought me inside. By the time I felt better and got ready to go, he just stopped me and gave them to me. I guess he figured I might like them since I'd commented on his collection of comics. They were on the shelf in his living room." I was not understanding why the urgency in her voice, nor the way that they were both acting. Along with my high anxiety about being late for class that was starting to wear on me, it was all making me seem flustered and impatient, something I really didn't want to unleash on them just then. They had only just met me for cripes sakes. I didn't want them already thinking I was strange.

"But who is he, Jett? What is this man's name?"

Frustrated and confused, I quizzically shouted out, "Mr. Scroggs. His name is Mr. Scroggs!" at which point, Mag's mouth fell wide open, and Jojo dropped his lunch tray on the floor.

Chapter 4:
Do You Know Sorrow?

Mr. Scroggs had a history in our little town of Mims. The mere mention of his name conjured up tales that were just spooky enough to whisper around a campfire. Yet no one could really tell me exactly what proof was out there to give a solid backbone to the fodder that graced the lips of the old biddies that played cards on their front porches while watching over the neighborhoods. Or what was whispered about on the playgrounds in the middle of a treacherous game of dodge-ball. Back then, I had no way of knowing that my new friend was a person whose name, when uttered, made stomachs lurch, and made the mamas clutch their children's sweaty little hands a little bit tighter as they passed the old man on the street.

Even if I had known, I can't say that it would have made much of a difference. I was always drawn to the outcasts like myself, and I favored the dark corners of the world where I didn't have to make myself so small. Besides, I owe that man too much now to ever wonder about any different outcome.

"Oh God, Jett… you have to stay away from him!" I

can still hear Mags shouting at me in fear that afternoon while sitting in that sticky cafeteria while kids around us started to throw sideways glances our way, something that I had always tried to avoid. Mags was staring at me just then, her eyes beginning to glisten with pools of tears as she bent forward while trying to pick up the dropped remnants of Jojo's lunch. For his part, Jojo was still just sitting in stunned silence and staring at me like my hair was on fire, or like I had just unearthed some mystical, ancient secret of the world.

"He's cool, guys. I don't get it. He manages the trailer park, and someone has to take the lot rent over to him, right? He has so many cool things in that trailer, so many things that you just wouldn't believe!" I tried to tell them but without leaving much of an impression. Jojo cut me off again, blurting out the words that would haunt me for the rest of the afternoon, at least until we were finally able to meet up after school once again and they could give me the full rundown of the lore that was Mr. Scroggs, that inky dark veil that hung above all of the town's well-meaning, yet cynically curious bystanders.

"Look, Jett, although he seems like a harmless old man, he has a backstory that no one can really explain. He has been questioned multiple times over the years by the cops," Jojo trailed off, looking down at the sticky tile where the remnants of his spaghetti had been, now smeared across the cracked gray tiles.

I just laughed. "Questioned? Scroggs? What the hell would he ever be questioned for? I mean, sure he's kind of odd, but I just don't see that skinny old man robbin' or rapin' anybody while dressed in his perfectly pressed suit! I mean, come on you two! You can't be serious!"

"No dude," Jojo started in a hushed tone, pausing to look around to see if anyone was even paying attention to us anymore. Satisfied that we were out of earshot from any of the curious onlookers, he leaned in towards me from his chair and almost whispered, "He makes kids disappear."

With no time to react or carry on the discussion any further, I hurriedly threw what was left of my lunch away as the bell blared out and walked with Mags towards the next class. My heart was fluttering in my chest and waves of nausea were rolling through my guts. Too much in shock from what I had just heard, I opened the door to the classroom for Mags as Jojo wheeled on by our room hollering out, "Dude, after school at Fox Park! We will fill you in then!" Mags just nodded her head in agreement while still looking like she was in a stunned state. We went into the classroom and took our seats.

It had been just another hot Florida day, made a little stickier by the fact that our school's air conditioning system was older than Scroggs and just couldn't keep up. As if trying to pay attention to economics in the suffocating heat while your T-shirt was sticking to you in all of the wrong places and making your anxiety shoot through the roof wasn't bad enough. Throw in the added drama of our lunchtime conversation and I may as well have just skipped class that day. Let's just be honest here. Every day that my ass even graced a seat in a classroom was an anxiety-driven battle of my own making. So the added anxiety didn't do me any favors. At least we only had two dreadfully long classes to make it through that afternoon, economics and then music, before school was out for the day and we were released back into the wild.

Music class wasn't something that I had elected to take. It was a state of Florida requirement in an effort to make all of us southern heathens into more well-rounded individuals who appreciated the arts. Lucky for us, our music teacher had only been out of college a few years himself and had stayed pretty current as to what we were listening to on the radio. He tried to pick music that fit into our everyday lives so the work that we had to put into the class felt much less like work. Although I wasn't great at singing, I could listen to Mags sing for hours. She didn't have a pretentious bone in her body, even way back then. That girl could sing, even though if you told her she was good she would just slug you in the arm and tell you to stop making fun of her.

Looking forward to listening to her sing was what got me through that damn class. Heck, after some time went by, looking forward to seeing Mags is what got me through a lot of things in my life.

After a few songs and a lecture on how to behave at the yearly choral field trip to the local college, we were blissfully released for the day by the sound of that chaotic screaming bell. I couldn't get out of that classroom fast enough. The thing is, normally I would have had my guard up. Normally, I wouldn't have fallen prey for what was waiting for me right outside of the classroom door.

I had been too preoccupied and antsy, worrying about trying to get out of class and over to Fox Park Woods to find out the story of Mr. Scroggs, that my normal hypervigilance of my surroundings had fallen by the wayside, one innocent mistake that I would be sure not to make again.

As Mags and I left the classroom and started walking

towards the locker bay area just a few narrow hallways over, I went flying. Not like I tripped on my shoelace, or slipped on the freshly mopped gray tile, but literally flying with a force that slammed my face into a bay of lockers that had been just a few feet right in front of me. I hadn't felt him shove me forward, but I sure as hell felt my lips and forehead split open as soon as they were forced into that cold orange metal locker by the asshole. As I closed my eyes and felt the hot blood slowly running down my forehead, I could hear him laughing as he kept walking by.

"Turk's such an asshole. You okay?" Mags questioned quietly as soon as she was sure that he was no longer within striking distance. I felt my face get hot with embarrassment and feared turning around to face the crowd that I was sure had already gathered to witness my shame. I had bit my tongue and caught my lip on my tooth, splitting that open as well. I could taste the blood that was now saturating my mouth.

Bravely, I stifled the hot tears that had embarrassingly begun threatening to fall. I backed out of where I had landed and turned to face Mags and the crowd. Being picked on was something that was not new to me, but it still broke my soul every time it happened. One of the most miserable and soul-smothering feelings on this mudball of a planet is to be singled out and made to appear weak, made to feel less than worthy… a sideshow, a freak.

With my mood dampened and my anxiety once again riding high, all I really wanted to do was get home and hide in the safety of my room away from the curious eyes of these new classmates, the people that I had been trying so damn hard to convince that I was just normal, just average, just a guy. I stood staring at her for a couple of heartbeats worth of a pause before blurting out, "Fuck him, let's go." To my relief, Mags only responded with a grin, and we were on our way to Fox Park Woods.

It was only a ten-minute walk or so to where we were supposed to be meeting up with Jojo, but sixth-grade-me was dumbfounded by the fact that I was strutting along the edge of the road with a girl. Mags wasn't just any girl, either. She was cool as hell. As we walked, we became heavily engaged in a debate as to who was the superior comic book villain before stopping on the side of the road to investigate a massive fire ant pile that had formed around someone's half-eaten, discarded glazed doughnut. I had wanted to destroy the mound, reasoning with Mags that those little bastards were no good, and some unsuspecting animal or person was going to meander into them and be in a world of pain. (Fire ants don't just bite. After those little suckers attach their jaws to you, they shoot a pretty painful stream of venom into your body as well, leaving painful puss-filled blisters in their wake that you will spend the next week or so feverishly scratching, then popping for relief). "Do they deserve to die because they cause you pain?" Mags squealed in panic as she pulled me away at the last second before I attacked that little colony with a stick I'd picked up from the ditch. "Think about it," she kept nagging. "There they are, trying to build a little home and carry on about their normal little lives, when all of a sudden, something tries to destroy it all, them included! Wouldn't you be pissed? Wouldn't you fight back?" She argued while leaving me and the ant pile behind, heading on towards our destination.

Dropping my stick and glancing back towards the fiery

little bastards as cars whizzed on by, I couldn't help but think to myself, *"Hell no, I wouldn't fight back. I would hide. Or at least, I would build my little mound further away from predators, further away where no one would notice. That way, if I ever did attack, no one would see me coming."*

Hopping away from the mound, I was adamant to catch back up with her, marveling at her long auburn hair that had been pulled up high into a ponytail yet was still long enough that it swept back and forth gently across her back as she walked. She was just so cool that sometimes little things like her hair stuck out to me, reminding me that she wasn't in fact just one of the guys. She was a darn girl; although, it would be a few years yet before that really came into play in our relationship, when Mags being a girl would be the sole cause for all of our paths being hurled into a whole other trajectory.

"Almost there!" she hollered over her shoulder, "We just have to cut down over the next street. Or," she paused, "if you think you are brave enough, I know a shortcut!" she teased.

I think I would have followed that girl into the fiery pits of hell, so it was no surprise that I blurted back, "I ain't scared of nothing in the wild. Let's go!"

Mags grinned and a wicked flame danced briefly in her eyes. I would see this little flame appear many more times over the years, mostly when she was excited about something, sometimes when she was pissed. That little wickedness that started as a twinkle in her eye and then spread to an almost smirk across her raspberry-glossed lips was always full force when she was out to prove someone wrong, trying to put someone in their place. On this day though, that someone was me.

She scattered off into the woods and stepped over pine needles nearly a foot long and razor-sharp palmetto leaves with nothing but her flip-flops on. She stepped boldly, with no care as to what slithering critter or scattering insects she may disrupt in her path. When we reached the small creek bed that ran behind the property, she paused on its banks just long enough to kick off her flip-flops, pick them up, and stick one painted cherry red toenail into the murky shallow water that was mysteriously calm. Not a ripple danced across the algae scum as she shouted over her shoulder where I was cowering next to a palmetto bush. "Ain't that bad! Thought it would be colder. Must not be very deep!"

"What if there's gators in there? There's some pretty nasty snakes that slither through that crappy water, too! I ain't scared, I just don't like not being able to see what is trying to get to me," I shouted out to her in awe of her complete disregard for the dangers around her that may be gliding just beneath the eerily smooth shallow surface.

When she was already in up to her thighs in the center of the creek, I could hear her giggle and shout back towards me, "Come on, Jett! Live a little! We'll get there much quicker by crossing here! Plus, the water feels dang good!"

I watched her slight silhouette walking gently through the murk, her hands holding her green and white flip-flops high overhead as her cherry red painted toenails must have been sinking with every step into the silky smooth, yet slimy creek bed floor. I looked both ways up and down that old creek and paid close attention to the banks, scanning for any movement of a gator or snake before I made the rash decision to go ahead and kick off my shoes and follow her towards a greater unknown. I too held my shoes and bag high overhead and gasped as I took my first step into the dark shallow abyss.

"Jesus!" I shrieked, just as I saw Mags make it safely across to the other side. I was trying so hard to be cool, so hard to act like any other normal sixth grader. But there was one huge difference. Where the water came up to the top of Mags hips at the center of the creek, it came damn near up to the center of my belly, which started to freak me out. I was dangerously close to having a panic attack. She had made it look so effortless, gliding across the shallow bed of murky water. Yet there I was, my toes sinking into what I instantly was imagining to be quicksand as I sloppily made my way across, trying to keep my head above water. Thankfully, the creek bed wasn't very wide, and I was able to clumsily scatter across it quickly. (I didn't allow my mind to wrap itself around any of the "what if's" that were dancing precariously close to the edge of my mind. Therapy must have been good for something in those early years because, as much as I had hated to go, I was able to cross a deep creek bed in murky water on the edge of the Florida Glades with no thoughts of snakes or gators whispering their way into my soul. Sure, even if I *did* still suffer from massive panic attacks, had begun a new fascination with washing my hands a billion times a day until they cracked and bled, and focused way too much on the organization of not only the clothes in my dresser, but also the way that the glasses and plates were arranged on the shelves in the kitchen cupboards, I had at least been making some kind of progress towards becoming society's depiction of a "normal" sixth grade boy.) As I crossed the creek, I focused solely on what had been right in front of me: the goddess to my sixth-grade heart with long auburn hair and tanned legs who had an avid love of comic books and all things a little odd, just like me.

She stood on the edge of the bank waiting for me, flip-flops in one hand, book-bag in the other, shaking off the water and brushing the sandy murk from her feet.

"We are almost to the backside of the park. Just have to wind around a patch of wild blackberries and pass through the tall evergreens and then we will be there. You gotta put your shoes back on though, cause the damn evergreens drop needles as long as the length from your wrist to your elbow, maybe more. If we're lucky, there might be some blackberries to pick, too!" Mags squealed, grinning from ear to ear, effortlessly sliding her flip-flops back on.

While I worked clumsily to brush the wet sand and slimy algae from in-between my toes, I shaded my eyes from the blaring sun with one hand overhead and looked towards the auburn-haired goddess that was Mags and blurted out, "Well how the hell is Jojo meeting us over there? He can't get around back here in his chair. There's just no way!"

Mags giggled and rolled her eyes my way before spinning around to head off in the direction of the park. "We are just taking the shortcut, silly. Jojo is going the regular way on his wheels. The sidewalk behind the school runs right over to the park. It just takes a little longer to get there." She stopped suddenly, spinning back towards me one more time with a look of disparaging caution furled upon her well-plucked brow. "Don't misjudge Jo-Bean though. His wheels never slow him down. He was a smart, but crazy kid before his accident and nothing has changed that. Nothing at all," she muttered, turning away from me again. "He could still kick anyone's butt if he had to..." she almost whispered before heading off.

"Hey," I shouted out while trying to scatter up to a standing position, forcing myself to just ignore the disgusting feeling that my damp and sandy feet had made into my pristinely clean shoes. (Once again, I was willing myself to push the feeling out of my mind, trying so hard to not let my OCD get the best of me, working at trying not to be the weird kid.) "What was it that actually happened to him? How did he land in that chair anyways?"

She didn't even turn around, just hollered over her tanned shoulder with the dark green terrycloth strap of her shirt slightly digging into her skin. "That's his story to tell, Jett. You gotta ask him about it. Seriously, he loves to tell it!"

I ran to catch up to her and we continued on, hopping over the dry pine needles that made up the majority of the woods' short path. As we rounded the last small clump of Palmetto bushes and made our way past an old fort that some kids had built out of well-worn pallets and a couple of broken down metal shrimping pots, I finally saw him in a clearing, his wheels parked next to a small batch of blackberry bushes, happily filling his face with their warm gooey sweetness, the juices staining his tanned fingers and spilling down his chin.

"Hey Jo-Bean!" Mags hollered out, taking off in a jog as her tousled hair bounced behind her. By the time I caught up to her, she too was happily munching on the warm dark berries, the juice now running down her own fingers, staining her lips and anything else that it came into contact with.

Honestly, I was never a big fan of blackberries. They had bumps and seeds and tiny little hairs on them that you could see when you squinted hard enough. Their texture alone was abhorrent, and when they were being picked and devoured directly off the bush after sitting out in the hot sun all day, their texture became warm, lending them to be a warm, albeit sweet mouthful of putrid mush. I hated them. Yet, there I was, cautiously picking those little bastards and flinging them into my mouth, trying to swallow them whole without biting down and bursting the warm contents all over my overly discerning tongue, grinning through berry-stained lips while keeping my teeth gritted in order to hold back any sign of gagging that was crawling around in my throat.

But those two, Mags and Jojo, appeared to be in heaven, dining on the warm little putrid delicacies, barely noticing that I was less-than-enthusiastically joining in. It was what I was good at, this way of hanging on by the fray, blending in just enough to not stand out, not calling any attention to myself or my shortcomings. I had done this thousands of times in my life and would go on to do it thousands more, putting myself through a type of personal hell for the goal of acceptance, the goal of blending in.

After swallowing a few handfuls of the putrid and gooey warmth, I cleared my throat and asked the question that had been nagging at my guts since lunch. "Ok, so you got me out here. Now, what's the story with Scroggs?"

Jojo stopped picking the berries and looked down at the small pile that he had built in his lap, pulling off the odd stem and flicking away any little bugs as he solemnly spoke. "Well, there isn't anything that has been proven. But I'm telling ya, that man's creepier than hell and the chatter around town about him has gone on for years..." he trailed off, popping a clean berry into his mouth, happily chewing away slowly like an old cow shifting her cud around, pushing it with her tongue from one side of her mouth to the other.

Mags stopped eating long enough to speak out into the air without looking at me, her eyes focused solely on the berry bushes. "He makes kids disappear, you know. No one knows what the hell he does with them or why. But there have been too many kids in this town that have gone missing, and somehow, every one of them has had ties that lead right back to that old man. He's just someone you should steer clear of, Jett. Just stay out of his way," she said without ever averting her eyes from her berry hoard.

I grinned and tried to shrug it off, laughing away the idea that the frail little old man whom I had only recently befriended had anything to do with kids going missing or anything even vaguely sinister. Letting out a laugh, I blurted out, "Man, you guys don't know what you are talking about. Scroggs ain't like that. The dude lost his wife, man. He's lonely. And he has some way cool things in his trailer."

"Whoa! Back the hell on up, Jett! Exactly how far into his place did you go? What exactly did you see in there?" Jojo blurted out, dropping most of his berries from his hands and staring at me, eyes wide and full of amazement. Mags stopped filling her face as well and turned, fixing her gaze directly on my face. An uneasy feeling began to churn in the pit of my already queasy belly. What was their problem? They couldn't actually be serious about believing the stupid rumors, I stood there wondering.

"You guys, he's just a little old man! He manages the trailer court and has a huge collection of cool old books and comics! I told you before, I took the rent check over to his place like my mama had asked me to, and it was so hot out! I wasn't feeling too good and must have passed out. Anyways, when I woke up, I was lying on his couch in his living room. There ain't nothing spooky going on in there, either. Just some old records and books and maybe some knick-knacks from his dead wife. That's it. Sorry I don't have a better story for ya!"

Their furled eyebrows raised, and no sound was coming from their stained lips as both of their jaws dropped. They silently stood there staring at me for a few seconds. With wide eyes, Jojo was the first to form a sentence. "He dragged you into his house?"

"Did he hurt you at all?" a panicked Mags quivered, her eyes softening as worry began setting in on her face. The thrill of the afternoon, the excitement of harvesting those vile berries had escaped both of my newfound friends' faces now, only to be replaced with looks of terror that were harboring a million questions.

"Geez guys, no! Scroggs didn't hurt me! That silly old guy doesn't have the strength to hurt a fly!" I began to argue but was immediately cut off by Jojo, whose face had become so animated that it was hard to stifle my laughter. Here he was, eyes of seriousness and concern, his stern, tanned browline pressed into heavy lines of stress... and his face was still smeared with blackberry goop.

"Boy, if you knew what this town thinks that little old man is capable of, you might just try a little harder to stay out of his way," he said in a hushed tone before leaning in a little closer. Mags just continued to stand stoically, her jaw still hanging wide open and her eyes frozen with a look of shock, like when you go to reach for your sneaker that you left outside only to find that a little black racer snake has curled up in the toe and made it his bed for the night.

"Did you notice that trailer down the way from the old man's house? The one with the caution tape around it that no one took down and the kids' bikes still sittin' out in the yard? Do you know which one I am talking about?" Jojo questioned. He wiped his berry-stained hands nervously across his jean shorts, staining the fraying hemline and leaving finger imprints across the front of his thighs that almost resembled blood. Almost. Except for that putrid blackberry color.

I didn't have to think about it. I had stood right in front of that place on the way to Scroggs' trailer wondering what the hell had gone on there, why no one was there, why it was left to look abandoned. "Yeah. Hey, yeah! I know the one. Why?"

Now it was Mags who jumped in, maybe to guard what Jojo was about to say and ease the blow a little. She knew that I lived just across the lot from there, and I still had to go home and try to sleep in a suffocating darkness that night with just the yellowish glow of the streetlamp on the corner creeping into the windows of our little trailer home. No matter what the lore was that surrounded that place, I still had to call it home.

"That's the James' old place. Have you heard about what happened to their son, Bradley?" she asked softly.

I acted only half interested, instead leaning back into the berry bush like I was looking for another ripe, disgusting berry. "I don't think so. What happened? He alright?" Part of me didn't want to know the answer. The caution tape had already led to wild nightmares rumbling around in my brain the night before, causing me to panic about every little thing that went bump against the trailer or ran across the flat roof. It didn't matter if the racoons were out digging through our trash again or the local cats were throwing each other's scrawny bodies into the sides of the place as they fought for food. To me, all those noises fed into my paranoia, my overactive and exhausted imagination.

"Well, his parents sure as hell weren't great to be around. His dad was a big-time drinker and would hit at the kids a lot. Bradley was a couple grades older than us, but his sister, Gracie, was in our class. She was home more than she was in school. Nice girl, though. She would come to school all banged up. Told the teachers she was just clumsy or that it was from wrestling with her brothers. But she told the kids the truth. Her mean old Pa would come home after a night out at the bar and get pissed off if the dishes weren't done or if there wasn't food waiting for him at the table. Their mama was gone most nights waitressing over at Charlie's Truck Stop out by the interstate, or taking odd jobs like cleaning the bathrooms over at the Visitors Center at night in-between the truck drivers stopping to shower or take a crap. Since Gracie was the next best thing, that mean old Pa would yank her out of bed in the middle of the night and beat her. When he tired of that, he would make her get up in the middle of the night and clean or cook for him before he would wander off and pass out on the couch." Mags' voice trailed off a little as it began to tremble.

"Eventually, Gracie and her younger brother Vernon

were taken in by her mama's sister over in the little town of Christmas. You know where that big old cement alligator head sits out by the highway? That little gator zoo? They don't live too far from there. Anyways, Bradley was too old to go. The aunt didn't have room for them all, and she had figured he was almost grown and could hold his own against his pa."

Stunned and with my stomach now churning from the lingering thoughts of such a barbaric story, I blurted out impatiently, "Well what the hell does that have to do with Scroggs? Did he get in a fight with the kids' old man or what?"

"No, man, it wasn't like that..." Jojo jumped back into the conversation. "Things got way worse around that place. Bradley's pa started beating his mama even worse after the little kids left, blaming her for destroying the family. She couldn't take it and took off with a truck driver one night and headed north, towards Wisconsin. No one really knows what happened to her after that. It pissed off his pa though. Soon, drinking wasn't enough and Bradley's pa started messing around with black tar heroin, which also led to him messing around with his dealer's old lady. That's the story that went around town, anyways."

"Ok, but Scroggs!" I jumped in with even more urgency for him to get to the point. This story was spinning on, and I knew that I had to start heading home soon before Mama knew I hadn't come home yet and would throw a holy shit fit. She is who I get my obsessive worrying from and why I knew even back then I would probably suffer from ulcers before I hit high school. Love that woman, and I always got why she worried about me. But dang.

"Scroggs came into the picture because Bradley started hanging around his place," continued Jojo. "Rumor has it, Bradley was out trying to score drugs off of that crazy old coot they call 'Pencil Man' down on the corner by the old gas station, you know the one that sells those deep-fried gizzards and quartered potatoes?" Jojo asked me. I couldn't answer though, only nod my head slowly up and down because the mere mention of "Pencil Man" prompted my tunnel vision, and I was now fearful of passing out in front of these two. I didn't need them to see me like that. I just wanted to look normal for them and fit in. I tried to focus on Jojo's words, staring once again at his berry-stained lips as they moved, calming myself down and backing further away from the brink of passing out and looking like a huge nerd.

"Well, after that, he started hanging at Scroggs' place. Him and Pencil Man go way back. Can't say why or how far back, but they go fishing and shrimping together a lot. People have even seen them head out to the Glades in the middle of the night! No one goes into the Glades at night man, without good reason!" Jojo finished before Mags took control of the direction of the story once again.

"Mr. Scroggs, he let Bradley hang out at his place a lot, I think to stay out of the way of his pa when things were bad. At one point, one of his dad's dealers even came looking for Bradley 'cause his pa owed him money and he was going to get it one way or another. A few weeks after that, Bradley disappeared."

I could feel the sweat rolling down the center of my back now, soaking my T-shirt. I no longer felt like I was going to pass out, but my mind was reeling with too much information, yet not enough. "That's it? Scroggs let the kid hang out at his house before the kid hit the road? What's so awful about that?"

"Jett," she slowly began again, "Bradley not only disappeared. The cops found blood. There was blood on Bradley's pillowcase, dripped across his bedroom hallway, and even on the front door handle of their place."

"So?" I shouted back at them, perhaps a little harsher than I had meant to. "Just because there was blood, that has nothing to do with Scroggs!"

"You are right, man," Jojo rushed in with his soothing voice to finish the story and calm me down. "There was nothing that led the cops back to Scroggs. But… this wasn't the first kid that had been in Scroggs' orbit to go missing. A couple of years before, a guy two streets down who was in high school went missing, too. And there was also the kid from Titusville that would spend his summers working for Scroggs, mowing lawns and stuff, and he went missing, too. Before that, when I was too little to remember, I also heard about the astronaut's kid who went to Scroggs for math tutoring and eventually started fishing and shrimping with Scroggs and Pencil Man at night, and guess what? CAME UP MISSING, MAN!"

"Come on, you guys! This sounds like the shit old biddies sit and squawk about over cards! How much of it is actually true? Don't you think that if he really did something to those kids that the cops would have something on him by now? Did they ever even question him? DID THEY?" I shouted, at this point too pissed to care that I was yelling.

"DUDE! Calm the hell down!" Jojo hollered right back. For being a smaller guy stuck in a chair, he was always one to make his presence known. The guy commanded an audience. "Of course they questioned him. Scroggs has always been on the suspects list whenever a kid goes missing. I can't tell you if it's the whispering in town that landed him on that particular list or if there is more that the cops know and they just aren't saying. I do know that it sure seems like a hell of a coincidence that he was somehow involved with all of those kids that went missing, in one way or another."

I didn't respond, just glanced down at my watch and shouted out to no one, "Crap! I gotta get going home! My mom's expecting me soon and if I don't show up, she's going to come looking."

"Yeah, I gotta get going, too. My mom will be home soon, and we have to run down to the marina and help my granddad clean some boats tonight," Mags said as she brushed her berry- stained hands on her bare, tanned legs, "You coming, Jo?"

"Yeah, I better get going, too. Walk me part way?" Jojo more stated than asked. I wasn't thrilled with having to walk with Jojo that day. It meant that we couldn't take the shortcut, just Mags and me, and that it would also take longer to get home. I hadn't been kidding either. My mom would come looking. Can you imagine that embarrassment of being a sixth-grade kid tracked down by your ma to walk you the rest of the way home?

I could never really hold it against her though. My mama has had to watch me fall further and further behind in life and then pick me up and force me to thrive more times than I wish to admit. That woman has worried for us both, even when I was too young to understand that there was anything I should be worried about. I suppose that when you grow this perfect baby in your belly for nine months and then he turns out to be not so perfect, her natural instinct is always going to be to try to protect me. I suppose that it had been hard for her to watch me go through so many surgeries, so many treatments. How many times had that poor woman sat at my bedside after another surgery hoping that this time, the outcome would be different. This time, it would work, and I wouldn't be the odd kid out in all social situations.

Hell, just a couple months before, I had gone through another hip surgery because the top of my femur had slipped out of my growth plate again. If my ass wasn't racing the clock to grow, it was busy falling apart while we kept mending my tired body parts back together again. My mama was a freaking saint. Except to a sixth-grade kid, I couldn't see that quite yet.

As we got Jojo turned around and back onto the compacted dirt path that led to the sidewalk along the edge of the woods, a thought struck me.

"Hey guys," I kind of quietly said into the humid breeze that was starting to lick our faces as it blew in off the water, "I don't know what to think. But I just remembered something else that I saw in Scroggs' trailer. There were newspaper clippings and pictures of some kids, all boys. Do you think it means anything?" I hated even saying it. Although I barely knew the guy, my heart was a kindred spirit to the man, the little oddball, like me. I was hoping that I was wrong, hoping that I would be able to somehow convince these guys, maybe even the town, that Scroggs was good… that being an oddball didn't mean anything was actually wrong with him.

Chapter 5:
Do You Know Suffering?

We started heading the long way back down the hot asphalt sidewalk that would wind around the edges of the park, past the small patch of woods, and eventually lead the three of us on home—I toward the trailer park, Jojo to the moderately-priced homes that sat near the edge of Port St. John, and Mags to the furthest destination, the beautiful plantation home that was her family's namesake sitting proudly on the banks of St. Johns River just a stone's throw away from her granddad's charter fishing business.

It would be a few years yet before Mags would confide in me about the horrors that sprung from that huge home with its wraparound porch and tire swing hanging innocently from one of the massive Cypress trees that lined the property. It wasn't until much later that I would come to understand why Mags was haunted by and hated the smell of the sweet old Cypress.

As we walked along, my sixth-grade reasoning had gotten the best of me, and I hatched a plan. I wanted so badly to prove the innocence of my new friend, so the three of us decided that the next Saturday when Scroggs went shrimping with Pencil Man, we would casually yet carefully sneak into his place and see what we could find. I needed answers, and I needed to clear his name. At the time, I had refused to believe that Scroggs was anything but a quirky kindred spirit. My naiveness that innocently went hand-in-hand with being a kid had blinded me, masking the view of wolves lurking just within the shadows.

"Dad! Hey, Dad! How much longer do I have to wear this dang thing anyways? It's so itchy!" I heard my son Nicky shout out, pulling me back from the warm path that my mind had just been wandering down. He had caught me staring out the window of the limousine that the Foundation had sent to drive us to the gala. (A goddamn limo. Pop would have gotten a charge out of that!)

Nicky had broken his arm a few weeks earlier when he and his brother were messing around on their bikes being fearless boys trying to jump over rickety ramps that the two of them had concocted. I was slow in answering him at first, pausing only to glance over at his brother, Vinny. A broken arm would be the least of our worries for him. Vinny didn't have a body that was as strong as Nicky's. Although I was able to spare him some of the issues that I had been forced to deal with growing up, I was unable to do anything about his growth plates fusing too quickly as he aged, or to shield him from the still-necessary surgeries that were needed to lengthen his femur bones in order to squeeze out just a couple more inches and get my boy to a society-acceptable height.

The odd thing was, Vinny had been through so many surgeries and so much trauma in his young life, yet he showed very little signs of discomfort or being disgruntled.

His brother Nicky, however, was given the merciful gift of a strong body that was born to run wild, yet his pain tolerance was near zero. My boys… as different as a turtle and a hedgehog, yet they shared a remarkable brotherly bond and a love of pushing the envelope.

Clearing my throat and letting a warm smile crawl across my lips, I glanced over towards my wife, caught her gaze and rolled my eyes. She had known what was on my mind. She always did. Her face beamed with light and as she smiled, warm creases graced the edge of her eyes. She was such a great mama. I don't think that I've told her that enough. Hell, I know I never told my mama that nearly enough.

"You still got a couple more weeks little man! Toughen up, son. That arm will be good to go soon, and you will be jumping ramps and climbing trees and giving your poor mama too much to worry about again before you know it!" I said, handing him my pen to shove down inside the bright orange cast so he could itch the parts that needed itching.

He let out a sigh of relief as he scratched away before asking, "Didn't you fall out of a tree once, Dad? I think I remember Meemaw telling us about that! Was it your arm? No... your leg! Didn't you break your leg from that, Dad?" Nicky asked before his brother mercifully interrupted, asking, "Are we almost there? I have to take a leak, bad!"

"We aren't anywhere near the place yet. It's at least a half-hour ride. Do you have to go that bad? Can't you just hold it?" I nervously asked, glancing down at my watch. I couldn't be late. There was too much riding on this, and my stomach was already twisted just thinking about the speech that I was about to give. My son just sat there, panic on his face as he stared at me with pitiful eyes, clutching his crotch.

I turned around to ask the driver to please turn off and pull over. We were on a stretch of highway that was completely surrounded by nothing but Glades and the ghosts of whatever may be lurking in the water. As soon as the limo pulled over, I flung the door open nearest the ditch and surveyed the water before hopping out onto the dry grass. The only sign of life that I saw moving around was a lonely armadillo slowly making his way down the waterline, searching for an unsuspecting lizard or cockroach to fill his belly.

"Okay, you can go here. Come on. Get on out of the car."

"Dad! Are you crazy?" Nicky squealed, "He can't pee here! A gator might get him! Or a snake! Or a scorpion!"

I just smiled and held the door as Vinny quickly got out to do his business in the privacy of the other side of the open car door where his mama couldn't see him. Absolutely no fear. He knew I would never let anything happen to him. As he peed, I stared off towards the ripples that were dancing across the top of the water, listening for a splash or any sound of movement, knowing that the hulking ghosts are always brooding, watching, and closer than you think.

He finished his business, and we hopped back in the car, my wife dutifully whipping out her hand sanitizer from her beaded black handbag that matched her satin black gown that she wore exquisitely. Damn. I was lucky.

I sat back, once again trying to calm my nerves by keeping my mind off the speech, instead, telling my boys about the time that I did, in fact, fall out of a tree. They sat staring at me wide-eyed, grinning in all the right places, trying to picture their dear old dad as a kid, carefree and brave. I left a lot of the story out, though. I didn't exactly fall. I was pushed.

The version of the story that I told them was close enough to the one that I told my mama when it happened. None of them needed to know the extent of brutality that was hurled towards me, or to experience the hurt that I'd endured. I tried my damnedest to shield my family from things that I wasn't proud of, much like I frequently did with Mama when I was a kid. I don't know which was worse, the burning feeling of embarrassment that radiates from red cheeks and swollen, crying eyes, or looking in the eyes of a person that you love and seeing pity staring right back at you.

As I sat there in the back seat of that limo with the warmth of my family huddled together listening to my tale of days gone by, I was well aware that the story I was shoveling wasn't even close to the hellish account that my heart was remembering. My boys didn't need to know that. My boys needed to believe that their dad was strong, that he could take on the world.

I had always been careful though, raising my boys, to be sure to let them know where my weaknesses lie. This was something that they needed to know in order to grow up well-adjusted and with a healthy dose of self-respect. They needed to know that perfection is just a ruse and that everyone is a little broken. After all, we were raising one son who was physically the perfect specimen and another whose body had decided to favor my genes. I liked to keep them on a level playing field. But that story, the one of how I really fell out of that damned old Cypress tree, was one that nagged on my soul every time I let it sneak up on me. With anger in my heart and embarrassment and shame lulling me back like a backstabbing friend, my lips told my boys one story, while my brain battled with another.

It was when we were walking home from the blackberry patch that day after school. I am guessing that the reason these memories are resurfacing and gouging their moral-less fangs into my stomach is because, seeing my son struggle with the pain of his little accident and the following weeks of adjusting to life with his cast, echoed all too closely to how fast things can happen, how quickly life, and the decisions you make to live or die can just hang in a dark cloud in the universe.

Jojo had been talking to me about playing football as the three of us were heading home, I do remember that clearly. That was the first time that he had actually spoken to me openly about the accident that had permanently landed him in that chair on wheels.

"I was a hell of a football player, you know? My dad had been signing me up for football camps and traveling leagues since I was old enough to carry the ball. Football was always his thing. He played all the way through college while he was getting his Aerospace Engineering degree.

Then I came along, and he figured maybe I would be able to take it even further, like I might be able to really be somebody," Jojo was saying until Mags impatiently interrupted him.

"Jo-Bean, come on, get going on the story before I get to where I turn off and head home. I like that part!" Mags giggled a charmingly wicked laugh. She and I kept walking along, transfixed by what Jojo was saying. I couldn't help but like it every time our hands would brush against each other as our arms lazily swung back and forth. We walked forward in a small clump, she and I, with Jojo rolling along right beside us. I had learned rather quickly that it was easy to get your toes caught beneath his wheels if you walked too close, or he would accidentally ram into your heels with his footrests if you were in front of him. Effortlessly gliding next to him while still giving him his space had turned out to be the best way to walk alongside good ol' Jo.

"Ok, Mags, but the boy's gotta know how dang good I was at ball to really appreciate the rest!" he argued.

"Yeah, yeah, Jo. okay, I think he gets it. Now go on..." Mags grinned.

"Well, although I was dang good at ball, I loved surfing, man. Controlling that board beneath you with every muscle in your body, there ain't nothin' that feels like that. My mom surfed too, so she was never too worried about me going out. I was always cautious of the tide and paid attention to the weather and if there was anything bad rolling in. If there were any shark sightings, I would move on to another beach for a while, and she made me promise to never go alone..." He paused there, kind of lost in thought for a moment.

During that pause, we heard some voices of kids running around in the woods just beyond where we had come from, laughing and hollering. They were probably smokin' or building a fort. We didn't mind them any and Jojo just went on with his story as we walked, the hot asphalt warming the underside of our shoes and radiating heat up onto our calves.

"The thing is, you can be so careful, so prepared, and still not see what's coming to take you out until your head's being held under water and your lungs have just about given up. I had been out at Jetty Beach with my younger cousin, Tabitha. We had paddled out and we were waiting on a wave to come in. Tabatha had been trying to decide if she wanted the first wave that was forming or not, so I had decided to ride it. As the wave swelled beneath me and I balanced myself, I didn't know that she had decided to go after the same wave. That's something you don't do. Our boards were too close. We managed to get up, but as the wave carried us towards shallower waters, her board nudged up against mine, throwing her off. I may have made it out okay, but an even bigger wave was cresting just as I had been knocked off my board. As I was upside down with my head about to hit the shallow sandy floor, one of our boards had become airborne and was hurled back down on top of me, cracking me right in the back and driving my head even further down onto the ocean floor. That was it man, there was no recovering from that," Jojo finished, seemingly wanting to end the conversation right there. I didn't push for more information, even though the idea of near death had always fascinated me. Instead, I remember asking him if there was ever any hope of being able to use his legs again.

"Oh man," he began, still rolling along and lost in his own story. "My mama sure thought there was. I saw specialists and therapists. They x-rayed me and poked me over and over until they finally told her there was nothing more they could do, and that I was lucky I didn't lose the use of my upper body too. My dad though, man. It had to be hard on him. There went his hopes for me doing something great."

Before I could even answer him, a face that I already knew all too well, one that haunted my brain and soured my guts every time I closed my eyes, lunged out of the woods at us, followed by his small group of ass-kissers. It was Turk. He was always such a dick.

I had wanted to run, wanted to get home as fast as I could behind the safety of the trailer doors where I wouldn't be seen, wouldn't be called out. I knew that I couldn't. I didn't want my new friends to see me like that, a sissy, a big baby who runs away. But I also didn't want to get the crap kicked outta me either, so I had found myself in quite a predicament.

Turk got up close in Mags' face and eerily whispered, "Hey, Mags! What are you doing out here hangin' with these losers, anyway? You should come over to my house. We're ordering pizza and maybe gonna steal my mom's boyfriend's car and take it for a joyride. He ain't home until next week."

For her part, Mags was usually pretty good at redirecting the monster away from easy prey, but on this day, Turk wanted her full attention. Truth was, he had always crushed on Mags, but when she would turn him down, he would get nasty, even calling out her own insecurities before moving on to some other poor kid. (This didn't stop in middle school either. He was a pain in all of our asses clear up through high school… until he wasn't.)

Mags had had enough. She began to turn away from him and continue walking home with us as she breathed over her shoulder in an icy southern tone that I hadn't yet heard emanate from her young lips. "My mama is pretty picky about who I hang out with these days. I wouldn't want to upset my mama by hanging out with boys whose sole purpose in life is to get in trouble. After what she's lived through, I can't put her through worrying about me. But thanks, though." Defeated yet again, the young Turk quickly flexed his jaw as he clenched his teeth together.

There was a glimpse of humility on his face, like something that Mags had said may have edged a little closer to his heart like a fiery razor than he would have liked. He didn't argue with her, just spun around towards Jojo and I as we watched Mags slowly walk away out of our line of sight.

"Well, what the hell are you two doing, hanging around out here? You ain't out there eatin' my blackberries, are ya? Those are mine, you know..." Turk chided. Surprisingly, he seemed to be in a delicate mood all of a sudden, no longer giving off the vibe that he wanted to kick our asses.

Just being in the presence of that kid made my stomach knot up. I knew I couldn't let him smell fear. Hell, to us, he was more like a cranky old gator that got a kick out of first cornering its prey, then tantalizing it a bit before it snapped its snarled teeth and battle-scarred jaws around for the kill. I hated that kid. Hated him and pitied him at the same time.

Frozen in fear, Jojo and I still said nothing in response. Out of character for Turk, he somehow softened a little and put a hand on Jojo's shoulder as he began to maniacally giggle like a little kid. "Damn, you goobers look like you just pissed yo' pants! I'm just playin', those ain't my woods and they sure as hell ain't my berries. So, which one of you is sweet on my girl, Maggie?"

"Dude," Jojo slowly replied through an untrusting,

satiric, and forced grin, "Mags ain't like that. She ain't lookin' for a boyfriend or nothing. With her dad and everything, all her and her mama have time to do is help out her granddad."

Turk dropped his hand from Jojo's shoulder and almost reflected for a millisecond. Something Jojo said had stuck. There was something in Mag's past that somehow slightly softened the asshole. "Nah, she don't know it yet, but someday she will, and it will be me. So, you two goobers can just stay in the friend zone with her, you feel me?" Turk asked, almost quietly as he darted his eyes from Jojo over to me.

"Hey, new kid…" Turk blurted out, his millisecond of reflection now gone, only to be replaced with the air of asshole once again, "you any good at climbing trees?"

At first, I thought he was joking, and I stood there with my legs beginning to tremble and my nerves forming a familiar lead ball in my stomach. Why do your guts always deceive you when you are trying to be brave? I wanted so damn badly to run, but I knew he would just find me.

When you are a sixth-grade boy just trying to survive school and remain unnoticed, you don't need to be making enemies. Graduation was a long way away and that meant I would have to deal with this butt-munch sooner or later. I had found that with bullies like Turk, if you were lucky, eventually they would get tired of putting you through shit and when it wasn't fun anymore, they would move on to some other poor soul, at least for a little while. Turk wasn't even close to giving up on me just yet though.

I may have overcompensated with my answer, however, when I fired back, "Of course I can climb trees! That's the great part about being so short. I have awesome upper body strength and my legs are pretty strong."

I should have known that was the wrong answer as soon as the words were out of my mouth, and Turk began to laugh as his band of buddies started to whisper behind me. Jojo jumped in, "Guys, we really ain't got time for this. We have to be getting on home." As he went to roll forward, one of Turk's cronies grabbed the handles of his chair to make it quite clear that we weren't going home just yet.

"Well, show off, I got an idea! You and me are going to scatter up the old Cypress that sits on the edge of the berry bushes back there, the one with the big knots in the sides and the Palmetto bushes below. If I get to the top first, you stop talking to Mags."

It didn't take me but a second to shout right back, "And when I win?"

Turk just dropped his cheesy smile and calmly spat back, "That ain't gonna be a problem little man."

I fucking hated him. I hated everyone that called me those condescending words, and this was made even worse because I had somehow been forced into a battle that I wanted no part of just to keep my friend. Hell, I only had the two friends so far, and the thought of losing either of them made hot puke start to crawl up into the back of my throat like acid.

"We seriously gotta get going home, Turk. And Jojo can't get his wheels back there without turning around to go back towards that old path. He'll get stuck." I stammered, trying so hard to keep my twelve-year-old voice from cracking and quivering out of puberty, anxiety, and fear. God help me, I just wanted to get out of there. I glanced up the road where I had last seen Mags walking. She was now no longer anywhere to be seen.

"Come on, little man... your buddy can wait right here for ya. It won't take long for me to claim what should be mine. Let's go! Or are you a sissy? A little baby that's going to go crying home to your mama? Wait until the kids at school hear about this! Won't be much of a surprise, though.

Everyone at school already knows what a little freak you are. A freak with no friends. A freak who hangs out all alone and lives out in that skanky old trailer court. A weirdo who…" the asshole was taunting, and I, in all of my adolescent pent-up rage foolishly took the bait.

"Just shut up! You don't know what the hell you are talking about! I'm so sick and tired of this crap. Let's just go!" I shouted back with little fear, leaving Turk with a stunned, and dare I say impressed look on his face as I started off, stomping through the smaller razor-sharp Palmetto bushes and dried pine needles that heavily blanketed the floor of the little patch of woods. I am sure that Jojo must have tried to stop me, or get my attention, but I either hadn't wanted to hear him, or didn't care. I just hollered out over my shoulder, "Be right back, Jojo!" as I humbly made my way deeper into the thicket.

We didn't have to walk in too far to get back to where the old tree stood. As I walked, I noticed not only the sound of the asshole's feet stepping behind me, but also his gang of trolls scattered about in the underbrush. My mind knew that my poor choices were leading me right into something awful. But the need to defend the only two friends I had, the yearning to fit in and to just be fricking "normal" was so great, that I think I would have done just about anything Turk had asked. It hadn't occurred to me then that maybe climbing a big old Cypress tree so soon after the growth plate surgery on my hip maybe wasn't the best idea. It also didn't occur to me that I just may lose. I knew I was a good climber, knew that I was quick and had pretty good upper body strength just from being so short and having to adjust to life, overcompensating where I had to with my upper body to pull myself up onto shelves when I needed to, or to accomplish some other mindless task that my body wouldn't allow me to do.

We stood at the base of the old Cypress in the sweltering, late afternoon heat. I stared up at her trunk, trying to map out where the best knots were that I could grab onto for leverage. There were actually quite a few limbs that would make for the perfect footholds as I went, and the climb itself really didn't look too bad. In fact, I had climbed larger, more difficult trees with my brothers, just farting around in the woods. It didn't strike me as strange back then that Turk would have picked such an easy tree to climb for a purpose. I couldn't have guessed that it was all a set-up, a ruse to embarrass me even further and push me into an even darker, more soul-altering depression than any kid should ever have to battle.

Chapter 6:
Do You Know the Darkness?

"When I say go, you guys are going to start climbing, new kid on the front of the tree, Turk on the back. Everything is fair game. You can shake the tree, spit at each other, do whatever you damn well please, but just make it to that long branch about three-fourths the way up where that big clump of moss is hanging off. You guys got it?" one of Turk's cronies belted out while I stood by the base, staring up into the treetops. My guts were churning and there was a nervous tremor that was taking over my body. There was no time to be a baby. I knew I just had to suck it up. I swallowed back the acidic puke that was lodged in the base of my throat and stifled the hot tears of rage that were beginning to well up in my terrified eyes. The whole thing really sucked. But there was no choice. At least no other choice for a twelve-year-old boy who was trying to save face with his peers, no matter how big of bullies or pricks they were.

"Got it Turk? Got it little man?" the crony shouted out into stale air that tasted the way the great Cypress smelled.

I rubbed my hands together and kicked off my shoes,

figuring that I may have a better chance without them, using my feet like a monkey to help grip at the limbs and balance myself better as I made my ascent. Then I laid my palms against her bark, feeling the large scale-like pieces of wood that ran along her old sides. I watched my hands vibrate with a tremble and said a silent prayer to the universe to let me win this and not pass out from the toxic combination of heat, anxiety, and my low blood sugar. Jesus, at almost thirteen, I already had the mindset and health of a little old man.

I can't remember who yelled out, as not all memories are made to be hung onto, but I do remember that feeling of apprehension as I shot off like a rocket scattering up that tree. I was so focused on winning while operating beneath a thin, yet healthy veil of fear, that I didn't realize Turk wasn't climbing up the opposite side of the damn tree. He was methodically scattering his way up below me, on my side, cautious yet poised, like a red rat snake effortlessly gliding along the bark, searching out its prey.

I was too busy focusing on my hands, reaching for the next worn knots in the tree, helplessly searching with my toes for the next limb to precariously balance upon to notice the scattering of feet that were kicking around dry pine needles in the thicket below, or to hear the echoes of stifled giggles coming from their dark souls beneath me.

My core muscles were tense, trying to overcompensate for the tender hip that I was so vigilantly trying not to put too much pressure on as I glided about the tree, helplessly, from tree branch to creaking tree branch. But the great Cypress was old and wide, which meant that my hip had to flex a little more than what I felt was okay. I knew it was going to ache and be pretty fired up after this fiasco, but there was nowhere else to turn, so upward I continued to climb.

About three-fourths of the way up to the winning limb, not only was my hip begging me to stop putting my body through that hell, but I started to experience tunnel vision, something that I knew about all too well. Between my continuously alternating blood sugar, high anxiety levels and medication reactions, passing out was something that wasn't new to me, and it wasn't something that I could help. I could only try and manage it.

I suppose looking back, I knew the heat and anxiety were getting to me long before I even made it to the base of that old tree. I knew that my exhausted body was still recovering from the latest round of surgery and wasn't sure what it was truly capable of at that point. But at the time,

I was just a pissed off kid trying to find my way. It's not like I ever went looking for trouble, but damn, trouble always seemed to seek me out, draw me in from wherever I was hiding, and eat me alive, one bitter morsel at a time.

"Come on, Jett, let's go! Jojo's still out there waiting too, and this is stupid! Let's just go!" I heard the voice before I could see her make her way into the clearing. This was followed by, "Oh my God! Jett, look out," screamed at the top of her lungs as Mags wandered into the precarious predicament that she had now found me in.

I felt the rumble below me first, then a slight vibration, and clambered out onto the nearest branch as quickly as I could, in confusion, trying to assess what the hell was going on. Gripping the limb for dear life, I glanced below me on the tree where Turk was only a few feet from the ground, laughing a soulless belly laugh while grabbing the larger branch above his head, shaking it with all his might. Below him, a few of his buddies were shaking the lower limbs as hard as they could while a couple of other assholes were starting to throw smaller rocks in my direction, one pinging me on the shoulder.

"What the hell? Knock it off guys! Cut it out, I'm gonna fall!" I screamed out in an equal amount of fear and rage, my eyes locking on the one person in the world who I didn't want to see me cry, didn't want to see me in such a shameful situation.

Laughing, Turk just kept shaking the tree while the other turds kept lodging rocks my way as they took turns shouting out things that, to this day, still sting my soul and set fire to my belly, like, "Come on, ya big baby, CRY!" and "Don't be such a weenie, you aren't up that high!"

My tunnel vision was getting worse, and it was getting more difficult to hold on. My fingers were raw from gripping the gnarly old branch as best they could. I shouted out behind tears, "Cut it out, guys, I'm gonna fall! Something's wrong, I can't see good!"

But the laughter just kept going and I felt a pretty good-sized rock hit me just below my right temple. They were merciless, like a pack of wild dogs, screaming and taunting me. My face grew hot with embarrassment as I watched helplessly, still gripping the tree, and partially blinded now. One of Turk's cronies grabbed Mags by the arms to hold her back as she was kicking and flailing around, begging them to stop shaking the tree.

"What have I done to deserve this?" I can remember thinking, followed by, *"What kinds of monsters do this to people?"* right before the limb that I was clinging to, that had been my lifeline, snapped.

The thing about memories is that the more painful they are, the more haunting they become. This is the shit that keeps me up at night, these ghosts of my past. I had put these memories to bed long ago, yet here I was, trapped in them once again, no doubt brought on by the current scenario as I was riding in the limo with my son, reminiscing about my past. As I was trying to write my speech for the gala, I was reflecting, perhaps too deeply, about the events that had occurred in my life that had put me on the path that I was on today. Then again, would I have managed to come as far as I have without dancing with these ghosts from time to time?

I have come to believe that we all have a little evil tucked away somewhere that sits hidden deep within our psyche, pacified by small acts of dishonorable deeds, manifesting itself into a form of retribution that tries to rectify itself with words like karma, which is merely a gentler term for revenge. And although I believe everyone is fully capable of a little evil, the monsters that I had encountered in those Glades on that day were stirring up something in my bones that hasn't let go of me in all these years.

On that day, those boys became ghosts, their darkened hearts and soulless eyes intent on making me feel like a fool, intent on pissing on their territory and imposing shame on anyone who threatened to get in their way. These are the ghosts that would haunt my sleep, even years later, the ghosts that were always at the forefront of my mind and a driving force behind why I went into the business that I did with the Foundation. These were the ghosts that chased me still.

I didn't know then that anything good would ever come

of that afternoon in the woods, on the outer edges of the Glades beneath the old Cypress that was covered with moss. I couldn't have known.

As the tree branch sharply snapped, I could see many things all at once. I replay it in my head sometimes before I fall asleep. From that angle, higher up above the ground, I could see the tears streaming down Mags' red cheeks and her mouth frozen open, emitting a guttural scream.

Turk immediately had a look of absolute horror when he realized that the limb actually did break and I was falling mercilessly towards the dry earth. His cronies below had hurriedly backed away and I was closing in fast on a… dead boar?

Later, I would learn that their original plan was to just scare me before I made it up too high, make me cry and hope that I would jump down. To add to their planned embarrassment, they had dragged the bloated carcass of a wild boar beneath the tree to "cushion the fall." In reality, though, they were bullies who just wanted to embarrass me more, wanting me to land on the bloated carcass, making it explode, oozing its rank innards all over me in the collapse. Then I would have to run home humiliated and covered in pig stink and they could all laugh about it at school the next day. That was their plan.

But evil isn't easily controlled, and the best laid plans run awry. What those putrid young humans hadn't factored in was the heat, my already low blood sugar and anxiety, or my surgery that had left me with a weakened hip. I wish that I could have seen their faces when I landed, a loud snapping noise coming from where my hip had previously been meticulously held together by a surgeon's nimble hands and hope, and my eyes rolling back in my head as I fell unconscious. They thought they had killed me. So, they ran.

Thank the universe that Mags hadn't left like we originally thought she had, and that Jojo was still waiting on the edge of the woods and heard her haunting scream drift out towards him on a wave of humid, Cypress-scented, salty air. Jojo had no clue what was going on, but he knew it had to have been bad, so he rolled his wheels out into the street where passing cars would either hit him or have to stop. It was actually a volunteer Mims firefighter who slammed on his brakes, climbed out of his truck and started screaming at Jojo as he sat sweating and terrified, gripping the wheels of his chair for dear life, terrified that a car wouldn't stop, and equally terrified that one would. He told me later that he was scared they would find me dead.

There isn't anything else that I remember about that day. My memory doesn't pick back up again until a few days later while I was lying in my dark room, high on pain meds and willing my damn hip to heal while simultaneously begging the universe to just let me die.

My body was sore, but nothing I hadn't felt before. I was lucky that my hip hadn't actually been pulled back apart where the surgeons had manipulated the growth plate. But the muscles around it that had been trying to reattach themselves took a nasty setback as they were ripped back away from the bone again and my healing took an unfortunate step backwards to square one. It wasn't the pain that was bothering me. I had been through enough physical pain in my young life that I had learned to tolerate it. I had been through much worse than that pain from previous surgeries on my hips, my shoulders, my knees, my teeth, hell, even the lumbar region of my spine had been manipulated by that point. It wasn't the pain that kept me bedridden for those few weeks. It was my lack of will.

I had always tried to keep my mama from having to go through any more pain herself. As an adult, it's easy to look back on stupid things, hurtful things that I have said to her that I wish I could take back, things that, as a father myself, would make my skin crawl and my heart ache if my boys ever said to me. But back then, I tried so hard never to let her know just how bad school was getting as far as being bullied. She had been forced to watch me go through so much pain in life that I never wanted to add to that. At that point though, after being shaken from that damn tree, there was no more masquerading around in front of Mama that everything was fine. Her knowing just how bad things had gotten for me at school laid a whole other suffocating veil of shame and embarrassment down upon my shoulders, which were already exhausted from frantically struggling to keep my head above water.

My frustration, grief and pain had begun to fester into a blind rage, coupled with a healthy dose of exhaustion and self-pity. I clearly can hear my own voice screaming at my poor mama that I wanted to die, that I just wanted to grab my pop's gun and blow my frickin' head off. I screamed at her out of hurt and anger, all of the emotions that I had been swallowing for so many years, blaming her for the bad DNA that put me on that hellish road in the first place. Tears rolled down her face as she sat on the edge of my bed in silence, listening as I lamented about never being able to be good enough, never feeling normal, and not seeing any other outcome for myself in this life except to leave it all behind. I told her I was damaged; I was a freak; I was tired; and I wanted out.

For my part, the realization of the gravity of what I had just laid at my mama's feet and weighed down on her heart wouldn't be fully understood until I was a father myself, all these years later. But I did feel shame and guilt almost immediately as I watched my sweet mama silently stare at me, and then cry, as I spoke.

For her part, and bless that woman 'cause I have no idea how she held it together at the time, she calmly wiped her face, grabbed my hand and stared into my eyes, firing warning shots at my slightly darkened soul.

"Now you listen to me, Jett!" she began in a stern but hushed tone. "I don't know what God's plan is for you on this planet, but I think I know where I fit into it. I gave birth to one of the most kind, funny and loving souls. It's my job to make sure that you live out your life and fulfill the journey that God has laid out for you. You are smart as a whip and have such courage, Jett! This was only a bump in the road. You will have even bigger bumps. Of this, I am sure. And you can hate on me all you want, but I am your mother, and I will only keep pushing you forward. Your soul has darkened a little today, my sweet boy, but I ain't letting go." And with that, she leaned in and kissed me on the forehead, the smell of her Avon Amari perfume still sweetly lingering in the air of our little trailer. She got up and headed for my bedroom door, pausing before she walked out, speaking casually from over her shoulder. "Better pull it together and change your mood. Your friends will be over in about half an hour."

As a parent, I have no clue how she was able to hold herself together or remain so calm. I don't know if, as an adult now, I would have been able to handle a situation like that with such strength. For all I know, when she walked out of my room that afternoon, she could have gone back to her own room, locked the door, and sat at cried a thousand tears. Maybe she incorrectly thought I was bluffing.

The words that hurled themselves at my mama that afternoon did bear weight. I hadn't launched them furiously at her out of just pity or anger, but they were an actual warning shot fired off to my mama's ears. I was begging for her to see just how deep into the well of depression I had fallen into.

The truth was, she hadn't known about the times in the past that I had seriously attempted (or maybe just half attempted, if we are being honest here), to end it all, to take myself out of this pit of misery.

Once, about six months earlier, I thought I could end it all by taking a big overdose of allergy medication. I took a few, waited, took a few more, waited, took a couple more … and fell into a deep sleep. The thought I had right before I finally fell asleep wasn't one of fear or regret, but relief, as my swimming mind rationalized, "At least it will all be over."

Months before that, we had gone swimming out at Playalinda Beach and I tried to hold my breath beneath the waves and pass out, aiming for a merciful drowning. The tide, however, had other plans and kept washing me ashore to shallow waters, so I wasn't able to stay under long enough to effectively execute my death plan.

A year before that, I tried to hang myself with a jump rope from the clothes pole that hung in my closet, but the damn thing snapped out of the brackets on the wall as soon as my body weight bore down on it.

So, maybe my mama thought my threats of suicide had been feeble warning words, cries for help. But what she couldn't have known was that I had already been headed down a path of destruction, disillusioned with the life I had been forced to live, and was actively looking for a way to escape.

My outlook on what had been my current situation of despair and embarrassment was turned on its head, however, when Jojo and Mags came knocking on the door that afternoon. It was only then that I learned a little of the background story of Mags and the hell that she had walked through. That was enough to make me never want to put anyone, especially her, through something so volatile and course-altering as ending my own life, ever again. My mindset was shifted that day, and I had Mags to thank for it.

She and Jojo made their way over around dinner time, and Mama was already planning on having them stay for dinner. With two more mouths to feed, my mama was quick to pull together a meal of her famous chicken alfredo, which was lovingly made with whatever cheap noodles she had found on discount and stored in the meager pantry closet next to the kitchen, a couple of cans of chicken she had bought on sale and stored the same way, and a cream sauce that she made from scratch with the milk purchased with food stamps. All of this was bought and coveted because it was part of her old life, the life she used to live before I entered her world with all of my insurance draining, money sucking abnormalities in tow. She traded the neighbor a few of our garden tomatoes for a few stalks of their garden broccoli, all from small container gardens, of course, that sat simply behind our trailers.

I hadn't felt like visiting with anyone really, but when Jojo and Mags showed up, intent on seeing me and staying on for Mama's supper, what choice did I really have? Looking back though, it was that visit with them that would change my trajectory in life.

I could hear the knocking on the door, the murmur of one of my brothers answering it, and the vibration of the floor as Mags walked and Jojo rolled his way back to where my room was. The doorframe of my room wasn't wide enough for Jo's chair though, so when he made it that far, he lowered himself down and belly crawled with his arms across my floor over towards my old green beanbag sitting in the corner, positioning himself in it and then staring at me. I had never seen him out of his chair at that point, and it was truly the most majestic, yet spooky thing that I had ever seen. My mind was blown away not only by his upper body strength, but his utter lack of giving a crap as to what anyone thought about the way he looked. Jojo had purpose and a mission in this life, and he was getting on with it, legs be damned.

"Well, Jett, how's it feeling? You doin' okay?" Mags gently asked, taking a seat at the foot of my bed, pushing off a stack of my comic books to the floor. She noticed my reactive wince as she did that. "Oh, calm down, I didn't bend the pages. Those old things are just fine," she said, reading my concern like only she ever could.

"I'm doin' okay, I guess. It don't hurt that bad. I'm just so sick and tired of all of this shit, ya know? I'm tired of assholes like Turk. Honestly, I'm just tired of it all, ya know? This ain't the life I want anymore. I make my mama sad; I can't make my pops proud cause I can't play sports like he wants me to be able to. I'm just so dang tired of trying. I just want to be normal, ya know? And if I can't force this goddamn body to thrive, then maybe I don't want to do it anymore," I spouted off, clearly unaware of the shit storm that I was dipping my toe into.

Jojo cleared his throat and answered first, as Mags calmly looked down at her feet and the worn shagged blue carpeting beneath them. As Jojo spoke, Mags stood and walked over to the small plant stand that stood propped against the wall across from the foot of the bed. It held a small fan and she clicked it on, dissipating the stagnant and depressed air that had been hanging in my room. I felt the forgiving breeze mercifully crawl up my body, beginning at my toes and making its way up to my injured hip. There was a relief that I felt that I wasn't aware I needed. "Dude! Look at your boy here!" Jojo began. "You think my life is a freakin' cakewalk? Don't you think that I was tormented at school for a while? Hell, my dad still ain't sure what I'm capable of and I am pretty sure that I have heard my mom cry in the bathroom at night in the shower when she thinks we're all asleep and can't hear. Jesus, man. You gotta know that no one's life is easy."

Staring over at my new friend as he was perched on the old green bean bag with legs that had deceived him in this life, I knew that he was right. I wasn't looking for a pity party, though. I truly did just want to make the darkness, the loudness, the pain of this life stop. I was so exhausted at that point, so stressed out, that I truly couldn't see any other way out. Then Mags spoke.

"Jett, has anyone told you about my pa?"

I hesitated, curious as to where this was leading, recalling that when Mags' dad had been brought up in conversation in the past, everyone got all weird about it, even the asshole, Turk. "Not really, Mags, no. But it's okay. You don't have to talk about him if you..." I began to say before she cut me right off in the middle of the sentence.

Sitting back on the foot of my bed, half blocking the breeze from the fan, she began to speak, staring past me out the window above my head. I could hear Jojo situating himself over on the beanbag so he could listen, as his body weight shifted causing the little foam beads to slide around beneath the casing, making a soothing white noise type of sound.

"My pa had a rough life, you gotta know that first of all. He was raised by his uncle when his own mom and dad died in a train accident when he was a kid. His uncle wasn't very nice, and expected a lot out of my pa, making him work for his construction company when he was like ten or eleven. His uncle always kind of saw my pa as just another mouth to feed at a time when money was tight, so he expected him to actually work for his supper.

That old uncle was also where Pa picked up the habit of drinking. He would grow up in a house where that uncle would work all day, go out and drink all night, then come home drunk as a skunk. He would beat all the kids pretty bad when they would get in the way of him beating on his wife. He also hung out with a rough crew who would steal from people and think nothing of cheating on their wives." She stopped talking, lost in a simple thought as she was still staring out the window above my head. Jojo and I said nothing, and soon enough she spoke again.

Noticeably rubbing her hands together out of nervous energy now, she began again in what seemed to be very calculated words. "When my pa met my ma, her dad, Granddad, never thought he was good enough for her. No matter what he did, he couldn't outrun the stigma of how he grew up. Granddad always thought that Pa was just around for Ma's family money and the boating business and Pa could never convince him otherwise. Ma had a rough go of it and argued with him a lot as the years went on. One night when I was like seven or so, I walked in on him yelling at her and when I tried to step in and get him to stop, he spun around in a glorified drunken rage and with all of the power he had in the back of his hand, he hit me across the face with such force that I flew across the room, knocking over one of my late gramma's antique lamps. It shattered into a pile of twinkling pink carnival glass on the wood floor. The lamp split my head open above my right eye, and Ma had to run me over to the ER for a few stitches. Granddad beat the crap outta Pa, and Pa wouldn't hit back 'cause it was Granddad. It scared Pa though, to realize he had it in him to hit me. It scared him bad. He stayed away from the house a lot after that. They were still married, but he tried not to be around as much as he could. I just don't think he trusted himself anymore around Ma and me.

Anyways, one day last year in the spring, I was getting ready to go down and help Ma with a fishing charter for Granddad and forgot to grab one of the new nets we had bought, so I ran back up into the house. When I ran through the breezeway, I noticed Pa's work boots were next to the door, which was strange because he had taken off early in the morning after a fight with Ma. I called out for him and immediately heard a gun go off somewhere upstairs. Mom and Granddad heard it too and came running, but I made it to him first.

In Ma and Pa's room is where he decided to do it. Although maybe the plan hadn't been well thought out at all. Maybe he just did it out of embarrassment of what he had done to me, or maybe fear of what he may do. He didn't even leave a damn note. I walked in and saw him lying on the floor in a wicked little heap in front of their bedroom window that faced the water. I imagine he must have seen me running back up to the house and went into a panic to hurry and get the deed done," Mags paused, blinking wildly out of whatever pull the window above my head had on her before clearing her throat and carrying on. "Anyways, I just wanted you to know that we all go through some shit. Some worse than others. But everyone has crap that we like to hide. And yeah, other kids can be assholes about it too, but that's on them. Hell, most of my friends stopped talking to me altogether when it happened. Some, I would guess, just because they didn't know what to say to me, and others, probably because of the rumors swirling around this little town about my family, crap like that. But Jojo never left me. And look, now I have you!" she innocently lowered her gaze to me and smiled before going on.

"But the other point I wanted to make is that you think things would be easier for you if you died. Believe me, when shit was going down about my family, I can't say that I didn't think about it myself. When your heart lands in that dark place, it feels like there will never be a way out. Like you can't breathe. Like you just want to make all the noise stop. I get that. But, Jett, I have also been forced to survive the other side, to crawl through the aftermath of what my pa had done. Do you have any idea what that did to my ma? Sure, Pa tried to stay away a lot, but they were still married, and she still loved him.

After his death, they had to put Ma in the hospital for a while because she said her heart was so broken that it hurt to even comb her hair. She didn't want to eat; she slept all the time and barely came out of her room. Now she takes medicine twice a day to, like she says, "Make the pain stop and chase his face away." She's not the same person that she used to be, but heck, neither am I.

They didn't make me go away after it all happened. The police came and took his body away, then Granddad made some calls to have the mess cleaned up. I sat out on my swing while I watched the coroner's office wheel in an old metal cart that looked like a bed on wheels across the wide front porch of the house, and could hear the clanging of the wheels of the cart bounce back down the steps inside as they hauled out the black body bag that held what used to be my pa. After they loaded the bag into the truck, one of the men who was dressed in scrubs and cotton footies that covered his shoes so he wouldn't get any of Pa's blood on his feet, noticed me sitting alone in the swing and tried to smile, raised one hand to wave, and then jumped into the back, swinging the door shut behind him. That was the last I saw of Pa. Mom had him buried at the cemetery over by the school, but Granddad wouldn't allow a funeral.

So, see, Jett. Don't you be talking to anyone about wanting out, about wanting to make everything stop. You would never want to put people, especially your poor mama through something like that, having to watch as the little metal cart rolls you out of this trailer and your brothers sit out on the porch waving goodbye to a hearse.

Don't you ever do that!" Mags sternly shouted at me, her emotions getting the best of her and letting one rogue tear make its way down her soft cheek, before slapping it off with the back of her hand.

I couldn't breathe. I knew that she was from a wealthy family and hadn't really understood why she didn't have more friends. Being a kid, I just figured she must have liked things outside the norm, like her love of old comic books and deep literature, so kids just kind of treated her like an outcast without really picking on her, per se. After all, her family had money and did a lot for the school and community. I couldn't have known the nightmares that she had lived through or just how deeply scarred she had already been.

"Supper in five!" my mama's voice bellowed down the hallway, my brothers' feet already running down the hall to claim their spots at the antique dining table that Ma had managed to convince Pop to keep when we were "downsizing" and selling everything we had of value to pay for my treatments. It was her last reminder of what our lives had been before the money ran out, before the treatments began to cost so much, before me at all.

Breaking the awkward silence, Jojo started back in, but this time, about the other issue that was gnawing at our twelve-year-old brains. "So, about Scroggs…"

"Yeah, when are we going over there?" Mags asked, seemingly happy to lift the darkness that she had created in the room.

My heart was relieved that we had something else to focus on besides me, and I decided that I would be better off focusing my time on clearing my friend's name than wallowing in this abyss of self-pity that I had created.

Let's be honest. Would I ever actually carry out these half-hearted attempts at ending it all? I highly doubted it. At least not when I had those two around to help hold me up and remind me what an asshole I could be.

"Look guys, I am telling ya, it wasn't him! He didn't have anything to do with those kids disappearing…" I began to beg, but was once again cut off by Jojo who, at that point had already begun belly crawling army-style back over to his chair to get ready to go eat.

"If it wasn't him, let's prove it then! I don't know what's worse though, knowing he did it or that he didn't."

"Why the hell would you say that?" a stunned Mags shot back in his direction towards the doorway.

"Think about it guys… if we can for sure say that we absolutely know it wasn't him, then that means someone else in the area is out there snatching kids. At least if it was Scroggs, we would know who to keep an eye on, who to watch out for. But if not him…. then what?"

Shivers crawled their way up my spine. It was a good point that none of us had thought of.

Chapter 7:
Do You Know Redemption?

I had spaced out there for a little bit while telling my boys the edited version of the tree incident as we rode along in the car. I decided to go over my notecards again one more time. The boys had retreated in their seats, once again staring down at their phones, one drooling over whatever the newest gaming system was while the other was aimlessly scrolling through his socials, a little perturbed that we were cutting into his social time and still a little salty that he was going to miss a birthday party this evening for one of his best friends down by the beach at one of their favorite hangouts, the Gator Shack.

Just thinking about the old shack made me smile, and my wife caught a glimpse of it. "What are you over there grinning about?" she questioned playfully, the toe of her high-heeled shoe playfully reaching across and nudging me in the shin.

"Just looking over my notes and thinking about good old Scroggs," I half lied, which was a good enough answer for her as she buried her nose back into her book.

Staring at my notecards seemed pointless, as I knew

what was on them by heart. I knew what I wanted to say, what I needed to say in order to get the Foundation recognized by the higher circles so our funding wouldn't run dry. Instead, I stared blankly at them, letting the voices of my childhood lull me back to the time we thought we had good old Scroggs right where we needed him to be.

It had been a couple of weeks after the tree incident and my poor mama was finally letting me back out of the house a little more, mostly just to get to and from school, but she seemed to be okay with me leaving to hang out with Jojo and Mags as long as I didn't stay out too long.

I knew which days of the week the old man walked up to town for his weekly supplies and pretty much knew the schedule of when he and Pencil Man went shrimping or fishing. We were on the bus heading out for the big choral field trip to the local community college when we hatched our plan.

Scroggs should have been heading into town that afternoon for his supplies because he didn't like to do that on the weekend when all of the old biddies would be off work doing their shopping. He always chose to do his shopping on either Wednesday or Thursday afternoon after school was out, but before people were off work. He would stop by to talk with Pencil Man about their upcoming fishing plans along the way. (I had watched this same pattern quite a few times the previous couple of months and couldn't see why he would suddenly break it.)

We had decided that we would all just be hanging outside together, riding bikes around the trailer court until we saw him walk on by. Then, we knew we would have about forty-five minutes or so to snoop around.

"Now Jojo, with your wheels, I don't think you would

be able to make it around very good on the inside of his narrow singlewide, so I was thinkin' you could wait outside as a lookout and Mags and I will run inside," I explained on the bus as we rode along. Mags and I were in the seat behind Jojo, who had a larger space where his wheelchair snapped into place for safety. "Cool, cool, man. Yeah, I can do that. But how ya'll gonna get inside?" Jojo questioned, just as we were pulling into the college.

"Scroggs has a key right under his doormat. I've seen him grab it before when he comes home from shopping. I'm sure it's there. It always is."

"Okay, that sounds good. But what exactly are we looking for?" Mags asked as the bus came to a grinding stop, the air brakes squealing to a halt.

"Anything that proves he didn't do it, I guess," was all I could think of to say.

"Or anything that proves he did!" Jojo rebutted with a sly grin.

We waited for everyone in the class to get off the bus before we attempted it too, since getting Jojo off was a lengthier process involving opening the door on the side of the bus and releasing the ramp for his chair. As we were waiting for our turn, the kids all filed by, chattering on about the field trip and how grateful they all were about being out of regular classes for the day. There was a brief moment when my stomach was in knots, though, as Turk and his buddies waltzed on by.

"Hey kid, good thing you kept your freaky little mouth shut," he snidely said under his breath as he walked by, stopping long enough to ask Mags if she wanted to go ahead of him. "I'm good," was all she responded, and he kept on walking. I noticed that as he got off the bus, he paused for a second, staring back at the bus as if he were stunned that she had turned him down, yet again. There was a secret satisfaction that I carried with me that day because of that.

We made our way off the bus and into the big auditorium where we watched a musical that the college kids produced, followed by a presentation that was intended to nudge us into the arts when we made it to high school and then hopefully, enroll at the community college where we could be part of the choral department. It wasn't anything memorable, but it was an afternoon that we got to sit in an air-conditioned auditorium and miss math class, so I was happy to go.

After the program was over, we had a little break time to head over to the cafeteria before getting on the bus. Along the way, we walked through the main hall, which housed a couple of community bulletin boards and trophy cases. I hadn't paid much attention to them on our way to grab our sacked lunch, which consisted of a bruised apple, foil-lined cup of apple juice, jelly sandwich, and bag of chips, but I sure as hell remember what I noticed on the way back to the bus.

Standing in front of the bulletin boards while trying to peel the unrelenting foil from the little plastic cup of juice, I noticed a flier stuck to one of the boards. It was a picture of a kid who had gone missing, none other than Bradley James himself. That wasn't the interesting part, though. The thing that made me just about drop my sack lunch right then and there and almost piss myself at the same time was that the photo of the kid was familiar. I had seen it somewhere before in a different context. "Jesus Christ!" I muttered beneath my breath… that was the same kid that

I had seen in the photos at Scroggs' trailer. I was sure of it! After glancing quickly around at other fliers, including ones for lost dogs, a couple in need of a babysitter, and a free STD testing flier from the local health department, I saw a couple of other missing kid fliers too, mostly older fliers that had been buried over time beneath the newer ones. I quickly looked at six different fliers, all boys aged sixteen and seventeen, except the one that I recognized from Scroggs' place. That kid was only fourteen.

Scroggs sure as hell wasn't going to make this easy on me as far as trying to clear his name. In fact, standing there staring at the fliers with the possibility of what he had done swirling around in my head, I had even begun to doubt him myself. That was until I saw a familiar name in the trophy case next to the bulletin board.

I had to blink a couple of times to be sure that what I was seeing was true. There, on a plaque that sat on a shelf directly beneath the division football trophies, wrestling tournament titles, and blue-ribbon school award, was a bronze plate plaque. It was set in a dark walnut wood and leaned against the back of the cabinet next to a bronze medal that was nestled into a dusty blue velvet presentation case.

The plaque was etched with the title, "Educator or the Year" and the medal was emblazoned with the bold, flashy words of "Civil Courage Prize." Both had a name attached to it that I had come to know all too well. These awards had been given to none other than the questionable Mr. Scroggs.

"Jesus Christ…" I breathlessly muttered, staring into the dusty glass case, my mouth flapping open as only my own reflection peered back at me. How in the hell had a man who had obviously taught for years in this little town, and had even been awarded this medal for courage, fallen so far down the pecking order of society? Why did people now fear him and whisper as he passed by? It appeared to me, at least in my then sixth grade brain, that Scroggs had obviously been a well-respected and esteemed teacher at one point in his life. So, what changed? What had to have happened for his community to do such an about-face and now hold him at such an arm's length away, only to be passed by and be paid such little-to-no attention?

Squinting, I also saw a framed article that sat proudly among the trophies in the case, encased in a thin dark walnut frame. It appeared to be an article from the local paper when the award for the Civil Courage Prize was given. There was an old black-and-white photo of a younger Scroggs set against the backdrop of a fishing pier and the ocean raging in high tide behind him. He was grinning in the photo, the creases in his face only appearing around his eyes and his small smile. He had been a much younger man when the article was written. Although the wording had faded with time, my young and hungry eyes were still able to read most of the article.

The Civil Courage Prize was for an act of courage and humanitarianism. At the time, Scroggs had been a professor at the community college and there had been issues in that part of Florida at the time with some drug cartels moving in from Cuba and trying to take control of the shipping industry, leading to many young people having no other way to make a living than to be forced into a life working beneath the cartels. They would help load barges down with hidden kilos of cocaine and heroin, or push black market weapons into the streets. These younger kids would be lured into this dark underbelly of Florida with promises of wealth and protection, and many of the kids who joined didn't have much of a home life, so the protection aspect for them felt like home. So many kids at the time were products of single parent households whose parent was working multiple jobs just to survive, often leaving the kids to fend for themselves. Let's be honest here. Society doesn't slow down with struggles. In fact, when people are struggling, spending most of their time focusing on making money and getting ahead, it's the kids who suffer, the children who are forgotten. They become faceless ghosts running alone around town, not even garnering so much as a pitiful glance from families who haven't had the misfortune of struggling. This is when the ghosts that roam the streets alone at night are sought out by the monsters that slide effortlessly out of the Glades, offering these kids the promises of cash, cars, and a way to make it to the next level in life, even when that meant walking right into a dangerous shitstorm of darkness controlled by forces more powerful than they could ever imagine. They couldn't have known the true dangers; they didn't know who to fear.

The article continued to lightly touch on Scroggs' position on the war against the cartel, commending him for his work in launching a foundation called "Jake's Way Home," which paid homage to his son who had gotten caught up in the dark, soulless underbelly of street life when Scroggs was still teaching after his wife passed away. The article spoke gently of Jake, a once well-thought-of kid, and his journey into the streets when he found himself with too much time on his hands after his mama had passed away and Mr. Scroggs had taken to spending more hours at school and more away from home… and Jake. Jake got himself entangled in a local street gang and too soon discovered that there would be no way out. Jake had lost his life one night when he was supposed to do a drug drop with a known gang acquaintance at a local mini mart and was shot by rival gang members. The poor kid had lay in the gutter alone and bleeding out, until a local fisherman had stopped at the mart to grab ice and smokes and, seeing Jake, called the cops. The fisherman then sat with Jake, cradling the young kid's head in his lap as they waited for the police to arrive.

Despondent over the loss of his only son, Scroggs had vowed to fight these gangs and help strengthen his community. He started the Foundation, hell-bent on doing what he could to keep his local students off the streets and out of the long-reaching, gnarly grasp of the local cartel and gangs.

What's more, the article went on to say how Scroggs was awarded the Civil Courage Prize for his acts of Bravery and Humanitarianism for leading his newly formed foundation right into the mouth of hell, brokering actual meetings with the lead kingpin of that sect of the Cuban cartel, negotiating the release of a few local kids from their grip. In turn, he arranged legal deals between the cartel and local restaurants to buy shrimp and fish solely from the cartel's fishermen. It seemed to me that Scroggs had been a badass at one time, figuring out how to pay off the cartel in order to save some kids from ending up like his own son.

"Pretty damn cool, Scroggs!" I spoke to my own reflection in the glass when I had finished reading the framed article. I was staring blankly at the medal in the case when Mags spoke from somewhere behind me. It was lunchtime at the college and the hordes of passing students had caused a low roar to vibrate all the way down the hallways, making it hard to hear what she had said.

"Bus is leaving soon, man, we gotta go!" she impatiently shouted, waving her brightly colored pink nails in my direction.

"Mags, come here, read this!" I tried to convince her, but she seemed too antsy to slow down.

"Tell me about it on the way! Come on, we gotta go!" she shouted back, spinning around as she headed back towards the main entrance where the bus was parked. I dropped what was left of my lunch into the trash bin by the door and chased after her. (I already had enough to worry about as far as what everyone thought of me… I wasn't planning to add to the fire by having people watch me try to eat on the bus. Because of my annoying OCD lately, just eating had become a whole process of using hand sanitizer, making sure that I tried to eat things directly out of the wrapper without even my own hands touching the food, and God forbid if anyone was talking or breathing anywhere near my food, slathering their hot breath and germs all over it.) No, I just didn't need the hassle of drawing more attention to myself, so I ditched my food and hurried back to the bus, my belly already hollow and grumbling.

Catching up to Mags, I began to ramble on about what I had seen in the trophy case and Scroggs' awards. I was in the middle of expressing how impressed I was by Scroggs when she stopped me.

"Dude, Scroggs may have been good shit back in the day, but that doesn't mean he isn't capable of doing bad stuff now. You haven't been around here for long; you haven't seen the things that we have seen. I'm telling ya, it's better to just leave that man to his own doings and just stay away from his place. I don't think he is someone that you want to find yourself tangled up with," Mags said over her shoulder as she climbed the steps onto the bus.

I followed her, walking right past Jojo who had already taken his seat towards the front and strapped his wheelchair into place. He had been spun around in his space and was flirting with Monica Judd, who was sitting right across the aisle from him. Jojo had it bad for Monica, and never missed an opportunity to talk to her. As I passed by, I heard him laughing and once again telling one of his old surfing stories, causally throwing in some crap about almost being bitten by a shark. Trying to stifle my laughter, I just grinned and walked right on by, grabbing the empty space next to Mags instead. The brown pleather seat was dang hot. Mags had already jumped up to lower our window, trying to get any air movement that she could to make its way into the stifling bus that was already too crowded with kids.

Sitting back down now, Mags asked me what it was that I had seen in that trophy case anyway. As the engine of the bus roared to life and we pulled away from the curb, I told her everything I could remember about the awards, Mr. Scroggs being an esteemed teacher, and his involvement with the community, fighting against the dark side of the streets that were slowly moving into the area, preying on kids our age. Oddly, she still didn't seem overly impressed.

"Look, I'm not saying that Scroggs hasn't done some good for this town in the past. I'm not saying that at all. I'm just saying that things have a way of happening and he seems to be caught smack dab in the middle of them a lot of the time. I just don't think he's who you are hoping he is..." she trailed off, fishing around in her backpack for her hand sanitizer and lip balm. (It was raspberry flavored, by the way. Strange, the tiny things that you remember.)

Watching Mags apply her lip balm and then sweep her long hair up into the elastic binder she usually wore on her right wrist, my young self thought briefly about what it might be like to kiss her. I was crushing pretty hard on that girl, almost as much as Jojo was crushing on Monica Judd, who, at the time, I could hear over in the next seat giggling about whatever story Jojo had just told. "Here," Mags said. "Hand sani! God knows how many germs were creeping around in that school. I mean, God, imagine where all of their hands have been." She turned towards me, extending her little bottle of hand sanitizer and waiting for me to stick my hand out. She was a girl after my own heart. As we sat rubbing the hand sanitizer into our hands, Jojo paused with flirting just long enough to shout out over his seat, "So, we goin' over to Scroggs' place or what?"

Miss Monica Judd had overheard and begged to know where we were going and why. When I felt that Jojo was just about to say too much, I interrupted, shouting, "Yeah man, that works. You wanna head there tonight?"

Mags jumped in to offer her two cents. "I really don't see the point. I mean, what are you hoping to find? What could you possibly find that would convince you..." but her words were interrupted as something had been launched from somewhere in the back of the bus and landed on my thigh. Giggling could be heard from a couple of seats behind me as I looked down to see that a semi fresh dog turd had managed to make its way onto my lap. Anxiety and sheer terror began to fester in my belly the minute I saw that filthy dog turd sitting on my bare skin. I was trying my best to hold my shit together in front of everyone, in front of Mags.

Maybe it wasn't me who was supposed to be the target. Maybe it was an accident, and some other poor kid was supposed to be the butt of the joke. Just as I was trying to convince myself of that half-assed thought, another turd was launched, pinging me in the back of the head, making me dry heave.

"Are you gonna cry, you big baby? Let's hear the baby cry!" I heard the sinister voice of Turk taunting from a few seats behind me. I'm not sure why that asshole took to making me feel miserable all the time, but I knew that if I responded, he would be getting exactly what he wanted.

"Cut it out, Turk!" Jojo hollered out from the front row, fully aware that his wheelchair had made him pretty much off limits as far as an ass-kicking was concerned. I mean, even as kids, you had to be a pretty big asshole to hit a guy in a wheelchair, and Jojo knew it.

"Oh, come on, what's the freak gonna do about it besides cry? Are you crying yet ya big baby? It's just a dog turd. A fresh turd, by the way. Lighten up, it's just a joke, man." Turk shouted back from behind us, fully loving the attention he was getting when the other kids on the bus would snicker and laugh as well.

For my part, I just froze, embarrassed as all hell sitting on that hot school bus next to the cutest twelve-year-old that I had ever met, willing myself not to cry. Here I had been trying to just make it through the days unnoticed, because unnoticed was normal. Unnoticed was easy. But no, I had somehow still remained on Turk's radar, and he wasn't about to let me get by day to day just feeling somewhat normal. He got a kick out of calling me out, embarrassing me, and reminding me that once again, I didn't belong. I was the freak, the outcast.

As another dog turd was relentlessly tossed my way, this one with more force, hitting me hard enough in the back of the head to make a pretty good thud of a noise, the back of the bus began to roar with laughter. I hung my head in a fit of hot embarrassment and just closed my eyes.

I could feel the tears welling up in my eyes and the suffocating feeling of being trapped, causing me to catch my breath. The darkness had begun to shroud my soul once again, reminding me that I wasn't normal, I wasn't average, and that I was still an outcast. It didn't matter how many schools I transferred to, or how many friends I tried to make. I would always be different. I would always feel out of place.

These childhood memories are what would haunt my nightmares for years to come, even after the hormone therapy worked, even after I became successful, even after I had my own family. The things you are put through as a kid stay with you forever. The feeling of sitting on those hot pleather seats that day with my eyes pinched tight, feeling as if the whole world was mocking me, laughing at me, still finds me at night when I am trying to relax or when my mind begins to wander.

These types of memories from my childhood had propelled my wanting to die, convincing my confused adolescent brain that my tender and broken heart didn't deserve to beat in this world anymore. That I was no longer enough.

Too many times I had wanted it all to end, wanted to just be seen as normal, and not wanted to be put through hell on a day-to-day basis anymore. These kids were no different than the other kids at other schools in other towns. Kids are just awful towards each other and always had been. When you are the one being picked on, it feels like the loneliest place on earth… that there is no way out of the darkness.

I would like to be able to say that I was strong that day, that I was able to retaliate or stand up for myself in some way. But that's not what happened. What happened was, even though I had tried my hardest not to cry, hot tears burned a trail down my cheeks as I sat hunched over in my seat, my anxiety choking my chest and my brain going into overdrive trying to think of any way that I could just kill myself when I got home that day so all the anguish would end. I sat there blocking out the taunting by picturing myself slitting my wrists, stabbing myself in the chest, throwing myself from my mama's moving car, swimming out too far into the ocean… I just wanted it all to end. I craved the silence, the calmness. But then…

In the darkness that I had hurled myself into for protection, someone reached in to pull me back. As we sat there on that hot old bus, the skin on our legs sticking to the warm and unforgiving faded green vinyl on the seats, patiently counting the turns that the driver made, knowing how close we were to getting back home, I felt a clammy hand clamp down on my thigh and give it a squeeze. She didn't say a word. In fact, when I pried one of my eyes open, I noticed that she wasn't even looking at me, she spared me that embarrassment of eye-to-eye contact. I looked down again at my leg, where Mags had grabbed my thigh, tethering me to this world. She didn't move. She said nothing. But for those last five miles as we drove back towards the school, she made it known, her hand never moving, that I was okay. That she was there, and we would be alright.

Chapter 8:
Do You Know Statistics?

Mags still didn't quite understand what my need was to clear Scroggs' name, or why I had such an unwavering urge to get into his house and see what else I could find out. But she at least agreed to come with me. The plan was that Jojo would stand guard at the front door and I would be left alone to explore the house by myself. That was the thing about Mags. She was always ready to walk the line with me, even if she didn't understand the urgency, even if she may not have agreed with what I was taking a stand for or how I was going about doing it. She was, simply put, loyal.

We waited until Scroggs left, heading down to do whatever the hell it was that he and the Pencil Man would do in the Glades under the dark, creepy veil of night. Although we had been intending on going ahead with our little surveillance earlier in the afternoon, something had held Scroggs up, and he hadn't left earlier as we had hoped, so we returned, reluctantly in the late afternoon, knowing that evening was fast approaching and none of us wanted to be in his place in the dark. I had hoped he had just gone fishing, and that would keep him away long after the sun went down. Whether that was what he was doing, (he claimed nighttime in the Glades was the best time to fish for snook and largemouth bass, especially when the moon was full because the fish would come closer to the surface to feed under the bright light of the moon), or what the old biddies in town whispered he may have been doing, *("Doris, did you see old man Scroggs heading out to the Glades again with that other creepy man, probably going out there to feed more bodies to the hungry crocs so they don't get caught?")* we really had no way to tell.

Hiding behind a shed a few trailers over, Mags, Jojo and I sat for a good twenty minutes or so, watching his trailer for signs of movement, impatiently waiting for him to leave, and yet nervously hoping that he didn't at the same time. We were kids for Christ sakes... we were just as scared of getting caught as we were scared of what we may find in his lonely trailer.

The high-pitched drone of the mating cicadas and katydids in the trees became almost deafening when set as the backdrop of my own racing heartbeat. I wanted to puke. I wanted to run. I wanted to just go home. But we stayed, me watching the trailer intently while picking at the cracked dirt beneath my feet with a small stick out of boredom, sitting in a squatted position for so long that my toes began to go numb.

"Damn it!" I blurted out to my nervous crew when the realization of what time it was suddenly dawned on me. I reached into my jacket pocket for the syringe that I had thankfully remembered to grab as I was sneaking out the door from home. I hadn't intended to introduce my new friends to the insane medication schedule and expose myself to them so early on for what I was, a freak in my mind. At the same time, that syringe held my shot of normalcy, the only way that I could force my bones to thrive and grow. So, pride be damned, as soon as my fingers graced the auto injector's lid, and after a mini pause of hesitation, I grabbed it and started to unscrew the safety cap.

Seemingly horrified, the two of them stared at me with their eyes as wide as saucers in the glow of the haunting full moon, neither of them saying a word as I lifted my sweaty T-shirt to expose my belly, pinching a mound of flesh on the side and quickly holding my breath while I forcibly stabbed myself with the pen, injecting the magic potion that I had convinced myself would fix all of my problems.

Whether it was the heat, the fear, the anxiety, or a sloppy combination of all three, I immediately began to feel lightheaded and nauseous. After quickly recapping the injector pen and sliding it back into my pocket, I dropped to a seated position on my butt, leaning forward and letting my head rest on my folded knees. A cold sweat immediately began to trickle from my brow, and I felt the nape of my neck begin to pulse. The tunnel vision effect was nothing new to me, so I slowed my breathing and closed my eyes, trying to relax.

Still, they said nothing. We sat that way in silence for what felt like an eternity, me humiliated and just focusing on my own breath, because who the hell passes out when giving themselves their own injections? The two of them continued sitting right by my side, not speaking, just waiting for an explanation for which I couldn't find the words. I was terrified that this would be the end of our journey, that seeing me like this would put me in a category of weird that was even too much for them to handle.

As I sat there, terrified of their response, searching quickly for the words that would make what had just happened seem less odd, being pissed at myself for not remembering to take the damn injection before I got there, I felt a hand on my back that gently began making soothing circular patterns. Slowly, I turned my face towards my left to see that it was Mags who had scooted a little closer, still focused on staring down the street. In fact, Jojo was on the other side of her, intently lost in his gaze as well. Stunned, I said nothing. Instead, I glanced towards the trailer we were supposed to be watching like hawks scavenging for prey, and set my head back down on my knees, calmly waiting for the sick feeling to pass, and grateful that I had somehow managed to find a couple of friends whose lives had already turned them into such outcasts, such misfits, that they thought nothing of my oddities, my medical issues, or my weaknesses. I had found my tribe.

"There he goes!" Jojo whispered in excitement from his chair on wheels, as he reached down to release his brake.

The hand on my back stopped making circles and only the warmth of her skin remained on my sweaty shirt. Even today, I am able to will my mind to take me back to that moment, the feeling of belonging, the feeling of attachment, the first time I knew that Mags was going to be a bigger player in my story for a long time. The phantom feeling of her hand on my back would guide me through many skin jabs after that. She would become a driving force that kept me going every time I felt fearful.

Mags and I stood, slowly following Jojo towards

Scroggs' trailer, trying not to look obvious as we quietly crept along. Looking back, I have to laugh at that now, because how the hell couldn't we look obvious? A kid in a tricked-out wheelchair slowly rolling along with a couple of other middle school kids in tow, lurking around in the darkness. Somehow, no one saw us, or at least no one had bothered to rat us out that night.

Scroggs' place had a couple of steps leading up to the front porch of the trailer, so Jojo sat at the bottom step, innocently keeping watch and looking a thousand percent suspicious. Had anyone seen him just casually hanging out there, we for sure would have been outed, but, once again, either no one had paid any attention, or no one cared.

Making our way to the front door, the nervousness of what we were about to do crept back into my guts and I had to force the hot puke that was forming in my throat back down to my knot-twisted belly. For her part, Mags seemed as cool as could be, grabbing the screen door first, flinging it open, then putting her fingers on the old, worn, bronze doorknob and giving it a twist.

The door had been left unlocked, to our amazement, and we slinked our way inside. Stepping over the threshold, I whisper-shouted over my shoulder back at Jojo, "If you see him coming back, make some noise!" I didn't even wait for his response as I shut the door behind us.

We left the lights off, of course, but mercifully, Scroggs tended to leave on the overhead light above his kitchen sink so he could see as he was coming and going in the middle of the night. The trailer was small enough that the little light gave an eerie glow to the living room and dining area. Only the back of his trailer sat in complete darkness, its secrets tucked away behind faded hollow core doors which would always remain shut.

We stepped lightly around the living room, looking at his shelves of books and trinkets. Knocking over a small wooden humidor, cigars rolled off one of the shelves and onto the floor. Mags picked them up one by one and set them back in place. Before she placed the last one, she rolled it around in her fingers and pulled it up to her nose, taking a big sniff of the cigar. "Hmmmm, smells like the kind my granddad smokes," she said before placing it lovingly back in the box.

Mags didn't poke around much in the place. She just kind of tagged along with me, looking over my shoulder at what I may find. She did, however, find Scroggs' collection of books and comics pretty amazing and stood in awe for a while as she glanced it over, lightly running her finger over the spines of the titles that graced the shelves.

The trailer smelled exactly how I remembered it, an intoxicating smell of cigars, aftershave, and a homemade cleaner that smelled of witch hazel and lemon. Although a clear hoarder of books and mementos, Scroggs had a method to his madness. Everything in his place was clean and organized, even if the organization meant bookcases stacked next to bookcases of his favorite titles, or stacks upon stacks of old newspaper clippings. As a widower, his home still carried the stale remnants of a life gone by. The small trinkets of his late wife's life had been left behind, and the photos of his past life still scattered every shelf and wall.

"Hey, look at this!" Mags hissed at me from the opposite side of the bookshelf. She had happened upon the same photo I had previously seen, the one of the kid in the ball uniform.

"Do you know who that kid is? Does he look familiar?" I asked, hoping she wouldn't have some horrible tale to connect to the old photo.

"Actually, no. He doesn't look familiar at all. It looks like an older photo though, so maybe it's from quite a while ago?" Mags whispered, returning to look for whatever she might find on the shelf.

I walked towards the other side of the living room where Scroggs had restacked some piles of newspaper clippings. It was hard to read much in the dim light from the kitchen, even with the moonlight that was pouring in through the windows. But I was at least able to make out the photos in the articles. They were all articles about young kids, kids our age, and all boys. At first, I debated showing them to Mags, fearful that she may be able to connect the dots from those pictures to some awful tales that had been going around town for years. I didn't want the whispers of him to be true, to know that my beloved fellow oddball had something sinister to hide. I just wanted to clear his name and get my friends off my back about stopping by and visiting with him. I wanted to prove that being an oddball didn't make you something to be feared.

I didn't have to make the decision to show her or hide them from her, because within a few seconds of finding the newspaper clippings and standing there debating what I should do, she was right next to me, looking over my shoulder.

"Who are they?" she asked, reaching forward to thumb through one of the stacks.

"I don't know. They just look like newspaper articles about baseball games, point standings in basketball, awards that some of these kids have gotten. I don't see any of the articles that I thought I had seen when I was here last time. These just don't look like anything exciting..." I trailed off, pawing through another stack of paper. Although I didn't say it out loud, something in my brain clicked. Something felt off in that moment. I knew what I had seen when I was here before. I knew I had seen articles about missing kids and different pictures, but now everything had been organized differently, things had been removed, laid out differently, almost as if he had known we would be coming.

It was a strange frustration because on one hand, I wanted more than anything to clear his name and not have to worry about what he may or may not be up to. But on the other hand, as Mags had warned us, if he wasn't the one causing all the malice that had taken place in this little town, who else should we be paying closer attention to? Who else should we fear without even knowing it?

It has been said that every average person will pass by thirty-six murderers in their lifetime. That's a number that always freaks me out. I mean, how are you supposed to know who to fear? "Hey, look at these!" Mags whispered, leaning over towards me again, her warm breath on my cheek and the phantom feeling of her hand on my back once again lulling me into a false sense of security, making me forget momentarily what we were doing there in the first place.

I leaned over towards her to get a better look at what she had found. It was an old album, kind of like a photo album, but for larger documents. It looked very ornate and was bound in a heavy dark leather, held closed with thick leather straps that were buckled by the coolest little bronze clasp. Unclasping the buckle and flipping through the pages, we discovered that the eerie looking book was nothing more than Mr. Scroggs' teaching certifications, licenses, and degrees that he had amassed throughout the years. He had been a highly awarded teacher for many years, so at what point did his community turn so darkly against him? There was something that we weren't connecting, something that we were missing. But what? And really, did I want to dig any deeper?

"So, he was a teacher for a long time," Mags began, the wheels in her brain also starting to spin. "But at some point, after his wife died, he must have stopped teaching… and then what? What changed for him? What did he really do to make this town turn on him? I just don't know, Jett. There's really nothing important here and I'm not sure where else we should be looking. I mean, all we have found are some articles of these kids which… hey!" She stopped mid- sentence, her mind rolling along faster than her mouth could keep up. "Maybe the articles of the kids were students, and he was just proud of them, proud that he had taught them? I mean, he did get those teaching awards that you saw on display over at the college, right? That would make sense."

I nodded my head in agreement while shrugging my shoulders, relieved that she hadn't seen anything else that would connect Scroggs to something dark or sinister, something that the people in this town had associated him with for so long. But there was still an uneasy feeling about this. I didn't tell her that night that so many things seemed to be missing from his trailer, things that were on full display when I had been in there before and were now nowhere to be found. I didn't tell her that I now had more questions than I had answers for. I didn't breathe a word of that. I didn't have time to because it was right about then that Mags zipped back over to the other side of the living room and picked up the framed picture of the young boy.

"This is the only picture that's framed. All the pictures of the other kids are just clippings and stories and awards from the newspapers. But this one is framed. It must mean something, right?" she asked, holding the framed photo at eye level now, trying to make sense of what she was looking at. She flipped the frame over and began to pry off the little clips that held the backing in place.

Nervous now, I questioned her. "Mags, don't wreck it. We can't get caught. What the heck are you doing?"

"Calm down. My ma always writes my name and the date on the back of my school pictures, especially the ones we hand out to other people, or at least my name and how old I was," she reasoned, which made absolute sense to me, too. She finished prying off the clips and slid the cardboard backing and the photo out of the frame. Flipping them over in the dim light of the moon, she tried to decipher the loopy handwriting that was there, just as she had figured it would be.

All the air escaped my lungs, and the walls of the trailer began to spin as I heard her read out the name on the back of the photo. I hadn't known then just what importance that name would hold later in my life.

"My God," she began, "I had no idea… but I suppose it makes sense…" she started as I was getting antsy with hesitation, hanging on to her every word with wild abandon, my heart throttling my breastbone.

"It says Scroggs. Jacob Scroggs, age 15. He has a son!"

His son. I hadn't thought of Scroggs as a family man.

Then I remembered the article I had seen about Jake in the trophy case the day of the field trip and realized I'd forgotten to mention it to Mags when we were coming home on the bus that day in all of the hustle. I had Scroggs wedged in my mind as a lonely, misunderstood widower that the town liked to gossip about… a man who just kept to himself. A father was something I hadn't imagined him being until I had seen the article on the field trip. After all, there were no other photos of this kid, of his family adorning the walls or shelves of Scroggs' home, no other evidence that this kid ever existed. Maybe someday, I would be able to ask him about it.

"So, there is nothing here that leads us to believe that Scroggs has ever done the things that the town accuses him of? No evidence that he has ever been anything more than a teacher, husband and dad, right?"

"Well, I suppose so. But, Jett, there is still something eerie about the old guy. I think you should still keep your distance," Mags whispered as she firmly tucked the photo back into its frame and secured the clips to the back again.

"I wonder what really happened to his son?" I asked, not expecting the answer that she quickly fired back.

"Why do you think anything happened to him Jett? Sometimes people just die for no reason," Mags said, no emotion hiding behind her serious words. It struck me as odd, because I hadn't yet told her what I had read in the article, that he was killed because of the darkened path on which he had become entangled. What had led her to jump to the conclusion that he was dead and not just out of the picture?

I was trying to come up with a clever answer for her when we heard Jojo's voice all too loudly from the front porch. "Hi, sir! Just stopping by to see if you want to support the local robotics team? We are trying real hard to make it to state this year!"

A familiar raspy voice fired right back in a questioning tone, "A little late in the day to be stopping house to house, don't you think?" came the voice of Scroggs, along with heavy footsteps as he made his way up the steps to his trailer, passing right by our trusty lookout. My heart was in my throat as I heard the screen door open. Mags and I darted for the back door beyond the dining table that led out to a little cement slab, lined with potted tomato and pepper plants that Scroggs enjoyed tending to.

"I know, sir, but I had homework to finish up before I could make my rounds. That's okay, I can come back another time, no problem," a nervous Jojo could be heard saying as Scroggs grabbed on to the old door handle and flung the door wide open.

"No, no, that's just fine. I was heading out to fish and realized that I had forgotten my fishing license and had to circle back home. Let me grab you some cash. Hang on, boy."

Mags and I carefully slid out the back door and slowly latched the door shut a mere few seconds before Scroggs entered the trailer flipping the living room light on. We were that close to being found out, a hair's space away from being exposed. It was exhilarating! We ran over to the side of the trailer that was closest to where Jojo was now waiting and collapsed to the ground, trying to stifle the wild giggles that were emanating from our bellies. The relief of not finding anything of merit within the walls of Scroggs' trailer, combined with the comedic scene that was playing out in front of our eyes with Jojo and Scroggs had our emotions running on high.

For his part, Jojo was trying to make his lie stick, patiently waiting for Scroggs to come back to the front door with some cash. I whistled over from where I was sitting to let him know all was good, that we'd made it out unscathed. He quickly glanced over and grinned, then focused back on Scroggs as he emerged once again from his trailer to give him some cash for his "robotic team fundraiser." No one was going to say no to a kid in a wheelchair just based on principle alone, but Scroggs still had to have questioned why he was actually there… must have wondered what the hell was actually going on. But he didn't act like it. He simply handed Jojo some money, leaned in and whispered something to him, and started back down the street with his pole again, whistling as he meandered along.

Jojo reversed his chair and wheeled himself slowly over to where we were crouched against the side of the trailer, ensuring Scroggs had turned the corner before he spoke to us. "Dang, you guys, that was too freaking close, like WAY too close. What did you guys find?"

"What did Scroggs say to you?" I blurted out, the excitement too much and the feeling too high from the adrenalin that was now boldly coursing through my already weakened veins. For his part, Jojo just looked at me quizzically. "He said he had forgotten his license and had circled back home, said that he would run in and get me some money," Jojo answered, unapologetically leaving out the ending.

"No, Jojo, not that. When he was getting ready to go after he handed you the money, he leaned into you and whispered something. What did he say? Are we outed?

Does he know?" I questioned again, curious as to why my friend was leaving out this part of the conversation that I had clearly witnessed.

"My dude, no he didn't. He literally handed me the money, told me to get home, and walked away," a perplexed looking Jojo answered, the blatant lie on his face. I felt my stomach churning, like I had entered a nightmare that I wanted to escape. I began trying to sort it all out in my head, questioning why Jojo would be lying to me and what it was that he was trying to hide.

Frustrated, I turned back towards Mags to ask her what she had heard, to ensure that I wasn't losing my mind. Surely, she had seen with her own eyes what I had seen. Surely, she would want to question Jojo to get to the truth as well. But as I turned my head her way, the most unexpected and mind-blowing thing happened to my already irritated and confused preteen-aged self… Magdalene D'Andrea leaned in and shut me up by kissing me. My first kiss. The kiss to end all kisses and the one that made me forget all the questions I had about that night.

For the first time in my life, I felt like an average teenaged kid, doing normal teenaged kid stuff as I stood there that hot Florida night beneath the light of the moon as Mags' soft raspberry lip-balm-flavored lips pressed against mine.

"Awe geez, guys, gross…." Jojo laughed and began to roll away.

The kiss was short, and I was temporarily stunned as she pulled her face away and simply looked at me and said, "What a rush tonight was, right? Gotta get home, Jett! See you later!" And that was that. There I stood alone after she had taken off, too, standing on the side of Scroggs' trailer house wondering what the hell had just happened. Trying to sort out the events that had just unfolded, I decided that I didn't care. I knew Scroggs was no one to fear. I had been right about that. I still didn't get why Jojo was fibbing about Scroggs whispering to him, but I quickly forgot about that and focused on the hell of a kiss that Mags planted on me.

Unfortunately for me, it would be a few years and many adventures later before Mags would kiss me again. But I patiently waited for it.

Chapter 9:
Do You Know Pride?

Blinking wildly out of the limousine window, I recognized the old diner that we had just turned by, knowing that the event center was just a few miles ahead. Tucking my notecards back into my jacket pocket, I turned to see my boys now content and wildly coloring in a notebook.

"Almost there, kids! You guys want to start picking your things back up now? We'll be there in just a few minutes," I told them as my wife flung the lint roller into my lap.

"Is it that bad?" I asked, grinning at her from across the car.

Rolling her eyes and grinning, she shot back playfully, "Jett, we have two boys, two dogs and a very needy cat, so yeah, your tux is full of hair, crumbs and little boy goobers," she laughed, diving right back into her book before I got a reply in. Dutifully, I began to roll away all the lint, fuzz, hair, and food that had accumulated on my tux in the short space of time from when I got dressed to where I was now.

"It's important to look your best you know, lots of eyes

on you this evening, Jett," she spoke towards her book, intrigued by whatever words were dancing off the page, not even glancing my way. That was okay though. She didn't have to look at me. I froze momentarily to look at her, this stunning creature who I get to walk next to, who I get to have on my arm for all the world to see.

"I know dear," I began to agree, wickedly grinning at the object of my affection without her even so much as receiving the glance. "Looks matter. They set a precedent," I spoke towards her, mindlessly rolling the lint roller up and down my tuxedo jacket arms.

"Looks set a precedent" I echoed in my own brain, something that had been taught to me long ago beneath the helpful guise of Scroggs and the Pencil Man. *"To dress like you want to remain invisible, well, that only will do the exact opposite. My boy, what you need to do is look sharp, stand out, and let the world know that you are not one to be overlooked. You are not one to be easily forgotten. You, my boy, owe the world more than that. You owe your sweet mama more than that."*

It was my junior year of high school and I had just had another nasty run-in with the bully that never relented. Although Turk would fade in and out of my life throughout my middle and high school years, I would never know when his infatuation with Mags would ramp back up again or when his disdain for me would kick back in. That's not entirely true. Turk always seemed to get pleasure from insulting me and making me feel inadequate, but those feelings would ramp up whenever he would make a move on poor Mags and she would shoot him down, yet again. He would see me and Jojo hanging out with her, as we regularly did back in those days, and focus all his hostility towards me. I suppose when it came to Jojo, even the biggest of assholes wouldn't dare come after a kid with wheels for legs, no matter how much he also hated him, so it always made sense that I was the easier prey.

It was just another sticky Florida day when I showed up to Scroggs' trailer, fury burning through my veins and looking for a way to stand my ground against Turk. I had been harassed at school again, this time in the parking lot, right in front of everyone. It had been humiliating.

I had gotten a new car. (Not new, per se, but new to me. In reality, it was an older car, nothing special, and I had saved up for a couple of years to buy her. I was proud of that, to have gotten something on my own that I had truly worked for, and depended on no one to get it for me. I had been a big enough financial burden on the folks for so many years with my medical issues that the thought of asking them for a car had never even broached my mind.)

It was an older, white Chrysler LeBaron with a dent right above the rear right tire from a previous owner's brush with a supposed grocery cart. It was only driven in the south though, so there was no rust around the fenders like you would find in the north, where their harsh weather requires loads of salt to be laid down on the roads, causing massive erosion early on in the lives of their cars.

Although she had no rust, her burgundy interior had faded to a dull mauve from the years of Florida's harsh sun rays shining in. I didn't care though. It was mine. I was proud. I washed and waxed that thing every weekend and had just installed a new sound system, even if that just meant me installing a new speaker that hadn't blown out and updating the radio to one with a high-tech removable face that could even play my collection of older CDs. I loved that car. I was proud.

So, you have to imagine the embarrassment and pain I felt the day that class was over, and Mags and I were walking towards the parking lot after she had just turned down an invite from Turk to go to prom with him. We saw a crowd formed around where I had parked my car.

The first thing I saw was that asshole Turk's car parked right next to mine. It was no secret that the car he was driving wasn't exactly his, and that the cartel his mom was running with had Turk running small errands for them, delivering weapons and small batches of black tar heroin to buyers in the area. As a "thank you" or just to keep the kid intrigued and make him feel like he was part of a bigger family, they let him use this car. The car, a brand-new Dodge Stealth, black with a V-6 engine and not a spot on it, was too fast for a kid like that, obviously commanding attention and respect. The sick part about it was that he didn't even respect that poor car, much like he didn't respect most things in his life.

Walking out to the lot, there he sat, clad in blue jeans with metal rivets on the pockets, perched on top of the hood of the Stealth. My imagination began picturing the scrapes that he was grinding into her poor hood without even caring or realizing it. But that was not his concern. The spectacle, the show that he had orchestrated was my poor car, which now sat sadly on four deflated tires, no doubt thanks to Turk's switchblade, and a lip-sticked drawing of a dick on her hood. I knew the hood damage wasn't permanent and I could patch her tires for the short term, but it was the sheer embarrassment that he was after. He wanted a scene. He wanted me to cry.

But for too many years this bully had gotten the best of

me, everything from pushing me out of a damn tree and shoving me down in the hallways, to toilet-papering my locker and throwing dried dog turds at me. The taunting had been relentless, and I had reached my boiling point. I had learned how to reflect, learned how to be funny at my own expense in order to survive the hell that could be high school.

At the risk of looking like a fool if Mags had responded any differently, I looked around in the sea of laughter and dropped to one knee in front of her, much to the astonishment of Turk. "Mags," I shouted loud enough for all the surrounding crowd to hear, "Would you want to go to prom with this deflated dick?"

She didn't even laugh at the reference. She just smiled, gave a glare of death with a twinkle in her gorgeous green eyes over towards Turk, still perched atop the hood of his car, and replied equally loud enough for all to hear, "There is no one that I would rather go with!" and hugged me in front of everyone.

Turk was pissed. The audience began disbanding and the show of utter embarrassment that he had intended to create in order to soothe his own broken soul had crumbled around him. All he could do was slide into his car and take off, revving his souped-up engine as he did. I knew what I did had gotten to him. I knew that I had caused him pain. And I knew I would pay for it, yet. "Sorry about all that, Mags. You don't really have to go with me. I was just trying to get that asshole off my back. Really, Mags, you…" I began, but was interrupted by Mags kissing me again, for the first time in years, and this time like she really meant it.

"Shut up. I said I would go with you. Don't question

it. Wonder if Jojo is going? He really wanted to go with Monica. I wonder if he's gotten up the nerve to ask her yet?" she wondered, her arms now locked around my waist and staring slightly down at me right in the eyes. This girl was her own brand of crazy, a real force of nature not to be messed with, and I had always known it.

As horrible as the whole scene had been, as awful as Turk had made me feel, I gotta say that standing there in the parking lot with her hands around my waist as we leaned against the car and she spoke to me, made me feel so damn good. I didn't even realize until much later that she had been saving me, yet again. She stood like that, her hands around my waist, talking to me and looking me right in the eye, until almost all the kids had left the lot. Then, as if on cue, she dropped her arms, stepped back, and asked if I wanted a ride so I could let my mom know what was up and grab the jack and tools to get my wheels off so they could be patched. I happily climbed into her granddad's old Ford truck, and we took off. It wasn't the first time that Mags had shielded me from pain and embarrassment, and it for damn sure wouldn't be the last.

After I patched the tires and washed the lipstick dick off the hood of my poor car, I first tried to clear my head and went out to the docks, bumping into Pencil Man himself, not saying much, just helping him unravel his fishing nets. His long slender fingers worked quickly, and I imagined that he only used his sense of feel to know when his nets or lines were being tugged on. It was always a mystery to me how that man operated, yet he never did ask for or need help from anyone in this world. And for whatever reason, there wasn't a soul in that town who would ever say one cross word about him… unlike poor Mr. Scroggs.

He let me sit next to him in the warm evening sun on the shrimping dock and blissfully didn't have much to say. I just sat next to him, gazing out at the glistening ripples that danced on the surface of the water, trying to cool my rage and focus on something, anything that would help me calm down and focus on what came next. Jesus. Prom. Had I just done that? Did I seriously just poke the bear and ask Mags to prom right in front of Turk? I grinned a little at that thought. It was either the bravest or stupidest thing I had ever done, but just like always, Mags didn't waiver and played her part. Whether she really wanted to go with me to prom, or she agreed to it just to get me out of the pickle that I had found myself in, I was grateful. Once again, she saved my ass.

After a while, Pencil Man seemed to be content focusing on the bobbing of his nets, so I thanked him for letting me sit with him and headed over to Scroggs' trailer. It was there that I spilled my guts to him about just how bad things had gotten at school with Turk. As any good teacher would do, he tried to get me to see things from another perspective, reminding me of how awful of a homelife Turk was trying to survive, a dark world that I knew nothing about. In true seventeen-year-old fashion, I told him that I didn't give a shit and that Turk got what he deserved. I did, however, want to see him squirm.

I didn't care what the reasoning was that Mags had said she would go to prom with me, but I did know that seeing us together was going to cut Turk deep and I salivated for that payback. I needed to look the best that I could, and that included not only what I wore, but also what I showed up in.

Sitting on Scroggs' trailer floor, shooting myself up

yet again with the hormones that would hopefully will my deprived body to grow just a few more inches before the puberty clock stopped ticking for good, he asked me something I found difficult to answer: "What is it boy? What do you really want? More than anything, what are you trying to accomplish here?" the sweet old man asked as I lay near passing out yet again on his shag-carpeted floor. The crease in his pants had always and still amazed me, and the smell of his cigars just felt like home.

Innocently and in a flat tone I answered, "I don't need to be great, Scroggs. I just want to thrive, to be good, and for that God-damned Turk to get what he has coming to him. I want him to feel the sting of pain that he's been forcing on me for all these years. I want him to get what the universe has coming for him," I shouted back as tears rolled down my cheeks, much to my surprise.

I had been so tired of being tormented, exhausted from the years of being made to feel less than good enough. I no longer wanted to feel like the freak, the kid with something wrong with him. For once in my life, I wanted all eyes on me and Mags at prom, not to feel sorry for me or to laugh at me, and not even to envy me, but just to have the other kids see me as someone on the same playing field as them, to look at me and think, "Damn. Good for him." Oh, and I also wanted Turk to feel pain. For his part, sweet Mr. Scroggs just squatted next to me, patted me on the back and said, "Son, then we gotta go see the Pencil Man. It's past suppertime. He should have made it back home from fishin' by now."

Over the few years that I had lived in that town, I had come to understand that somehow, Scroggs and the Pencil Man had grown up together. They seemed to trust each other and help each other out from time to time. Besides fishing and shrimping with one other, I found out that Scroggs would run Pencil Man to various appointments and pick things up for him that he needed too, since Pencil Man couldn't see and wasn't able to drive anymore.

What I hadn't known yet was that at one time, Pencil Man could see, and he loved to drive. In fact, he had quite an infatuation with cars and still kept the best of his secrets hidden in a storage shed behind his house. Sometimes, he would go out to his shed in the early evenings, slide the cover off of his old GTO, and sink into her seats, turning the ignition on long enough to feel the engine idling beneath his feet while listening to a couple of songs on the radio. Then he would cover her back up again to protect her from prying eyes. He would tell me later that this was when he felt most alive, most connected to the person that he once was, the person before "the incident," as he would call it.

I never asked about his sight, and it would be years yet before I would find out what had really happened to him, and how Scroggs was involved. As a young man, Pencil Man's older brother had pissed off some pretty prominent people and had a large debt that needed to be paid, so they cornered Pencil Man when he was just a seventeen-year-old kid, pinned him down and poured sulfuric acid into his eyes as he screamed in debilitating pain. His brother never got over the incident and spent the rest of his life looking to get revenge on the family that stole his brother's sight.

Scroggs was Pencil Man's best friend growing up and stayed by his side even after his loss of sight. But I didn't know any of this back then. At the time, they were both elusive characters to me who held so many mysteries. I found them more amusing than anything else. Looking back, I should have feared them both. Had I known their true origins, I should have feared them all.

On that day though, Scroggs and I pulled up to Pencil Man's house, a huge old home that reeked of family money and sat high on a hill, surrounded by old Cypress trees and low-lying Palmetto bushes. My first impression was that for someone who couldn't see, the home was well taken care of, right down to the gardens. Obviously, Pencil Man had come from money, and there must have been someone else running the show.

"Wow. This place is unbelievable!" I marveled as we put Scroggs' old Thunderbird into park and climbed out into the driveway. "I don't get it, Scroggs. If he's loaded, why the hell does he sit on a corner selling pencils all afternoon, acting like the town crazy?" I asked, still drooling over the huge home and fancy front porch that we were making our way up towards.

"Because, my boy, appearance is everything. Sometimes, you want the world to know who you are, and sometimes, you want to be hidden in plain sight. You, for example, are at a point in your life where you want to be seen a certain way. You don't want to stick out, you just want to fit in, appear normal, right?" Scroggs asked, giving me a wink as he stepped onto the front porch.

He spoke over his shoulder towards me as he reached for the screen door. "Well, sometimes people need to be thrown off your trail, need to forget that you exist. It's a whole lot easier for Pencil Man if everyone just thinks he's a crazy old fool on the corner than to remember who he really was and where he came from. For God's sake my boy, people need to be able to sleep at night in this town," Scroggs snorted, maniacally laughing before he shouted into an open doorway,

"Hey, Luca, you in here?"

I followed Scroggs into the breezeway of the estate-like home, in awe at the grandeur of what my eyes were witnessing, and also in awe of Pencil Man's actual first name. The town kids had always just referred to him as Pencil Man. The place was immaculate with large pieces of what I had assumed to be artwork on the walls in the foyer, pristinely polished old walnut plank floors, and a bronze chandelier that hung high above our heads. I was at a loss for words, so I just stood behind Scroggs with my mouth hanging open and my soul hungry for the part of the story that had been left out. For men that had done such a great job hiding who they were and what they were up to, I couldn't help but wonder why the heck Scroggs would bring me here, why he would be willing to allow me a brief glance of their world, the one that they keep safety tucked away from prying eyes.

"Well ain't 'dis something! Scroggy, my boy, you know I can't see much, but I sure as shit can see a shadow of someone here with ya! Now, do tell, who have you brought up to my humble abode?" Pencil Man's voice echoed and vibrated against the elaborately wallpapered rose motif walls long before I ever saw his slight, yet tall frame appear off to the side in the den.

The den. Now that was a place of magic and mystery. Just glancing around at the red velvet gaming table and the elaborate walnut bookcases that framed a large metal safe big enough to walk into, I got the feeling major dealings had gone down in there. The spookiness and mystery of the room deepened even further as I noticed the old gun collection that graced the walls. Not just a few guns, and not just simply old shotguns and rifles either. I mean, these were museum quality pieces that I was sure had not been easy to come by. Yet there they all were, taking up space on the walls, right out in the open with no fear of anyone trying to steal them.

In fact, that was one of the things that really stood out to me about the place. Here was a blind older man living on the outskirts of town, no fancy gates or security systems. Not even the door was locked when we first came up to the house. The home had an immense presence to it that commanded respect. Anyone passing by would know that there would be untold riches that graced the inner walls of the place. Yet here it was. A treasure trove of wealth and history, art, and artifacts that just sat in this grand, yet unlocked home on display. Yet no one dared to break in and rob the old guy? Surely he had people who helped take care of the house and did his cooking and cleaning for him, drove him places when Scroggs didn't. And yet no one had ever tried to walk away with any of his goodies knowing that he can't see and wouldn't know what was missing anyways?

While I was caught up in this complex riddle, standing in the foyer of a home that seemed forgotten by time, I paused in awe as I watched the verbal exchange between these two old friends. At least I had assumed they were friends. That line was sometimes blurred with these two and it's hard to tell. I had gone fishing and shrimpin' with them from time to time and ran into Pencil Man down on the corner or bumped into him at the store, but I never really wondered about where he lived or what his story was. I only knew, back then at least, that the two of them were bonded somehow, and I had never really taken their friendship for anything more than its face value. I didn't know shit about their world. That had become glaringly clear. "Luca, this is the kid that I had told you about before. Jett. He's the one who fishes with us sometimes. He's also the one who's been having a tough time with that kid at school, you know the one, the kid that runs all over town in that hot black Stealth? He's been getting some attention out there on the streets too, and it ain't been the good kind. Anyway, this kid here has had his own share of misery, the big stuff," Scroggs said, taking Pencil Man's slender arm and leading him to where I was standing until he was damn near within inches from me.

"Is that right?" was all that Pencil Man had to say as he stood in front of me, looking directly over my head towards the beams of light that were radiating in from the front door that we hadn't bothered to close.

"Hi, sir..." I began to stammer, no fear in my belly, just pure shock from the whole situation that made me at a loss for words. I said the only thing that my seventeen-year-old brain could concoct, "I been shrimpin' with ya. In fact I was just up with ya on the docks this afternoon for a bit."

"Sure, sure..." he began, a grin crawling across his bronzed face as a light seemed to flicker in his grey eyes. "Don't say much, do ya? Say, am I right in thinking that you hang around with that little Magdelina girl? And the kid on wheels?"

Perplexed at how he figured that out, I simply shot back a nervous and quick, "Yes sir, I do. They have been good to me since we moved here a few years back."

Feeling my curiosity, Pencil Man just smiled again and

spoke into the air above my head. "No one's business is private out here in these parts, boy. And the good ol' dogs like us, well, there isn't much that we don't know, or can't find out about. Hoo-wee! Ain't that right, Scroggy?"

"You got that right," Scroggs began, shifting his wire-rimmed glasses on the bridge of his nose and reaching into his breast pocket of his dress shirt to retrieve a finely pressed handkerchief to blot his sweating brow. "Damn, it's an ass kicker out there today. Got any beer?"

"Awe jeepers cripes, what the hell kind of a question is that?" the unusually jovial Pencil Man retorted before feeling his way down to my shoulder, giving it a tight squeeze right above my collar bone. For a slender older guy, there was no mistaking the power that those hands still held, and I once again wondered what his world used to be like, a world of old family money and a fancy house. A world where he had been envied and possibly even feared? To me, that power held so much hope.

"Boy, run into the kitchen just beyond that hall and grab some beers, would ya son? You go right ahead and get yourself one, too. We are gonna head out to the back porch," he ordered, steadying himself as he turned around. It was almost mesmerizing to watch him walk the hall back towards the back porch, as if he was doing a dance, knowing exactly how many steps that it took to get there and stopping right in front of the glass before lowering his hand to turn the old bronze handle. I could hear their voices pattering back and forth at each other as I made my way to the kitchen, which was just past the fancy dining room that boasted a large woodburning fireplace big enough to swallow small children. And no one would have been the wiser.

The dining set was an expensive, heavy wood that was pieced together in planks and accompanied by a handful of old heavy chairs, their seats cushioned in a rich blood-red velvet. It was garish…. and to my seventeen-year-old brain, it was also sickly cool. I hadn't even wondered why a single old man would have such an elaborate set up, or why he even needed entertaining space for so many people. Looking back from where I am now, there were all kinds of signs that I had missed as a kid, all sorts of glaringly obvious things that should have stood out, things I now know revealed that there had been so much more to this man's story. I was painfully unaware of just how much power that gentle old soul held in the world.

Grabbing three cold beers from the impressively stocked double fridge, I spun around to head back out of the kitchen when something on the counter by the sink caught my eye. Showcased in a small ornate bronze frame, there was an old photograph of a much younger Pencil Man sitting on a boat with a young girl, all of maybe five or six, helping her hold a fishing pole that was hilariously too big for her, as the wind blew her hair around wildly and she stared down towards the water, leaving only the top of her forehead visible.

"Hmmmm. A daughter maybe?" I thought to myself, trying to make a mental note to look around and see if there had been any other pictures anywhere out in the open. It was odd because he had never spoken of family. Then again, it wasn't like we talked too much when we were fishing, and he was a private sort, much like Scroggs. Those two always kept their pasts close to the vest, creating an aura of mystery that surrounded them with just the slightest possibility of mayhem, enough to

make townspeople leave Pencil Man alone and whisper about Scroggs.

I suppose Pencil Man's perceived wealth is what bought his privacy. In a town as small and poor as Mims, solitude was easily bought, and history just as easily forgotten. Money was scarce around those parts and the ones who had it were able to buy off the ones who lusted after it.

Swinging the screen door open and stepping out onto the back porch to join them, I was first met by a welcoming breeze on which the scent of Cypress lay heavily. The evening pig frogs had begun to bellow, and the skeeters were only just starting to bite. I sat the beers down on the table that was perched between the two co-conspirators and grabbed the skeeter spray bottle off the decking beneath it, lathering my exposed legs to ward off the biters.

There are two things that I never get sick of smelling: the sweet scent of Cypress and that bug concoction of Scroggs'. He would always bring it with him when we were fishing, and I noticed that Pencil Man used it, too. The smell was sweet, and the ingredients were simple, supposedly one last remnant of Scroggs' life with his dearly departed wife. He told me that it was her blend of part witch hazel, part isopropyl alcohol, and some lemongrass. Besides the bugs hating the stuff, it stung like a bitch on open sores but dried them up pretty good while warding off infection, too. It was like a cure all, in that I had also watched Scroggs use it to shine the chrome on his Thunderbird, wipe off the vinyl seats, and leave the windshield spotless. He would even use it to soak his clothes and get the stains out if he'd dripped fish goo on them. Plus, it smelled great, almost like coming home.

"So now, boy…. what's got you all riled up now?" asked Pencil Man, as he gently tapped his foot on the creaking wood porch, effortlessly swaying his old cane rocker back and forth while taking his first pull of the icy cold beer.

I sat down on the steps in front of him, much like a kid in front of Santa, or some poor kid at a Sunday service, looking up at the preacher man for answers that were too big to be asking.

Taking a hearty swallow of the icy cold swill (and almost gagging), I spoke without putting too much thought into the harsh words that crawled out of my soul. "That asshole Turk deserves the same embarrassment that he has been making me feel. Hell, I have put up with that son-of-a- bitch for so long, I just won't do it anymore. And who does he think he is anyways? Why does he get to walk around and be a jerk and no one does nothin' about it? It just ain't right!" I half- shouted up at Pencil Man.

For his part, he tried to warn me, tried to talk me down and dilute my plans of retaliation, reminding me that sometimes a person is a product of their upbringing. I didn't care what type of life the kid had or what kind of dangerous shit he had gotten himself caught up in. All I knew was that I had had enough, and prom was going to be the perfect time to put him in his place. "You don't get it!" I continued to lament to the two old beer drinkers who were casually relaxing in the setting sun on their old cane chairs, effortlessly gliding back and forth with such little concern for my predicament that it was beginning to piss me off. "My whole life, guys like that have belittled me, picked on me, gotten a good laugh at my expense. And for what? They're assholes toward me just because I don't fit their fuckin' mold?! Why do I have to hide?

Why do I have to fear turning a corner or sitting in the lunchroom alone? I'm just so sick of this shit! And now that same asshole won't leave Mags alone either. He keeps bugging her and pestering her, trying to get her to date him. But she don't want no part of that. He's starting to take things way too far, and I'm done putting up with it!"

Scroggs said nothing while Pencil Man raised one of his greying and furled brows and simply responded, "There it is," and chugged what was left of his beer.

Confused, I spouted back, "There WHAT is?"

"The fire in your belly, boy! You ain't stood up for yourself yet, not once in all these years! You have been pushed around, spit on, shunned, humiliated, yet you kept stuffing it down, choking on the pain, letting the resentment gnaw on your soul and hold your head right below the surface, where you stayed, struggling to breathe, begging for a merciful soul to just end this pain instead of handling it on your own. For such a big part of your life, you weren't even willing to take a stand, to fight for yourself. Now finally, you have a reason…. Miss Magdeline D'Andrea!" Pencil Man said, rising up from his chair as he did so, letting out a small, and what I felt at the time, condescending chuckle.

Misunderstanding the sentiment behind his words, I defensively jumped up and began launching into some sort of a tirade about him not knowing what he was talking about and that he had no idea the hell that I had been living through. I stopped just short of those words.

Instantly, I realized that it was impossible to yell at a man who had lost his sight about the daily ridicule that I faced with my stature. Taking a deep breath, I exhaled a sheepish apology while staring down at the ground.

For his part, Pencil Man simply walked over towards the edge of the porch steps and hollered over his shoulder towards Scroggs. "Well, should we get him what he needs, or what?" to which a wickedly grinning Scroggs rose from his old cane rocker, spun on his heels, clapped me on the back and said, "Okay kid, whoo doggy! Show's about to start."

Chapter 10:
Do You Know Confusion?

"Shit, we're here!" I blurted out to the kids, reeling myself back in from wherever I had been subconsciously traveling as I gazed out the window, mindlessly staring at the Cypress trees whizzing by instead of focusing on my acceptance speech that I was still terrified to give.

Having money never changed the fear. Being successful was never enough to change my past. The years of standing out while just trying to fit in and the torment and humiliation that I faced at the hands of assholes like Turk had scarred my soul, searing my edges just enough so that no matter how great my cause, how noble and prosperous I had become, I was still at heart just a dejected and defeated kid. So the thought of standing in front of a room full of well-wishers and spectators would always terrify me, always leave my stomach in knots, and always knock my ass right off of any small pedestal on which I had tried to steady myself.

"Okay boys, suit jackets back on please," my wife directed the kids. "And remember, this is a proud moment for your dad, so let's try not to be assholes in there, alright?"

For their part, I was surprised to see that, instead of her requests being met with groans and whining, they were filled with excitement and wonder as they gazed out the windows of the sleek limousine, gracefully parked now by the curb as our driver opened their door. They may be too young to really understand the significance of this day, blissfully unaware yet of how cruel people can be to each other, and the depths of hell I'd had to survive in order to get to this point. They would never know my true self, the one who still doubts my value in this world and never enters a room without feeling like I am being stared at, silently holding my breath for the snide remarks to start flowing, keeping my armor up and ready to deflect any harsh words that may be hurled my way. All they know me as is their dad, a guy who spends way too much time at fundraisers and in his office; a guy who goes out of his way to help other kids escape their own demons; and a guy who tries hard to be a person they can be proud of. As the boys climbed out of the sleek black car, waving to the cameras and the groups of people who had gathered in the walkway, some with familiar faces and some who have yet to become a part of our story, I calmly ran my hands down the front of my slacks, grinning at the freshly pressed crease lines which, for a fleeting second, brought dear old Scroggs back to the forefront of my thoughts once again. "Okay kid, show's about to start," I heard him whisper in my ear, as if the years hadn't passed at all and I was a seventeen-year-old kid again.

"Well, let's give them what they want," my beautiful wife sighed through a toothy grin, a sly glimmer sparking a flame in her wickedly taunting green eyes. "All you have to do is be gracious, accept the award, give them a good story, and they will be happy to throw more cash out towards the Foundation." She leaned in close, dusting off my shoulders and straightening my tie, then brushed her berry-colored lips quickly across my cheek before breathing into my ear, "He may have helped to set you on this path, but you built the fucking empire. This is yours now. Don't you dare forget that!" She then backed up to look me right in the eyes, her hands squeezing the top of my thighs, and gave me a wicked little wink before exiting the car.

Swallowing the ball of nervous energy that had formed in the back of my throat, I watched her graciously step out from the car and heard her voice greeting old friends, this persona that she feeds the public, such a far cry from the homebody and quiet soul that she is in private. What the public sees of my wife is a finely crafted persona that she has created, one that has been instrumental in helping to build my own brand, and a far cry from where I came from.

Taking a deep breath and nervously grinning to myself, I slid forward in my seat, getting ready to make my own exit, when I noticed that her book had fallen to the floor as she'd scurried out of the car. Leaning down to retrieve it, my heart caught in my chest, and I remembered once again where we had begun as I saw the title on the old worn cover of her favorite play, *Macbeth*.

As I clumsily climbed out of the car, she was the first thing I saw, which is no big surprise as she is always the first thing I look for in any room, in any setting, in any nightmare. She quiets my soul and reminds me that the world can be good and that not all people are monsters. She has seen me through some pretty tough times in this lifetime, and is the only thing, at times, that keeps my lungs breathing and the monsters that lunge at me from my past at bay.

Looking at her standing there in the curve-hugging, black beaded gown, her auburn hair piled gently on top of her head with whisps of loose curls cascading down and resting on her shoulders, I felt like a nervous kid again, the kid who wanted nothing more in the world than to impress her. Once again, I stood in silence, questioning my worth, my value in her world, feeling like I wasn't good enough for this beauty, trying my hardest to be who I perceived that I needed to be in order to fit into her world. Someone that she could be proud of. It was just like prom all over again.

Junior year was when our lives became a kaleidoscope of confusion, or should I say that it was when the messy inkblot that was our lives became rearranged and set back into focus again, changing the trajectory of where I had thought my life was headed and instead, putting me on the course to be… well, to be enough.

As she had promised, Mags made good on her vow to go to prom with me that year, even if I thought she was just doing it to get a little payback at Turk and help me save a little face with the kids at school who had witnessed the insanity of what I like to simply refer to as, "the parking lot incident," when my car had been vandalized and Turk was the one pulling the strings. When I had gone to Scroggs, begging mercifully for help in getting revenge, in making things right with the Turk situation at school, I hadn't yet known his and Pencil Man's full story, the truth about who they were, or understood how, in a tiny town such as Mims, easily lives were intersected and truths, half-truths and legends were easily blurred.

Pencil Man's wealth should have tipped me off. And if not, then certainly the way we were treated like royalty—or maybe even feared—in the shop when the two of them took me to be sized for a tux for prom should have. But I was just a kid looking forward to having a good time and just doing something that every "normal" teenaged kid did as a rite of passage… go to prom. Well, that *and* I had really wanted to rub Turk's nose in the fact that Mags would be sliding into my car that night, hanging onto my arm at Grand March, and laughing at my stupid jokes all night long and not his. I hadn't wondered yet why on earth these two older guys would go so far out of their way to help me, other than just because maybe they saw a kid in need and figured they would do their best to help out. I had no way of knowing who they actually were, or why they were so intent on guiding me and my friends through the turbulent waters of adolescence, offering all that they could to make our time in that town suck just a little less.

I just knew that when Scroggs and Pencil Man offered to take me a couple of towns over to Merritt Island to help me order a tux for the big night, and to even pay for it, I didn't hesitate. I mean, hell, my family couldn't afford to shell out any more money for me cause times were already tight as it was. And I wasn't about to show up to Mag's granddad's waterside estate home without looking like I belonged there. She deserved more than that. She always deserved the best.

It caught me off guard, though, when the shop owner greeted Pencil Man by name, Luca, which I hadn't heard anyone call him before outside of when Scroggs had greeted him at his home. Until that day, Scroggs never spoke of his real name. And it wasn't just his name that threw me off. It was the way that the shop owner acted, like there wasn't enough she could do for him. Then again, she was around his age too, so maybe they had known each other growing up or something, even if it must have felt like lifetimes ago.

There the four of us stood in the little shop, picking out patterns and taking my measurements as curious passersby peeked in the windows past the sign that said, "Shop's Closed, Come Again." Mags had already told me that her dress was black, so all I had to do was match that. With the shop owner's careful sense of style and the impressively deep pocketbook of Pencil Man to back it up, she chose a brocade pattern that was deep-set in a luxurious black sheen of fabric, highlighted by a deep crimson pocket square, vest, and tie that would of course match the corsage and boutonnière flowers called in to the florist down the road who didn't dare question the order. All she had to do was merely mention Pencil Man's name on the order and all was set. Although I hadn't yet questioned his authority in this little town, I did realize that he commanded respect, which was something that I very much craved.

The evening of prom, I pulled up in front of Mag's granddad's estate in Pencil Man's beloved car, a four-door 1969 Chevy El Camino that was finished in a matte black with a pissed-off white stripe running down the center of the hood. The night before, he'd had me rev the engine and drive him through town after we'd gotten her all shined up and filled her belly with gas, just so he could feel the rumble beneath the floorboards once again and remember what it was like to truly feel alive. He was all too eager to lend me his car, almost giddy like a kid at the thought of someone really admiring her again, much like a kid showing off his favorite toy.

Stepping out of the old muscle machine, the humidity hit my lungs with every suffocating gulp. In my flurry to get here, I had forgotten to administer my injections. Even though my medical team had thought I would be done with those by seventeen, I was a late bloomer, so my growth plates still hadn't completely fused, allowing me a few more gracious months to try and eek out another inch or precious few inches. Fortunately, years of practice had put my brain into auto-pilot mode, and I'd tucked both injectors into my dress shirt pocket on the way out the door, one for my hormone issue as well as the insulin injector that kept my already fragile and struggling system from going into diabetic shock or coma from all the damn hormones being pushed through my kidneys and liver. As I'd hurriedly grabbed them, I heard Mama hollering at me as I squealed out of the driveway, reminding me to stop back over for pictures after I'd picked up Mags.

So here I now stood, my heart thunderously clapping beneath my stressed ribcage, the back of my shirt already drenched in sweat. What the hell was I so nervous about? I had known Mags for years at that point, and she was one of my closest friends. So why the hell did getting all dressed up change anything? With trembling hands, I delicately slid my black brocade jacket off and laid it gently on the hood of the car, fumbling to roll up my dress shirt sleeve so I could quickly access those spindly veins and quickly inject the magic potion that my body was begging for. I paused, still not sure that I wouldn't pass out from the injection, because there was usually a fifty-fifty chance of that. It was still something that I could never fully get used to. Deciding that I was already shaky from the nervousness alone, I decided to gently lean against the trunk hood of the spotless car to steady myself.

"So that's how you treat a legendary classic, is that right?" I heard a heckling cackle coming from somewhere over my shoulder, emanating up from the banks of St. John's River where Mags' families charter boats all sat, bobbing against their docks. Another voice laughed at the same time, one that was all too familiar. Pausing midair with my auto injector in hand and my sleeve rolled up, I turned to see the weathered faces of Pencil Man and Mags' granddad, Ernie. What a sight I must have been! Leaning against this beautiful old car with my sleeve hiked up looking like I was about to shoot up with a little black tar, something that was all too well-known around those parts. I froze, stunned at the sight of them and not knowing what I should say. "Hello Mr. D'Andrea, and Luca. What are you fellas doing out here?" was all that I could muster, still frozen in a strange position with my hand midair clutching the injection pen. It felt awkward but kind of nice saying Pencil Man's real name out loud, like a rite of passage in which I had been allowed to partake.

"Well, go on boy, shoot it up! Don't let us stop ya," Ernie barked, more of an order than anything else.

"No, no, sir, it's not what it looks like! I ain't into drugs or…" I had begun to ramble but was mercifully stopped by Pencil Man.

"That you, boy? Ain't you picked her up yet? Thought you two would have been off to dinner by now," he spoke, stopping only to take a swallow of the beer he had been holding in his tremoring left hand.

"Yes, sir. I mean, no sir... I was about to go get her, but I forgot to take my shot before I left, and Mama would have my head if I forgot it. Heaven knows that woman would walk right into that gym, right out onto the dance floor and shoot me up herself," I offered with a small grin as I looked back down at my arm, trying to decipher where my spindly little veins were hiding from this time. Just as I eyeballed one of the little bastards, promptly stabbing myself with the needle, Ernie's voice bellowed through the Cypress-scented air again. "It's alright, boy. I know of the troubles that you got goin' on. No matter. That hurt ya much?"

Finishing up with my injection, and methodically rolling my sleeve back down, I kept my head down, eyes closed for what felt like forever, willing myself not to black out, praying for the strength to open my eyes and answer this man. Softly, I spoke, "The pain is always there, I guess. There's never really a point that I get used to it. I just know that the pain has a purpose, so I guess I just gotta rise above it. But no sir, it ain't too horrible, I guess. Did Mags tell you about what's going on with me?" I questioned, walking back to the hood of the old car to retrieve my jacket.

I had met Ernie a handful of times over the previous couple of years, but Mags, Jojo and I tended to just try to stay out of his way. He was working a lot, and when he wasn't working, he was in his study working on bills and what-not, so we tended to just leave him be. Honestly, he always seemed intimidating, whether that had been his intent or not. Not scary, just a tough old grandfather who seemed to have worked hard and seen some shit in his days, who didn't take gruff from anyone. Intimidation and fear are separate monsters, and although I had been intimidated by Ernie as a kid, I had never been smart enough to fear him.

"Boy, you have been hanging around my granddaughter for a few years now. Do you think I would ever let that happen without knowing the ins and outs of you?" the old man laughed before lowering his tone and adding, "I know exactly who you are and where you come from."

I didn't know if I should be terrified or pissed at the way he made it sound. Was "who I was" not good enough for his granddaughter? Suddenly, the trailer park that I called home felt a million miles away from the front lawn of the sprawling estate on which I now stood. I slid my arms back into my tux jacket, straightening my vest and tie while simultaneously trying to figure out what the hell I was supposed to say in response to that last remark. Staring down at my freshly polished and borrowed shoes, I tried to muster up the courage to defend myself. "Sir, my folks are good, hardworking people and I…" but I was cut off before I even got started, startled by the sudden movement of Ernie stepping forward and raising his arms to brush dust off the shoulders of my jacket, the sheer size of his muscular arms not lost on me.

"Listen kid, you don't have to convince me of anything. Like I said, I know all about you. Hell, if I didn't think you were of a decent upbringing, you wouldn't be standing here in my driveway with a borrowed car, borrowed shoes, and a paid-for tuxedo shootin' the shit with me when you should be making your way on up to the house to pick up my granddaughter, whose mama has been helping her get ready," he said matter-of-factly. He stopped only to wave up towards the house at Mags' mama, who waved back from the window, surely wondering what the hell was taking me so long to make my way up to the house.

"Now boy, Luca here has been telling me a bit about the troubles you've been having with this Turk kid. Ain't he the one that's been running with the Cuban cartel? What kind of trouble has he been giving you kids?"

Nervously, I told Ernie about the infatuation that Turk had always seemed to have for Mags, and the jealousy and hatred that he had projected onto me. I didn't want Ernie to see me as weak, didn't want him to think that Mags wouldn't be safe with me. "I can handle it though. For years I have just tried to avoid him, tried to stay out of his way. I'm done hiding from him. I won't do it anymore. But if it came down to it, sir, just know that Mags will always be safe when she's with me."

He stood, looking me right in the eye while Pencil Man ran a hand over the trunk of the car, admiring the smooth lines with arthritic fingers. "Is that right? Well, I'm glad to hear it, boy," Ernie grinned, reaching around his back into his waistband, dislodging from a holster that I didn't know had existed. A 9mm handgun with a surprisingly hefty weight was thrust into my sweaty hand.

Not knowing what to say, I froze in fear as we stood there, his hand in mine, staring into my soul. "There are very few things in this world boy that are worth defending. My granddaughter happens to be one of 'em. I trust you, but I don't trust them. You will protect her, yes?" were the last words he spoke before our little moment was interrupted by Mag's mama hollering from the front porch. "Dad, leave the kid alone. They have to get going!" as though he was just out there giving me the playful jabs of an overprotective grandfather.

"On our way up!" he hollered back, dropping my hand and spinning around to start walking towards the house. Pencil Man spoke softly as he walked past me, following the sound of Ernie's voice, "Just stash it in the glovebox, kid. Don't bring it up to the house."

My intent was to safely store the gun in the glove compartment, but I was fumbling around too much to even get it opened, so I stashed it beneath the driver's seat instead. Quickly, I followed behind them as we made our way up the drive towards the house where Mags was waiting for me. We had almost made it up to the porch when something struck me as odd. What *was* Pencil Man doing there?

"So, are you guys fishin' buddies too, then? I mean, I usually see Pencil Man, I mean, Luca with Mr. Scroggs, but this is a ways out here for him to just come and fish," I questioned, trying to talk about anything that would calm my nerves and keep my mind off not trying to look like a dork to Mags.

The millisecond that the front door swung open and Mags was revealed, standing there in the floor-length satin black gown, two things happened. First, as I stood there on the grand front porch in my borrowed shoes with sweat running down the nape of my neck, the cicadas singing, and the humid breeze wafting in through the Cypress trees, my world became deafeningly calm and my intent clear. Standing before me was my best friend, but I saw her differently now. Gone was the goofy girl who climbed trees and collected odd comic books. Gone was the girl who would venture out with me to the wild blackberry bushes, eating her way through story after story that Jojo or I would tell. The person who I was looking at now no longer resembled the one who held such a prominent space in my youth. Although I knew that I had begun to crush on her long ago, that evening on that porch with a serenade of pig frogs somewhere out in the water, I felt my heart explode, and it was then that I knew that Ernie was right… some things were worth defending.

As I stood there, lost in her beautiful smile as her mama ran to grab her camera for pictures, the second thing happened, and when it did, my life would take on a whole new trajectory.

"Yeah, we like to fish too. But I suppose we can let you in on the secret now, kid. We are brothers," Pencil Man softly whispered in my ear, his hand gently on my shoulder, guiding me forward towards Mags.

Chapter 11:
Do You Know Deception?

"You can't be mad at me, Jett. Please don't be pissed!" Mags begged as we sat safely back in the car after a few rounds of pictures on the front porch at her house. We were now heading back to my house for a few as well, otherwise my mama would have had a fit.

We had been discussing the bombshell that had just been dropped about Pencil Man being her uncle. I couldn't understand why she had never told me.

"In the beginning, when you were new here, it was nice that you didn't know who my family was. I liked that you didn't pity me because my dad offed himself and that you didn't think I was strange because I had the weird blind uncle who hung around with the other town misfit," she began, referring to Scroggs. "And then, I just didn't know how to tell you the truth. I didn't want you pissed at me. But really, Jett, does it even matter?" a desperate question echoed into the air of the silent car. I wasn't sure what to say. So much didn't make sense.

"Look, Jett. You and Jojo are my very best friends. We hang out, we laugh, we have fun… it's just easy. I didn't want to complicate it," Mags retorted, her last defense had been hurled before she retreated back into her seat. As we made our way toward my home, she sat nervously looking out the passenger side window at the Glades that were slowly disappearing as they made way for housing developments and trailer courts.

"Mags, I get it. Believe me, I do! I just think at some point within the last few years, you could have found a way, or trusted me enough to tell me about it! I just can't believe that you…" but it was pointless. Glancing over at her, I knew that I couldn't stay mad at her, and really, what was I so pissed about? I spent the good part of most of my childhood hiding from people, trying to be average, someone that no one noticed. Maybe that's all that Mags was after too.

Pulling up to our trailer house, I decided to let it go. After all, this was prom, and even though it really didn't mean that much to me, at seventeen, even I understood the significance of this night to a teenaged girl. Putting the car in park, I turned to face her and put my clammy hand on her shoulder. "Mags, I get it. No worries. I know that you would never try to hurt me. Just forget it, okay?"

She turned to me then with an astonished look, almost as though she thought she had lost me for good. "Jett, seriously, I'm so sorry," she whispered before throwing her arms around my shoulders to hug me. That was a hug that I never forgot. The seconds seemed to last an eternity as I felt her warm breath on my neck and could feel her chest pressed into mine, her heart echoing in sync with my own. She was nervous too.

I remember a flurry of pictures being taken here, too, by Mama, much like the flashbulbs that go off now when

I arrive at benefits, fundraisers, and awards dinners. My dad had come outside as well, marveling at how good Pencil Man's car looked and telling us to have a good time. I remember waving at my brothers in the yard as we pulled away and the easiness that took over my soul, the normalcy that I had been chasing for so long that seemed to have finally been attained. For once, I was just one of the guys heading off to prom with his girl, like any other kid.

We met Jojo and Monica for dinner at The Depot, a fancy restaurant on the edge of town that sat along the banks of the Indian River. We were seated out on the deck and laughed and ate burgers and calamari as we watched for gators out on the banks. We, being who we were, decided to swing over to the shrimping docks on our way to the school before the dance. It was all innocent enough, just a group of kids hanging around in the moonlight, waiting to see the shrimp electrify the water. It didn't matter how old we got. It still seemed like magic.

When we got to the docks, Jojo and Monica had already beat us there. Jojo was rolling up the path with her by his side, heading over to the little ice cream shack that sat at the base of the docks.

"I don't care where I end up in this world, there will never be ice cream from anywhere better than this. It's just so smooth and…" I had turned to talk to Mags before getting out of the car but was interrupted by her lips on mine. Stunned, I didn't know what to do with my hands, so I just kind of sat there awkwardly while she kissed me, her soft raspberry-flavored lips gently locking onto mine for just a few seconds. But that was all it took. She had me. We had officially crossed the friend zone. And my night of finally being normal continued on.

There was no oddness between us. Nothing would have seemed any different if you were an outsider. We still just looked like two goofy teenagers headed off to prom. Even Jojo didn't know. Well, he didn't know quite yet anyways. That would come later.

When we got to the dance, I made sure to park the car under a streetlight in the back of the lot where no other cars had been parked. That car was like Pencil Man's baby, and I was honored that he had entrusted me with it. I got out and walked around to the other side to open Mags' door. I took her hand and helped her out of the car, making sure that her dress was fully out of the car before I slammed the door, just like my mama had told me to do. Jojo and Monica were waiting at the sign-in table when we walked in.

"Music's pumpin' in there, my man! It's gonna be good!" Jojo said, his date grabbing Mags and taking off to the bathroom. "Be right back!" she hollered over her shoulder as they wobbled down the hallway in heels that they still weren't used to walking in. Jojo and I entered the gym, which had been transformed into an "Under the Sea" themed ballroom, thanks to thousands of strands of Christmas lights and green and blue balloons tied to everything that would stay still. "How's Mags doin?" Jojo asked, my friend looking me dead in the eye like he suspected something.

"She's good, man, she's alright. She's the one who wanted to come, ya know, so I…" I began, knowing that I wasn't fooling anybody.

"Shut your face, dog! You ain't gotta tell me that you like being here with her. I can see that. I've seen it coming for a long time, man!" Jojo said, just grinning his goofy grin like always. "I don't know man, all I know is she's the same Mags as always, but somehow, she ended up here with me. Now I don't know if it's just out of pity for me or..." I had begun to try reasoning with Jojo, attempting to list all the reasons that there was no way that a girl like our Mags, a girl from such a high-status pedigree, would see anything in a guy like me for more than just friendship, more than as a wounded dog she could protect. I had thought of all these things but didn't get a chance to tell Jojo any of them because we were interrupted by the girls' giggling as they returned from the bathroom. Suddenly, I felt nervous again, realizing that we were about to walk out into the big reception area of the gym, the strands of lights glowing from above our heads and the sea of blue and green balloons hugging clusters of fake foam and cardboard palm trees in our own little version of paradise… or teenaged hell, depending on whose opinion you asked for.

For me, I had spent much of my childhood and adolescence hiding out in the shadows, trying to remain unnoticed. With Mags on my arm as we walked in, followed by Jojo rolling on in behind me with Monica Judd by his side, we really were the spectacle that no one could look away from. The anxiety was forming a lump in the back of my throat, and beads of sweat were beginning to roll down the center of my back, leaving a trail down my freshly pressed and newly paid for shirt. (Thank the good Lord almighty that I had a vest and jacket on too, so at least no one would see me sweat like a stuck pig out on the dance floor.)

Oh crap! The dance floor. I hadn't given the thought

of actually dancing much of a ponder because I was so focused on looking good and playing the part. But now that we were there, now that the music that the live DJ was spinning came crackling out of the old speakers and the vibrations were trembling up from the gym floor and finding their way to the uneasy feeling that sat in the lower part of my gut, all of my nerves began to fire up and I had suddenly wanted to be anyplace but here. We had made it to the entrance of the dance floor, right past the fake palm trees, when I felt my legs begin to tremble and my hands start to twitch in defiance. For her part, Mags either didn't notice or just wasn't going to call me out on it, believing that I was braver and more self-assured than I had ever believed myself to be. That was her, though. She was always the strength that I needed when I couldn't find the courage to push myself further. She would always find a way to get me across that threshold, the one that I all-too-often found myself teetering over, that bridge from who I was then, to who I was destined to become.

Pausing only briefly while she looked around to see which familiar faces were dancing and which were just standing around like lame ducks, she grabbed my hand and led me out to the dance floor. It didn't take any convincing on Jojo's part to get him and Monica out there as well. We must have been a sight out there, nervously bobbing around to whatever song had come on, while Jojo kind of sat in his chair and spun the wheels back and forth and from side to side. After a while, Monica even took a turn or two sitting on his lap as they spun in a quick couple of circles, laughing and having a great time, no care as to who was watching.

It had been a long time since I had felt so normal, so

average and so free. That was the magic of those two friends. They made me forget the darkness and step into another world a little bit at a time, and I liked it. I found that once they pulled me out of my comfort zone, once I let go of the anxiety and fear, there was a whole other life out there just waiting to be taken, and I wanted all of it. I wanted the easy laughter and the oddly-timed inside jokes, the high-fives down the hallway and the discussions over the lunch table about what we were looking forward to that weekend. I didn't have to be a spectacle, didn't have to sit out on the sidelines all alone. Our crew may have been small, but we were all that we needed to be happy.

Everyone acted upset when the good old chicken dance was being played, but we all laughed and ran in circles doing it anyways. Then there was an old Elton John song about a crocodile that some teachers had requested that somehow got everyone out on the dance floor, flailing their hands around in a chomping motion like maniacs and ended with the kids lying on their backs and laughing hysterically beneath the twinkle of cheap strands of Christmas lights. We were a school that bordered the Everglades, and our mascot was, of course, the crocodile, so you do the math on that one.

Lying on the gym floor, listening to the end of the song with Mags sprawled out next to me, her head on my arm, I knew then that whatever happened after this night, she was who I wanted to do all of life's adventures with. Her granddad was right. That girl was worth saving.

"Hey Jett," Mags softly spoke, turning her head so that she was no longer staring up at the cheap twinkle lights, but was now staring right into my eyes and manipulating my soul. "I really am happy you asked me here. There's no one else that I would rather be here with, you know?" She threw her net and reeled me in, my own eyes lost in her stare.

I had wanted so many things in life, but because of my health, I always wondered just how much I would be able to accomplish, how far I would be able to go. Growing up, I feared that I would never be able to do all the "normal" kid things like playing sports and having parties, dating girls and raising a little Cain. Too small to play football, too short to play basketball, and just not built to run, I replaced sports with my love of all things tech-related and my love of movies and comic books. I may not have partied too hard or dated a lot of girls, but lying there on that gym floor with Mags at prom, I realized that I could have everything that I wanted out of life. I just had to stop thinking that I wasn't good enough. Sure, my life may look a little different, and I may not have a lot of friends, but the ones I did have were true and we had a lot of fun together. As for Mags, sometimes you don't realize who is staring right back at you. "You are the only girl who would go with me, Mags, so it was a good thing I asked!" I tried to joke with her as I stood up from the floor, dusted off my pants and extended my hand to help her up too. The song had ended and a slower one had begun to play. Jojo and Monica had already left the floor and headed over to the snack table that was an elaborate spread of cheese and crackers, those little rolled-up pinwheel looking sandwiches, cakes and cookies, and of course, a giant punchbowl filled with a greenish colored punch that we had already watched a couple of guys pour a fifth of vodka into. Jojo was already two cups deep by the time Mags grabbed my hand to pull me back out onto the dance floor, laughing at my lack of desire to go back out there. "There's hardly anyone out there now, look! Most of the kids are just standing around the edge of the floor, eating, and talking. People will be watching us, Mags!" I half joked around, making my real desire to hold her close less apparent.

"Oh, come on, Jett," she chided right back, pulling my hand along as she walked, me playfully digging my heels in where I stood. "I like this song, and I don't give a rat's ass who is lookin' at us anyways."

All of my anxiety dissipated, leaving only an ache in my chest, a longing to be close to her. For seventeen years, I had struggled with self-acceptance, self-worth, struggled to find my way. I had survived the pits of depression and the crippling effects of anxiety. I blindly made my way through a nightmare that had spanned most of my childhood, never knowing what life would have in store for me, not knowing if I would make it here, to this sweet spot that I had now found myself in, standing in the middle of the dance floor at prom, finally not giving a shit who was looking me, proud to be standing there with Mags. We walked back out to the floor. She wrapped her arms around my neck, and I grabbed her by the waist. My heart was beating a new rhythm in my chest, but it felt so different than anxiety, so different than fear. I held her tightly, nervously swaying side to side, unsure as to if I was doing it right, but in that moment, not really caring either. I wanted to dance with her, hold her like that forever, with no one around who cared. Just she and I.

But there was someone else around. I had hoped like hell that he wouldn't get a date, or that he would be too busy with his "family business" to bother coming at all. I didn't want to face him that night. I just wanted the night to be perfect for Mags. And it was. Until it wasn't.

I saw him crossing the dance floor right behind Mags, his expensive purple silk shirt peeking out from his equally expensive black tux, being sure that his gold ring and chains were visible. He walked with purpose to where we stood locked in an awkward embrace, Mags blissfully unaware of the dark entity that was about to intrude on our teenage dream.

His voice bellowed out above the soft tremble of music that was wafting through the humid air in the old gym. "Hey Mags, you look hot!" the asshole breathed into her ear as he leaned in close, putting his hand on her back. "Wanna dance with me?"

Startled, she didn't even look at him, instead, looking right up into my eyes, trying to engage me, to let her intent be known to me that she wasn't going anywhere. We were both right where we wanted to be. "No thanks, Turk. I'm good right here," came her response, spoken into thin air, not even giving him the courtesy of a glance his way, her green eyes still desperately staring right into my face.

Turk took a disgusted step backwards, still staring right at her, his eyes like daggers into her back, yet flaring with the rage of a pissed off two-year-old. "Come on, Mags, it's prom night! You don't want to spend it hanging out with this freak, do ya? I know a couple of people who are throwing a huge ass party later out by the dunes. The whole school will probably be there. We could roll on down there in my Stealth. It would be dope. Come on, you don't wanna miss it." Turk had tried his best to entice the girl with whom he had been obsessed for the better part of his adolescence. But she didn't flinch as she turned her head to face him and politely declined. "No thanks, Turk. I'm good here. Besides, your date is looking for you..." Mags retorted with a smirk as she watched the girl, who was obviously not from around there, come staggering in the side door of the gym, calling Turk's name and stumbling along, obviously high on something. Her makeup was heavy, and her dress curved in all the right places. As she moved in closer, it was obvious that she wasn't a high school-aged kid at all, but a woman possibly in her early twenties with faded bruises on her right cheekbone and old track marks running along the inside of her left arm. Turk was quick to grab on to his prize in a thinly veiled attempt to make Mags jealous. This woman, this poor strung-out soul, draped her arms around his neck and cooed into his ear, "Come on, baby, let's go. This is so boring here. Why don't you and me take a ride and party."

Turk clearly liked the offer, but was still offended by Mags, the one thing in his life that he wanted to claim as his own. But she still sat delicately on a pedestal that would forever be out of his reach. Clearly trying to make Mags jealous, he turned his attention back towards the woman in the too-tight dress, her cleavage fighting to stay covered, put his hands on her tiny waist and purred, "Oh baby, that does sound good, let's go." Turning one last time towards Mags, he questioned yet again, his one hand on the woman's waist and the other obviously sliding down to her ass cheek, giving it a squeeze. "Offer's still good Mags. You sure you don't want to come party with us?"

Slightly perturbed and disgusted, she shot him a look that had a flicker of fire in it and said, "Thanks, but no, Turk. You look like you've got your hands full. I'm doing just fine right here with Jett," and as a wounded Turk looked on and the cheap Christmas lights hung over our heads, Mags did something that I didn't see coming, something that would not only prove a point to our nemesis but would change the trajectory of all our lives. She turned back towards me, grabbed my face with her soft hands, and kissed me, a slow, gentle kiss, as the music played on, and we swayed side to side.

I'm not going to lie. It felt like time stood still or that we were in some cheesy teen movie. Maybe it's just how I remember it, but I think about that kiss often, even now. In the seconds that it took for her to kiss me, her warm raspberry-flavored lips pressed against mine and her heart once again beating against my chest, in sync with my own, I felt the eyes staring at us from all over the room, the jaws falling open and time standing still. For the very first time in my life, I was the center of attention, the one that everyone was looking at. But this time, I was enjoying it. I wasn't hiding. I was proud. I was finally proud of who I was and what my place was in this world. I didn't care who was staring at me, what they were thinking, or what would happen next. In that moment, all I cared about was her, my Mags, the one who pulled me out of my shell, dusted me off and exposed me to the world. We had just become us. And from that point on, it was us against the world.

But someone *did* care. Someone *was* hurt. As Turk roughly grabbed the woman who had followed him in by the top of her arm and spun around to leave, he gave me one last long stare and shouted out, "You're gonna regret this, boy. You don't know who you are fucking with."

"Go to hell, Turk," Mags blurted out, as I stood there,

too stunned from all that had just happened to know what to say. To that, Turk momentarily paused as a creepy smile crawled across his lips and he said loudly in her direction, "Careful there, kid. Don't you forget where you come from. We are two of the same, girl. Don't you forget that," before he calmly sauntered away, back out the side door of the gym.

"Man, that kid's such an ass!" Mags said, rolling her eyes and leaning back into me, once again placing her hands around my neck as we continued with the slow dance, or what was left of it that she was trying so hard to rescue.

"Why did he say that, Mags? Why did he say you were two of the same?" I asked, knowing full well that I wasn't going to get a satisfactory answer. I had only begun to scratch the surface of knowing who this exquisite human was, and at that point, she kept the darkness of her past pretty guarded, only offering a meek explanation. "Who knows with that asshole. He barely knows who *he* is most of the time."

I knew I was getting myself into something pretty deep, attaching my heart to that girl, but it felt so good to just be normal that night that I simply didn't give a damn. I didn't want the feeling to end. We continued laughing and dancing, talking, and just hanging out for the rest of the night. At one point, I was starting to feel pretty shaky and realized that I had been dancing and sweating for hours and maybe my damned blood sugar was starting to take a dip. I tried to spike it quickly by slamming down a piece of cake, but that only made me feel worse. I didn't know where the night was going to lead, but I knew that I didn't want to have to cut out early because of my health. I didn't want to be reduced to the weird kid, the freak again, not when feeling normal felt so right.

I reached for the insulin injector that I was sure I had stashed in my pocket earlier when I was in such a rush to get out of the house and get to Mags on time. "Shit," I thought, realizing that it was no longer in my jacket pocket. "What the hell, I know I grabbed it…" I thought out loud, as Mags began noticing that something was wrong.

"Hey Jett, you okay? You're looking really pale all of a sudden, almost gray. Can I do anything? Get anything for ya?" the angel sweetly asked. Damn it. I didn't want the night to end, not like this. I tried to think of the last time I knew I had the pen stashed in my pocket. It would have been at Mag's house 'cause I had injected my hormones there in her driveway when her granddad and Pencil Man came out to talk to me. I had been in my pocket then. Shit. Ernie. He'd handed me that damn gun. I'd leaned back into the car trying to get the glove compartment open, and when that didn't work, I leaned further down to stash the damn thing beneath the seat. "Shit," I said out loud, realizing that the insulin pen must have fallen out there, in the car. It must be on the floor of the driver's side, rolling around somewhere. As crappy as I was beginning to feel, I couldn't send Mags out to the car to grab it for fear that she may see the gun, and then I would be the one having to come up with satisfying answers that thinly veiled the truth. "What is it, Jett? What's up?" she questioned; a look of concern perched on her perfectly tweezed brow line.

"I think I'm just due for insulin, that's all. I'm gonna run out to the car quick. Be right back in!" I tried to tell her, hoping to just run out quickly and not cause any type of commotion, not wanting to draw any further attention to myself, especially the wrong kind… pity.

"I'll come, too!" she shot right back, getting up from her chair at the table where we had been sitting and having snacks with Jojo and Monica.

"No, no. It's fine. Just stay here with them and I will be right back!" I retorted, jumping up from my chair a little too quickly, causing the room to start to tilt and almost losing my balance. I suppose the spiked punch that we had been drinking wasn't helping my cause. Mags jumped right up, throwing an arm around my waist to steady me, and told Jojo and his date, "He will be fine. I'll just go out to the car really quick with him to grab his pen and we'll be back in."

Seeing that I wouldn't be able to argue with her, I relented, relieved to have someone in my corner. We turned away from the table, her arm around my waist and mine thrown over her shoulders. "Okay, be right back in Jo," I said over my shoulder.

"Right. Sure. See you in an hour. You two better stay outta trouble out there…" a mischievous Jojo could be heard wickedly giggling as we were walking away. "Insulin. Sure. There's an excuse to get her out in the car... alone," he kept chiding. Without looking back and quietly grinning ear to ear, I raised my left hand in defiance to flick Jojo the bird. I knew he was kidding, but it felt so damn good to just be seventeen. He was still laughing as we walked away.

Chapter 12:
Do You Know Guilt?

Leaving the safety of the gym, I was a little nervous. First, what if this was one of those damn times when my blood sugar dipped too damn low, and I passed the hell out? Then what? I didn't want Mags to see me like that. Secondly, what if we got to the car and Mags *did* want more while we were out there? I didn't know what the hell I was doing. I obviously hadn't had any experience with girls before, and I didn't want to be embarrassed by my lack of knowledge or skill when it came to making out.

"This is stupid, just calm down," I told myself in my head as we walked towards the back of the lot where the car was parked beneath the light post. I was coming off such a high from the night and refused to let my anxiety get the best of me. I just focused on the first step, finding that damn auto injector. Unless I found that first, nothing that followed would matter anyways.

The humid night air hung thick with the sweet scent of Cypress, and Mags' heels made a funny clip-clop noise as we walked across the warn asphalt towards the car. Funny how small things like that get lodged in your brain like it was only yesterday. Clip-clop, clip- clop… I can hear them even now.

Walking towards the car, we noticed that it no longer sat alone, that there were a few other cars parked close by as well, all of nicer quality and also probably trying to avoid being door-dinged or scratched. I was still pretty shaky when I reached the driver's side door, and by the time I got the damn door unlocked with my shaky hands, I was damn near getting tunnel vision, knowing that passing out may very well be in my future if I didn't hurry up and find that dang injector pen. Flinging the door open, I leaned down to feel around on the floorboards, my fingers reaching cautiously beneath the driver's seat, gently grazing the 9mm that still lay nestled there.

"Shit! I can't find it!" I frantically called out in a shaky voice, trying my best to hide the panic that was now starting to creep into my soul. Where the hell was that damn thing? I slumped to my knees on the warm pavement, feeling the baked-in heat rising up though my pants and into my skin. I reached further beneath the seat, then swung my hand around by the foot pedals, praying to the heavens that my trembling fingers would bump into the pen before things went from bad to even worse.

"Hang on Jett, let me run around and see if it fell out and rolled to the other side, okay? Just hang on a second. Stay calm, okay? Jett, are you listening to me?" a panic-sickened voice emanated from Mag's raspberry lips. She reached for the keys that I had laid on the seat and ran around to the other side of the car to unlock the passenger side door. Scrambling with the keys, I heard a pause and a very faint, "Oh my God..." before the door flung open and I could see her stunned face, her eyes wide with an amalgam of equal parts fear and anger. She leaned into the car and started systematically feeling around on the carpeted base of the floor, feeling her way around beneath the passenger seat and the floor on that side.

"What is it? What was that about? That face you made? You okay?" I managed to get out before my body started to shut down. One of the last things I remember was seeing her scream out my name and lunge at me from where she had crawled into the car on the passenger side. The last thing I remembered feeling were her fingers gracing mine from under the seat of driver's side when, as she was searching for the very thing that would keep me alive, she touched very thing that would lead us right into a hell of our own making. The damn gun.

I woke back up sitting on the ground right next to the car with my head leaning against the rear quarter panel of the driver's side. The door was still flung wide open, and the dome light illuminated the face looking down at me.

"Oh, thank God, Jett! Thank God..." Mags let out a relieved cry, collapsing herself right next to me, leaning back against the car as well, her left hand on my leg and the insulin pen still lodged in a death grip in her right hand. I could hear her sniffle and felt her body shutter as she began to softly cry. It took me a minute or two to come back from wherever I had been, and in that time, this goddess of a friend got back up on her knees and reached back into the car, procuring an opened can of pop from when we had stopped earlier in the night at the shrimping dock.

"Here, drink this," she said, her voice returning to its normal tone, but her fingers still visibly shaking as she put the can in my raised but weak hand. I happily drank the flat pop, knowing that the magic of the sugar in that can combined with the insulin bolus that I had just been injected with should bring me back around from the corner of death pretty quickly. I was grateful, of course, that I had avoided a diabetic shock or coma. But the real shitty part was that I knew my night would be over now. No more late-night talks or fumbling around anxiously in the back seat of Pencil Man's old car, even if I had wanted to. After an episode like this, I knew that a heavy exhaustion was on its way, and that there would be nothing more I could do about it other than sleep it off. I just needed to get home.

We sat there for a few more minutes like that, just she and I leaning against the beautiful old car, before Jojo and Monica came to find us and see what the hell was taking so long. "What the hell, guys? I half expected to find ya both in the back seat, windows steamed up… not sitting out here on the ground. What happened?" Jojo asked, wheeling himself over to the passenger side of the car, presumably to shut the door which had been left wide open.

"Holy fuck! Who did this?" his voice screeched from the other side of the car. "Oh my God!" Monica gasped.

Confused, I asked what the hell they were talking about, and right about then, bells went off in my mind, a faint echo of a memory that crept its way back to the frontal cortex of my dazed and foggy brain. Right before my lights went out, Mags had said something to the same effect when she had climbed into the passenger side of the car.

"What the hell are you guys all talking about? What's wrong over there?" I shouted, Mags just squeezing my leg and looking down at the warm asphalt.

"Jojo, we had a tough time finding the insulin pen, so I climbed in the car over there and found it. Jett damn near passed out before I could stab him with it! He ain't seen that side of the car yet…" her voice trailed off and was then interrupted by Jojo's anyway when he rolled along the back of the car and shouted out, "Damn, dude, not the taillights too! Those assholes! Jett, don't worry, I'm sure we can get this back to my dad's and he can help us fix it before you gotta take it back. Just stay calm my man."

"Jesus guys, can someone please just tell me what the hell is going on?"

Mags just kept squeezing my thigh and calmly spoke to no one as she stared straight ahead into the darkness. "It's my fault, Jett. It has nothing to do with you, really. Turk's just pissed that he can't have his way. I shouldn't have kissed you in front of him, shouldn't have pushed him into going there. Now he's pissed. I'm so sorry, Jett!"

Wanting to see the damage to the car myself, I clambered up to a standing position, my head not agreeing with the decision, almost causing me to pass right back out again. I steadied myself against the car momentarily before slowly walking around the car from the backside, a hot knot of nerves and fury beginning to squeeze my intestines and a ball of fire sitting directly in the center of my chest. I saw the broken taillights first, obviously shattered by a stick or something heavier like a bat, since there was some denting along the bumper as well. I was sickened and honestly had to swallow the puke that was fighting to come up into my throat. I inhaled a shaky breath before turning the corner to see the side of this damaged and beloved piece of history. Not only did the asshole swing a bat into the front quarter panel on the driver's side, but there was a long scratch running from the middle of both doors on the passenger side. At first, I thought it was from a key, but quickly realized that it must have been something more along the lines of a screwdriver because the scrape mark was wider and deeper, making it next to impossible to just buff it out.

I stood staring at the wounded car, rage building up in my soul. "Who the fuck does he think he is? Who does shit like this?" I screamed out, wanting to cry, but not wanting these guys, especially Mags, to see me cry.

Mags came running around to my side of the car, standing next to me with her hand on my back, just saying nothing.

Jojo just offered his help again saying, "My dude, we got this. No problem. My dad's a wiz with machines, we can fix it…" but his voice was slowly drowned out by a rumble coming from the rear entrance of the parking lot. Sure as shit, a shiny black Stealth pulled in, gliding over to a stop just feet away from where we were standing. The tinted driver's side window was rolled down, exposing the smiling face of the bastard behind the wheel.

"Well, what are you guys doin' out here? Mags, you done spreading your skinny little legs for this little freak? Look at him. Him and his piece of shit car. He doesn't' belong in our world, girl. You know that. Come on, kid, let me take you home. I'd love to have your sweet little ass in my car…" came the voice of a snake from the driver's seat.

I am sure he must have said more revolting things. I am sure he must have said something more that night that would have triggered me to unleash years of anger and pent-up rage. Looking back, I would like to think that I had more of a reason than just words to go temporarily insane, effectively signing my own death warrant. But I don't remember any of that.

I remember my anger blocking out the noise, my rage giving me tunnel vision and my diabetic shock leaving me feeling invincible. I was done. Done hiding from him, done feeling afraid.

Mags' granddad had been right. She was absolutely worth defending. I would protect her, if I didn't die first, that is.

I grabbed the keys from Mag's hand that was also still clutching the insulin pen, and without giving it a second thought, positioned them in my fist like brass knuckles. Methodically, I calmly walked right over to the driver's side of his car and looked at the snake in the driver's seat, noticing that he was now alone, no date riding shotgun, none of his cronies in the car either. It was just him. I stood there, staring at him and trying to decide what to say, what to do, when he beat me to the punch and spoke first. "Jesus Christ, you freak. Get the hell outta here. Don't be anywhere near my car. Did you hear me, little man, or are you just retarded too?

Those were the words that lit my world on fire. Slowly, I let a sinister grin creep across my lips and slowly echoed into the universe, "Fuck you…" as I punched my hand into the body of the car and walked down the side, the keys in my hand making a horrible scratching sound as I walked.

I knew I was dead as soon as I did it. I think I would have been okay with that, though, because somewhere in my seventeen-year-old head, I believed that I had won. I had gotten the girl. I was the one everyone envied on that dance floor. And there was nothing that Turk could do to me now that would take that away.

The next few seconds replay in my head like an explosion, all of my senses firing at once, the electricity coursing through my veins from fear as he quickly climbed out of the car. A roaring sound drowned my ears from the kids who had just ended their prom night and were making their way out to their cars to go party somewhere else, now noticing what was happening and screaming in excitement. But the only thing that I saw, the only thing that I wanted to see right before I took the first hit, was her beautiful face, my Mags, staring at me with a calm expression, tears rolling down her face. Had I let her down? Did I not do enough? These were the questions that haunted me when Turk slammed the first fist into the left side of my head. Already weak from the effects of the insulin, I could hear her screaming before he landed the second blow, this one to the center of my belly while I was already bent over in pain from the first blow.

"Turk, get off of him, you asshole! He's sick, goddammit!" She begged, as other kids stood around shouting inaudibly as well. Were they cheering for what I had done, or egging him on to keep going, giving me, the freak, what I deserved.

He had climbed on top of me now, and although my left eye had begun to swell, I was still able to see him out of my right eye as he leaned in close and whispered, "Now I'm gonna make her watch, make her see what a big fuckin' pussy you are. And when I'm done with you, I'm gonna take that sweet whore out into the woods and give her what she really needs," before lifting my head up and slamming it back down on the pavement. Once. Twice.

It was getting harder and harder to see and the world had begun to swirl. He was off of me then, standing off to my side, muttering something about his car and what a freak I was, right before I felt the toe of his snakeskin boot land a hard kick into my rib, then a pause before another landed right into my bad hip. The pain was so bad it halted the breath that I was trying so desperately to suck in.

What a poetically devastating way to die. Defending my best friend. What a scene it must have been though, me lying there on the warm asphalt in the parking lot, the overhead streetlamp shining down over us in a yellowish bath of light, blood spilling out of my head onto the asphalt, my finely pressed pants and newly-paid-for brocade suit in tatters as two cars sat off to the side, both damaged, while a crowd of onlookers cheered on. My brain sorted it out like a movie, but I wanted the fairytale ending, the one where I rose up off the ground and kicked the crap out of this asshole, effectively standing up for myself and saving the princess. That ain't what I got, though.

Instead, as I laid there, helplessly bleeding from my head and too weak to defend myself, I raised my right arm to shield an incoming blow to the face from his fist again. He was so full of pent-up rage that I didn't see an ending coming.

"Damn it, Turk! Stop it, you're going to kill him!" shouted Jojo, who was helplessly looking on from the sideline in his chair on wheels, effectively rendering him unable to help in the current situation.

Turk just smiled as he grabbed me by the lapel jacket and raised me up again with the intent to slam my head back down into the asphalt, probably for the last time. Realizing that I was about to go out, I closed my eyes and hoped for a merciful end, hearing his voice shout back to Jojo, "Good!"

Fireworks. I thought I had heard goddamn fireworks. I shit you not, for a split second I actually thought that the prom committee must have come into a cache of Turk's drug money or something, 'cause I damn near thought I heard fireworks shooting off.

The explosion was then followed by silence, and Turk dropped me, too stunned at something to continue beating me. "What the fuck, little girl? What are you doing?" he screamed out, still making no attempt to move from me, like a lion guarding his kill from the hungry hyena. I laid there in the warm blood and rolled my head over to where I thought I had heard the blast echo from.

Out of my one good eye, I saw her. She stood there, my Mags, calmly and with purpose, her thin arms raised high above her head pointing her granddad's 9mm towards the sky. I exhaled a sigh of relief and allowed my painful face one glorious smile.

"Leave him alone, Turk. Just go." Mags calmly ordered. If she was scared at all, that girl didn't show it. She had one hell of a poker face.

"Oh, you bitch! You don't know what you just did. Do you know who the hell you're messin' with?" Turk screamed back at her, obviously shaken, and pissed that he was put in a position in front of the entire student body that made him look weak and unstable.

"A better question to ask, Turk, is do YOU know who the fuck you are messin' with? Go ask your bosses and your cartel family who my granddad is you piece of shit.

You should know better!"

"Bitch, you crazy! I'm gonna leave, but you better be lookin' over your shoulder, girl. They are gonna come for you," Turk said as he climbed back in his car and peeled out of the lot. It was right about then that the school faculty finally made their way outside as he was leaving. Funny how that always works.

I was okay. Just bruised and banged up with a questionable ego. The school demanded that I be checked out at the hospital anyway, I suppose wanting to cover their asses just in case anything was seriously wrong with me and they could be held liable. Mags drove me over there and sat with me in a room while I waited for my pop to get there. I didn't want him to know, but when you are still under the age of eighteen, your life is oddly still the responsibility of someone else's, unfortunately. I had been their burden for far too long, and this was just one more thing to dump on the pile of disappointments.

Jojo took Monica home and came back over to the hospital afterwards. Rolling into my room, he found Mags sitting on the foot of my bed while a police officer finished taking the report. The story that we all gave him matched up, and they must have bought the part where we said it was really Turk who fired a warning shot, because at the mere mention of his name as Mags was telling her side of the story, the officer kind of quit taking notes. I guess some people walk on the wrong side of the law so deeply that even the local cops know that it's better to just let them twist in the wind than piss off people whose money runs the town.

"Okay kids, I think that's about all I need then. If you need anything else, just holler. Boy, I couldn't get ahold of your pa, but your mama is sending someone over to get ya soon. You should be out of here in a bit," the kind officer said, rather matter-of-factly before giving a quick wink to Mags and heading out into the hall.

"That was some night, my dude!" squealed Jojo in a low tone as soon as the cop was out of earshot.

"Not how I expected the night to go at all, but still happy we did it," I said solemnly as Mags gave my hand a squeeze.

"It was a pretty bad ass prom, wasn't it?" Mags blurted out, trying not to let a sense of pity fill her eyes as she sat surveying the damage to my face. Eighteen stitches ran beneath my left cheekbone and there were about twelve or so more tucked behind that ear. I had three cracked ribs and a bruised clavicle, a minor concussion, and a crack in the growth plate of my right hip. The nurses that cleaned me up said I was an easy bleeder and had worried that the damage was much worse when I first walked in.

I sat in awe thinking about how the night had turned out, which was a far cry from where it had started. All I wanted to do was have a good time with my friends, just blend in like all the other juniors and seniors. I had wanted so badly for everything to be perfect. Although, as time would teach me, even the most intricately structured plans don't always work out.

Feeling exhausted from the events of the night, I suddenly realized that it was a Saturday night, so my pop would have been working the extra shift over at the quarry as he always did every other weekend for a little extra cash. Mom wouldn't have left my brothers alone in the middle of the night at the trailer court, so I wondered who the officer had been referring to when he'd said someone was coming to get me.

His voice bellowed in the hallway asking a nurse for directions to my room before his thin silhouette appeared in the doorway. When Scroggs walked in, Mags instinctively jumped off the bed like she had seen a ghost and moved over to a chair where Jojo had set up camp.

"Well now boy, that didn't end the way you thought it would, now, did it?" he spoke in a calm demeaner, his words crisp, yet not in a chastising manner. Leaning in a little closer to survey my wounds, the old character almost whispered, "If I didn't know any better, I'd say you put up a hell of a fight, kid. Looks like you must have been battling pretty hard for somebody…" and he gave me a wink. The smell of his aftershave wafted through the room long after he left to see what he had to do to get me out of there.

"I'll take the car back for ya," Mags began, shooting a look over at Jojo. "Jojo can come with me too, right Jo-bean?"

"Yeah, no prob, Mags, I'll get you home. Takin' the car back to the Pencil Man? I think I know where his place is," Jojo replied, stretching as he finished his sentence with a yawn.

Scroggs walked back into the room as the two were discussing their final plans for the night, still perched over by the wall.

"I should go with you guys," I said. "I have to be the one to tell him the awful thing that happened to his poor car. Just makes me sick what that asshole Turk did to it. Pencil Man trusted me with it, and I let that happen to it. I gotta face that fire," I said, feeling sick in the pit of my stomach as I said it.

Scroggs interjected, "Now boy, I saw the car parked out in the lot and it ain't that bad. The body shop will have that shined up in no time, new taillights and all. Don't you worry 'bout it.

Besides, you aren't the one who did it. You aren't the one who will answer for it." He walked over to where Mags and Jo were still quietly jabbering on. "Okay you two, ya best be getting' on home before your families start to worry. I know it's prom night and all, but it's getting to be pretty late. What's the clock say… almost two in the morning?"

Looking up on the wall, the three of us were mesmerized when we realized how much of the night had just slipped away. We had been caught up in the excitement, the drama, and the brave tale that we would tell our own kids someday.

"Okay then," Mags said as she stood, her gown now slightly tattered and her eye makeup smudged from pissed off tears she couldn't will to stop. She walked over to me and awkwardly leaned over to give me a hug, obviously feeling strange being under the watchful eye of Scroggs just a few feet away from her. "See you tomorrow then. Mr. Scroggs, it was good to see you. Thanks for coming to get him," she said looking down towards the floor as she spoke and hustling by him as quickly as she could, noticeably making no eye contact.

"See ya tomorrow, bud!" Jojo waved over his head as he wheeled back out of the room. Then it was down to just Scroggs and me.

"The hospital talked to your mama, boy. They are ready to clear you so you can get out of here. Then I'll take you on home."

"Thank you, sir," was the only thing that my tired body was able to say. After the nurses came in to change my bandages one more time and give me wound care instructions, I headed out to the Thunderbird that was parked close by the front door of the hospital. Scroggs opened my door and got me situated, handing me an icepack for my ribs and a plastic hospital bag that held my vest, tie, and torn suit jacket. I slumped over in my seat as we drove away.

We were about halfway home and I could barely keep my eyes open. I felt like once I hit my pillow, I would be out for days. It was when I was in this tired and emotionally drained state that he decided to talk to me.

"You wanna talk about it, boy" he asked, hands at ten and two on the wheel and eyes laser focused on the road ahead.

"Not much to say, really. The guy's an asshole, I've told you that. He got what he had comin' to him, though." I said smoothly with my eyes pinched tight, my head throbbing, and my ribs straining with every breath I took in.

"Is that right? Well, if I'm a betting man, I would say that he's about to get a little more than what he had comin' to him. Woo-eee. He don't know what he's in for..." Scroggs laughed as we turned down the main drag over by the trailer court.

Confused, his words not really lining up in my swollen head, I questioned him, my eyes still blissfully pinched tight, hoping that sleep would find me soon. "What do you mean? What's coming for him?"

"Well, for starters, I heard that you keyed his car pretty good, that right?" Scroggs asked in a rather dry tone.

"You bet I did! I got it good and deep too!" I proudly answered.

"Well, boy, like I have told ya before, that boy's ma has been hanging around with one of those cartel boys, and he's been lettin' him drive that car. So that car comes with a hefty price tag.

That boy has been using it to run drugs and go on small gun runs for the cartel. Everything that he has, the car, the clothes, the cash, it's all just an illusion. That piss ant ain't the one pulling the strings." Scroggs spoke as he pulled the car into my drive, letting it idle as he hopped out and walked around to open my door and guide me out.

When I realized the possible ramifications of what I had just done, I got hot. I felt like my tongue was swelling up in my throat and I wanted to puke and pass out at the same time. I began to breathe erratically and with each breath it felt like my cracked ribs were gonna splinter apart. When my door was flung open, the only thing I could get out in my panic-induced state was, "Fuck, Scroggs! Those boys are gonna kill me! They're gonna hunt me down and kill me for sure!"

He looked at me in confusion before letting out a giggle, put his hand on my shoulder and told me to calm the hell down. "Listen boy, that ain't how the game is played. You won't be the one they will be after. You only put the wheels in motion. They are gonna take one look at that car and hold him accountable."

"Jesus, Scroggs, what are they gonna do to him? They gonna kill him?" I asked, sick at the thought. I mean, I *did* hate the guy, but I couldn't live with the thought that his blood would be on my hands.

"Can't say, boy. But I do know he will be the one to have to answer for what he has done. Now, let's get you on in to your poor mama. She's been worried sick."

Hobbling into the house that night, the last twenty-four hours seemed like a blur. I realized that what had started as an evening full of nervous expectations and teenaged banter could end in a possible murder. And it was my hands that held the blame, even if they hadn't been the ones to pull the trigger.

Chapter 13:
Do You Know Instinct?

I slept hard that night, although my sweet mama kept coming in to wake me up and then let me go back to sleep, fearing that I may die in the night from the concussion. When she was satisfied that I had made it through the night, she stopped waking me right around dawn and I slumbered well into the early afternoon. I suppose it was the trauma and the adrenaline from the fight, combined with my tanking sugar levels that really wore me down.

When I did come to, I saw my pop sitting in the corner of my room just looking at me. Startled, I bolted upright, asking if everything was okay.

"Of course it is, son. I just got home not too long ago from pulling extra hours on the overnight and your mama filled me in on how you were," he began, staring intently at me and letting a slight giggle escape his lips before continuing on, a crooked smile taking its place on his weathered face. "Sounds like you had one hell of a night, huh?"

I didn't know if he was going to be proud or pissed, so I banked on pissed and launched into a scattered tirade of an apology, outlining all the reasons Turk deserved what he got, and how I was just so sick and tired of him picking on me. I told him about what he did to the car, how embarrassing it had been that I was too weak to really fight back, and that Scroggs had sprung me from the hospital.

Pop just stared at me, not letting my words faze him too much at all. He ran his hands through his thinning hair and let out a big sigh. "And what about the girl, the one that you are always hangin' around with? She turn out okay?" he asked.

"Mags? Yes sir," I proudly said with a smile on my dopey hormonal face, still envisioning her in that dress, feeling her raspberry lips on mine as the whole dance floor watched. Carefully gauging the situation, I left out the part where she'd fired off the gun and actually rescued my ass instead of the other way around. "She made it out just fine."

"Well, did you at least have a good time before the shitshow started?" Pop asked, still half- smiling, so I knew I wasn't in trouble for anything... yet.

"I really did, Pop! That car was so fun to drive and the group of us danced and ate and had a ton of fun. Um... did mom tell ya that I almost passed out though from my dang low blood sugar?" I asked him, sheepishly hoping that he wouldn't launch into a lecture about being more responsible. But once again, he surprised me. Rising to his feet, he said, "She sure did, but you know what? You knew your body well enough that you saw the signs and knew what you needed to happen. You handled it, kid! I keep telling your mama that you are almost an adult now and I think you got yourself handled. She needs to quit worryin' so damn much. You scared me though; I don't like getting calls that you are in the hospital in the middle of the night. But you handled it, kid. Sounds like you had a good time, and you took care of the things that need to be taken care of, including that little gal of yours," Pop said, as he dropped eye contact and headed towards the door of my room to presumably go sleep the rest of the afternoon away before he had to be back at work the next night. Poor Pop had been working so hard that he usually only had Sundays off, and he spent most of those precious hours sleeping in front of the TV. But on that Sunday, he had stayed up long enough to make sure that I was alright. Even better, as he walked out of my door, he said the words that I had been chasing down from him for years. "Proud of ya, Jett. You did real good last night."

I could have floated out of that room, I was so pumped! The man I had thought I was such a disappointment to for all those years finally thought I had done something worthy enough to be proud of. But the excitement was short-lived, as he quickly turned back towards me in the doorway to put me on alert. "Oh, that asshole, the one who put you in the hospital last night? I heard your mama talking to the neighbor. He's gone missin'. They found his car parked out by the Glades next to the shrimpin' docks, but no sign of him. Ain't that something?" Then, as he walked away down the hall, he tacked on," The universe is a mysterious bitch, ain't she?"

My head was swirling, trying to make some sense of what he had just said. I had fallen asleep the night before, envisioning ways that he would get revenge on me or make my life a living hell. I had thought about what Scroggs had said to me on the way home from the hospital. That because of the things I had set into motion, Turk would have a bigger nightmare to answer to. I felt slightly guilty at that thought, not because he didn't deserve a disastrous downfall or at least to be knocked back down a couple of pegs on the food chain, but I didn't like the way that my guts felt. It didn't sit right with me that I would have another man's downfall on my head, my hands being the ones responsible for the pain that he would be forced to endure. I mean, of course I hated him, but the way any stupid teenaged kid hates an enemy. I didn't actually want anything too bad to happen to him, and I damn sure didn't want to be held responsible for wiping him off of this mudball we called Earth.

I leapt out of bed, maybe a little too fast, and threw on a change of clothes. I hadn't heard from Mags or Jojo yet, so maybe they hadn't heard or surely they would have filled me in. Passing my mama in the kitchen, who was trying to get a late lunch on the table for the heathens that were my younger brothers, I bolted towards the back door, intent on running over to Scroggs' place first to see what all he had heard, since it was Sunday and he would be back from running his errands in town and would have gotten his fill of the local gossip.

"Now hang on there, Jett. You haven't eaten, haven't taken your meds yet. You still have a concussion, you know! You haven't even told me about prom yet! Won't you please just sit down a spell before you take off?" she begged as she set down a plate of sandwiches on the center of the old blaze orange and chrome Formica dining table, the one she had picked up at a tag sale after having to sell her prized walnut dining table that she'd gotten as a wedding present and that we had sat around as kids, to pay off one of my medical bills last year. It killed her to sell that damn thing, but as always, we needed the cash for my medical treatments. My heart ached. She deserved to be rewarded with all the fruits of her labor, to finally hear me tell her stories of normal teenaged stuff, like school dances and crushes and boys being boys. I owed her that much.

I reached into the center of the table to wrestle a bologna and cheese sandwich away from my brothers and beelined to the fridge to grab my auto injectors. "When I get home later, Mama, I promise. I just have to get going now. I told Scroggs I would help him clean up Pencil Man's car from last night." She was pacified as I leaned in to give the poor woman a quick kiss on the cheek. "Don't forget to do your shots!" she hollered out as I ran out the door.

Like any other day, it was still muggy and blazing hot in our tiny Florida town. The walk over towards Scroggs' trailer was made all the more miserable by my head beginning to throb and my ribs feeling like they were going to explode with each step I took. I tried to just focus on eating the dang sandwich and quit thinking about the pain. Passing by Scroggs' neighboring trailer, the one where Bradley James had lived, I froze for a quick second, standing on the curb directly in front of the abandoned trailer from where he had gone missing a few years back. No one ever did move back into the place, and nobody ever came to remove it either, so there it still stood. The weeds had grown high around the old swing set and raccoons had taken over what had been the porch. What was the real story of Bradley? Where the hell did he go? It was even spookier to think that it was possibly happening again with Turk now missing. Goosebumps crept up my back and the empty trailer that stood in front of me offered no answers, so onward I walked over to Scroggs' place.

Pencil Man's poor old four-door El Camino sat out front. A bucket and sponge rested by her front passenger tire. The painful looking scrape down her side had faded to a dull sheen, as someone must have already started trying to buff out what they could. Focusing on the rear of her, I saw that someone had also carefully removed the pieces of the sad little shattered taillights, as well as the rear bumper to try and pound out some of the dents.

"Damn, Scroggs has been busy!" I thought to myself as I walked back around to the driver's side of the car to open the door, looking to see if the wrappers and napkins from our ice cream and snacks were still lying scattered about from the night before. I didn't want these two old guys to think that I was ungrateful or that I was a pig, for God's sake. Flinging the door open, the first thing that hit me was a familiar, yet pungent aroma that I would know anywhere… Scroggs' wife's bug spray concoction. Although I thought that was kind of odd, I figured Scroggs must have been wearing it this morning when he was working on the car.

Plausible, I convinced myself, because the bugs were out now that it was already afternoon. The heavy scent of witch hazel, alcohol and lemon hung thick in the air as I glanced around the interior of the car. I immediately noticed that it was immaculate. Not only had the dash been wiped clean of all dust, but the steering wheel had also been polished to a perfectly chromed shine, the windshield damn near sparkled, and there wasn't a speck of dirt on the floorboard carpet.

Something just wasn't clicking yet in my confused state. "Why the hell would he go to all the trouble to make the inside immaculate? Pencil Man can't even see to drive it and would never know if there was a little dust in there," I said out loud to no one as I leaned in to look around a little closer, suddenly wondering about the whereabouts of the gun. Lowering myself down to a crouching position, I put a hand on the fabric seat to lean over and look beneath it. There was, of course, no gun. I figured that there wouldn't have been… that Pencil Man would have already told Scroggs to do something with it. What threw me for a loop, though, was when I noticed that even the seat was damp.

"Damn it! Did I leave the windows down? Did it rain last night?" I stood in thought, staring at the car in utter disbelief and confusion. I glanced around the street and noticed that everything was still bone dry and dusty, no sign of water anywhere. I knew that if rain had somehow seeped into the beautiful car in this hot weather, surely it wouldn't take long until mildew or mold would set in, destroying the old fabric in no time.

I stood there realizing that my head was once again starting to throb, and my cheek had started to swell from being out in the heat. "This makes no sense…" I once again said out loud to no one, gently touching the stitches behind my ear to make sure they weren't oozing and that it was just sweat rolling down the side of my neck.

The strong smell of the witch hazel concoction was almost overpowering, and I lifted my hand to smell my fingers from where they had gotten damp on the car seat. It was pungent. My hand smelled just like the bug concoction. "Now why the hell would he have needed to clean the seats too?" I knew that we hadn't spilled anything, and I was so careful to not get any blood from my wounds on the seats last night on the way to the hospital.

That concoction was known to fend off bugs, mold, and mildew. It could bring out a shine and clean a windshield too. Suddenly a sickness attacked my soul and I felt like I was beginning to suffocate as I remembered clearly now what else that old concoction could be used for. I had seen Scroggs soak his fishin' clothes in it before when he had gutted fish and accidently sprayed blood on them. That's right, the sickly-sweet concoction of witch hazel, alcohol and lemon was great at oxidizing and lifting blood out of fabric. But if I was damned sure that I hadn't bled in that car last night, then...

Just about then, the screen door on the back of Scroggs' house slapped against its frame and Scroggs appeared in the doorway of the workshop, water sloshing out of the top of an old carpet shampooer. So, he *had* been shampooing the seats after all.

Startled to see me, he almost dropped the shampooer and said, "Cripes sakes, boy, I didn't think I'd be seein' you up and about today. How you feeling?" going right back to his work of cleaning out the car, not missing a beat.

Feeling like my brain was on fire, trying to hold my anxiety at bay, I quickly said, "Not too bad. Slept in real late after Mama kept waking me up all night, frettin' that I was gonna die. Dang cheek bone is puffing up again and I thought I'd be okay walking on over here, but now I ain't feeling so well again. Can I go in and grab some water and sit a spell? I promised my mama I would take these damn injections when I left the house."

Acting like there was absolutely nothing to worry about and nothing to hide, the slick Mr. Scroggs just said, "Sure thing kid, help yourself. There's some stew still warm on the stove from lunch," as he flipped the switch on the shampooer and kept right on vacuuming.

I let myself into the trailer and flipped on the TV in the living room, settling down on a pillow in the middle of the floor. I could hear the shampooer emitting a low buzz from outside as I rolled up my sleeve to once again shoot the magic potion into my veins. I wanted so badly to be done with it all, but at the same time, I had been proud for a fleeting moment that I was finally beginning to get a handle on my own life, that things had finally started to turn around for me. I held my breath as I jammed the damn needle into my arm and felt the old familiar pinch and burn as it went in.

The truth was, I was just about done on the journey to race my growth plates. Time was running out to keep tricking my body into growing just a little more. By the onset of summer that year, when I was seventeen, I had reached a height of five-foot-three, which, to most seems a little on the short side. To my mama, it was more than we had ever dreamed of. For so long, my growth had stalled, and we had setback after setback with surgery after surgery. When I was younger, we had tried to hold out hope that I would possibly hit the five-foot mark, but that took years of torment and frustration to get that far. For some reason, puberty held off just long enough, leaving a preciously small window of time for my body to thrive before the growth plates closed.

Although five-foot-three was short, my body had also

followed the normal ebb and flow of weight gain and losses that naturally came with hitting puberty. I was thankful that as the dosage of hormones had finally tapered off, so had my weight. Without realizing that it was happening, my body, which had fought me for so long, finally gave in that junior year of high school and gave me a bit of a reprieve, allowing me to look at my own reflection, and not cringe.

I pulled the syringe back out of my arm and laid back onto the carpet for a little while, staring at the white tiled ceiling and daydreaming about marrying Mags someday. I was crushing so hard on that girl, imagining us going off to college together in another year and what living with her in a dorm might be like. Jojo would move with us too, of course, and we would party our way through four more years of school. Lost in a feverish daydream, I barely heard the voices that were now rising to an arguing tone near Scroggs' workshop.

Wanting to see what the heck was going on, I sat back up, maybe a little too quickly, and flicked the TV back off. Hopping up, I slyly peaked out of the bayed living room window trying to see who was out there. I couldn't see anyone from that angle, so I made my way to the screen door in the back of the trailer. Just as I was stepping outside, my body defied me once again, my vision forcing a periphery of blackness, and my knees began to shake. I couldn't stop myself from dropping to my knees, then falling forward into a slumped position, stopping myself with my hands on the cement pad of the shop to prevent taking a nosedive to the ground.

"Christ, boy, you okay?" Scroggs' voice called to me from across the shop. I was barely keeping my eyes open at that point, fighting off the woozy lightheadedness that had attacked me, either a ramification of last night's events, getting up too quickly from the floor, a freefalling blood sugar level, or a nasty concoction of all three. "Awe crap!" I shouted, "I forgot to do my damn insulin again. Since they started tapering back my hormone injections and the other meds, it's just been a rollercoaster of a shitshow." I rolled over and sat flat on my butt on the dirty cement pad, pulling the other auto injector out from my pocket. As I was yanking the cap off in a sloppy manner, I noticed a car pulling away from the curb in a hurry, squealing its tires as it took off.

"What the hell was that about?" I blurted out to Scroggs, too exhausted to give a shit about niceties at that point, while grabbing a fold of skin on my belly and jabbing the injector in quickly. A painful burn made me shout out and writhe in torturous pain. "Oh, damn! That time it stung like a bitch! Must have gotten some air bubbles in there..."

"You know, you really should be using alcohol wipes to clean the skin before you shoot up with your little concoctions. Or even a little bit of witch hazel to clean your skin. You gotta be careful of infections, boy. You gotta take better care to stay well, you know..." Scroggs replied, ignoring my initial inquisition as to who the hell had just squealed out of there like their ass was on fire, simply going back over to his carpet shampooer to empty the dirty water into the drain of the shop floor. Watching the water swirl, I blurted out the obvious, "Why are you scrubbing down the car so good? We didn't get the inside of it dirty at all. I thought we were gonna work on the scrape and dents?"

I just sat there staring at him, waiting to see what his

reply was going to be. But just as I had expected, he simply said nonchalantly, "That poor old car hadn't been cleaned real good in years! It just sits there most of the time, collecting dust. So, I figured I might as well put a little elbow grease into her while I was tinkering on the outside, too. I don't have anything better to do anyways," he said, never even pausing to look my way.

"Did you hear about Turk?" I blurted out, making my way back up to my feet, slowly taking a few steps in his direction.

"I did! I heard the neighborhood old biddies whispering about him this morning over their morning coffee. You know, as they were doing their morning gossip walks around the neighborhood, slowing down right in front of my place, craning their old, wrinkled necks to see if I was doing anything worth gossiping about," Scroggs replied, tacking a little laughter on the end for good measure.

"Why do they all still have it in for you after all these years? Why the hell don't those old bags just leave you alone?" I questioned, a small ember of anger beginning to rage within my belly. I too had been the misunderstood outcast for far too long, and for the life of me I couldn't figure out why people had such a misunderstood and dark opinion where Scroggs was concerned. Why the hell was he so easy to peg things on? And why the hell didn't he ever take to dispelling the rumors and defending himself a little better? Acting odd sure as heck wasn't helping his cause. "Small towns need scapegoats, kid. Someone to pin suspicions on so they can sleep better at night. It wasn't always like that around here though, at least not with me. It wasn't until after my wife passed and I took to staying to myself more and throwing myself into my work more that the local nags took it as a sign that I was going off the deep end, possibly locked in some struggle with depression. They saw me as a recluse, a shut in. It just became easier for them to see me as a monster than to ever believe that there was real evil lurking their streets at night.

Truth is boy, the evil is usually hiding within their own four walls." Scroggs quieted down and walked over to his work bench, reaching for a roll of shop rags. I was still gripping my auto injector, which was now empty, and walked over towards the trashcan in the corner to throw it away. As I was lifting the metal lid, Scroggs had just turned around to face me, dropping his roll of shop towels and yelled out, "No, not that one, boy! That one's full! Just leave that one alone…"

His words hadn't hit the air in time. His intent to stop our worlds from unravelling any further were shattered the millisecond that I lifted that lid. The can was full, he hadn't been wrong about that. It was what was lying right on top of the garbage, on the piles of dirty shop rags and bloodied paper towels that would rip my world apart. I immediately recognized the blood- spattered gown that was balled up in there, and the only thing that made that realization worse was that I also recognized the purple shards of a silk shirt that had been covered in blood and torn to shreds as well, sadly nestled in right next to it. I frantically lunged into the trash, running my fingers over the gown as panic started to claw at my throat. My heart made a swift run for it as my brain started to rapid-fire facts. I hadn't heard from Mags since yesterday. Turk was missing. That fucking car had just been wiped completely clean and here I sat with my hands buried in Mags' and

Turk's bloodied and torn clothes. If that was the bottom of my well of torturous despair, my head was further held under when I slid the remnants of the silk shirt over to the side, exposing the contents of Turk's wallet, including his cut up driver's license.

Scroggs froze at first, then slowly began walking towards me with his hands held out in front of him, as if to tell me to hold on or to calm down. He was waiting for a reaction. The man I had wanted to believe in for all those years, the man I had considered to be a kindred spirit in our little club of outcasts, was wanting to see if he had poked the bear, if there was any kind of fight or flight left in my soul at all.

My words wouldn't come. My heart shattered within my body and in all the confusion, I watched my future hopes and dreams fall away, layer by layer. There would be no college for me and Mags, no dorm room, no wedding. Everything that I had held within my grasp just twenty-four hours ago had been violently ripped away, and there I stood, face to face with the monster I never saw coming.

I wanted to puke. I wanted to kill him. I wanted to die.

"Now, just wait a minute, boy…." Scroggs cautioned in a low tone. "You don't understand what you are seeing..." he said, attempting to soothe me, attempting to calm me down. My heart was crushed and my soul was having none of it.

"How could you! Of all the horrible people that you had to choose from. Turk, I understand. Hell, Turk, I probably wouldn't even bat an eye about. But Mags!!!! MY MAGS!" my voice was getting louder and louder, the panic and rage taking ahold of all logical thoughts that my swollen brain was trying so desperately to produce. Instinctively, I grabbed him by the throat and slammed him against the hood of the car, his arms immediately raising up to claw at my face, my neck, his legs writhing in an uncontrollable fashion.

The strength that I had from the adrenaline rush was like the stories you hear of a person coming up on a car wreck and being able to lift a car with their bare hands. I held him down by the throat, pinning him to the trunk of Pencil Man's beautiful old car, squeezing the life out of his greying eyes as hot tears ran down my cheeks, nearly blinding me in the process. I wasn't sure what hurt worse: the thought of losing Mags, or the thought of losing him, this old sage that I had likened myself to, had loved for the better part of the last six years like a father. I held his throat tightly, forcing the life to escape his body while mourning him at the same time.

There is a chill that encapsulates your soul when you are struggling to overcome a loss. Death saunters into a room and wraps her cold arms around your heart, tracing her icy fingers down your spine. You feel hollow, alone. There's a silence that deafens your ears and a darkness that drowns your heart. I had become a shell of a young man in just a few seconds, empty of empathy and void of guilt. I stared into his face, his creased forehead glistening with my tears, his dry lips mouthing the word, "Stop."

That was the last thing I saw before I felt the barrel of a gun jab into my side and my world was forced to a stifling darkness as a bag was pulled over my head.

Chapter 14:
Do You Know the Muffin Man?

"Dad, what do you think they are gonna have to eat? Do you think that I can get chicken nuggets?" my oldest son Nicky asked, skipping ahead of his brother, Mama, and me as we made our way over to the sign-in table. The table sat in front of a grossly oversized poster of myself, which was utterly embarrassing. My hands began to sweat as my youngest jumped into the conversation. "They better have ketchup, Dad! I hate eatin' nuggets with no ketchup!"

My wife let out an audible sigh, herding the boys along, not unlike lost little lambs. "Boys, let's not worry about it, okay? I'm sure that whatever we have will be great! Besides, did you see what's sitting across the room over there?" she questioned, pointing toward one of the most elaborate dessert banquets that I had ever seen. Sitting front and center was the overflowing milk chocolate fountain, the stuff little boys dream of.

She leaned over to gently grace her raspberry lips upon my freshly shaven cheek before grabbing the boys by the hands and proceeding to go exploring through the great hall, pointing out all of the exciting things along the way until it was time for them to take their seats. I could hear her voice echoing down the marble hallway as she made up stories of the art pieces that graced the walls and told them of great adventures when she would happen upon an old, elaborately framed photo of some poor sucker who had come before me.

My wife was great at this shit. She ate it up! She had always been a master of creating mystery and magic out of the monotonous and mundane. It was her way in life to carve out a little story everywhere she went. And our world was more colorful for it.

Clearing my throat, I apprehensively stepped ahead as my place in line had finally made it to the front. Out of embarrassment, the sweet older gal with the slicked back gray bun who had been in charge of tickets and registration hopped up quickly from her seat, damn near knocking over the glass of water that had sweated all over the white linen tablecloth, scattering a small pile of ceremony programs onto the floor. She stood right in front of me, mouth hanging open, eyes stunned, as if she had seen a ghost.

"Heavens, sir! What are you doin' out here standing in line with all of these people? You should be back in the green room! Oh my Lord, I apologize for making you wait out here! Had I known…" she continued, near tears, as though I had the power to end her job and wipe her from the planet right there. I mean, I had become pretty powerful. But that wasn't who I was brought up to be. Cracking a smile to soften the mood and ignoring the rest of her blabbering, I leaned over to pick up the programs that had spilled onto the floor, just as my mama would have expected me to do.

"Ma'am, there's no worries here. I haven't been waiting here for long and actually, I have enjoyed watching the guests arrive!" I handed her the small pile of rescued programs, placing my hand on her arm as a sign of my trust, a symbol, I had hoped, of no harm done. She just stared at me, her eyes brimming with a pool of tears that had formed, whether out of fear or embarrassment. But before she could force her lips to spew another empty apologetic word, there was a hard clap towards the center of my back, followed by the low bellow of a gentleman's voice. "Jett, it's so good to see you here! I am so proud of the work that your organization has done and honored that we can continue our work together," the low, gravelly, condescending tone came from the face that held no soul. I didn't have to turn around. I knew who it was.

I learned a long time ago that to make it in this world, sometimes you have to partner with people who may be heading in the same direction that you are traveling, but for different reasons. Sometimes, you have to choke out the voice in your head that's begging you not to get into bed with a crooked business partner, just to keep moving forward. Sometimes you have to focus on building yourself a decent line of credit, no matter what type of debt might be incurred in order to get your business off the ground.

Alvaro was one of those dark entities, the type of soul who had a much darker reasoning for wanting to be in business with me, but who was also able to see the good that I was trying to do and was proud to be able to bring honor to his Cuban roots. Although Alvaro liked to fly below the radar of his family's cartel lifestyle, he was a good businessman and able to convince his family that staying in business with me was not only profitable, but also brought them some clout within the local law enforcement and circuit court circles. After all, there were police chiefs, judges and lawyers in this town that sat on my board of investors right alongside of Alvaro, not even wincing when they broke bread. It felt powerful to be that close to the right side of the law, and Alvaro craved it.

Alvaro and his family weren't a new concept to me when he first showed up at my office to make a formal proposition. In fact, we went way back. I think I was just finishing up college when I ran into him back at the trailer court, after I had gone home to see Mama and Pop for a long weekend. He and his new wife had bought a trailer next door, and it took all of one night of drinking and hanging out around the firepit to figure out who he was and where he was going. His charm, charisma and embedded lack of fear weren't surprising. After all, he was considered to technically be Turk's stepbrother after Turk's mama ended up marrying Alvaro's old man. I didn't trust him, but I liked his head for business and his devotion to his family. After all, that was exactly what I was trying to do… build something great for my own family, a legacy if you will.

Oh, and I liked the fact that his name meant "mighty," and could even be interpreted as "warrior of elves." Karma always finds a way.

Spinning around quickly, I threw my arms around him in a lavish show of love and gratitude, hugging one of the most dangerous predators this side of the Glades. But on this night, it didn't matter. On this night, we were just two philanthropists, two stable pillars of our little town who were coming together to proudly boast to a roomful of well-wishers and big pocketed sharks how far our little endeavor had reached and to showcase our successes. In truth, however, the night still came down to money, something that was no different than hustling in the streets.

"It's been a hell of a year, my friend, a hell of a year," Alvaro spoke, lowering his tone and maintaining a stoic stance, although I was able to catch the slightest flicker of a muscle in his jaw as he clenched his teeth together, a trick that I had mastered long ago, something that I would do when I would try not to cry, try not to show emotion.

I knew exactly what he was referring to. He had just lost one of his own sons in a terrible show of retaliation from another highly organized local family. "Yes, I'm so sorry to hear about…" I paused, choosing my next words extremely cautiously, "the family…" I continued, only to be interrupted by the little older gal once again as she handed me my name tag and motioned for me to follow her, telling Alvaro that she would be right back and that his name tag was on the table. "From my family to yours, Alvaro, I truly am sorry, and with much respect. If there is anything that we can do, anything at all…" I half-heartedly was attempting to escape his eyes, the eyes of a man who knew exactly what he was after, which made the hair on my forearms stand on end and the coldest of chills crawl up my spine.

"No worries, old friend. I know where to find you. See you inside. I'll be sure to stop and see your boys," he spoke, his jaw relaxing and, dare I say, a slight smile fighting its way across his strained mouth. Following the little old gal with the tight topknot of a gray bun, I followed like a weak duckling, briefly looking back towards Alvaro, only to see him still standing there at the registration table, paused in time, his scowl begging me to come back, demanding answers. He nodded his head towards me once again and spun on his perfectly polished alligator boots, heading for the great ballroom where my family had probably settled into their seats, innocently waiting for me to take the stage, no notion of the ghost of my past that was making his way towards them to become "reacquainted."

As close as we were as business partners, I made no mistake in thinking that the arrangement made me any less of a target in his eyes, no less of a cash cow. Alvaro knew that his world, although a dark underbelly of the city that was infinitely prosperous, depended on my world maintaining the status quo of existing. His involvement with my Foundation, which provided us with lucrative amounts of funding for my nonprofit as well as a few other business ventures, came at a price. The more years I spent doing business and side deals with him and his family, the more I began to understand that the price was quickly outweighing the reward, and when Alvaro sent a subtle hint that he was going to check in with my family, I took that as a hint that there was trouble and that I would be expected to help remedy the situation. I would be expected to play along. I would be expected to look away or risk losing them all.

I had become so shaken by the sideways exchange that sweat was now beading on the tanned creases of my forehead, also running down the center of my back and settling into the waistband of my tuxedo pants. I dutifully followed the little gray-haired gal to the green room that sat adjacent to the side of the stage behind the plush velvet black curtain. Honestly, my brain was on fire and her voice had begun to sound like an echo far away. I had no idea what she was saying.

Nervousness and fear had conspired to attack my system and once again, try to take me down, no different from all the other times this had happened as a kid. But I was a man now, and this was damn embarrassing. The dark cones had started to attack my periphery and I was only able to see a small space directly in front of me as we walked, just enough to watch the back of her squared-off heels of her black, freshly polished shoes as they hit every other tile with a loud click. I just listened for that sound, those clicks, lulling me down the hall. Stopping at the door to the green room, she pulled the set of keys from the rubber cording wrapped around her wrist and her hand trembled a little as she slid the key into the door.

She reached in to flip the light on the wall, and I barreled past her, dropping into the nearest chair, my body collapsing, my head dropping forward, dang near to my knees.

"Oh, my goodness! Oh, my goodness! Sir? Sir? Are you alright? Can I get you something or go get anyone for you?" her frightened voice spoke from somewhere within the room, the tunnel of my vision tightening now, only allowing a small frame to appear in front of me.

I had been stuck between the battle of trying not to hyperventilate and gasping for air at the same time, frantically trying to form a few words to calm her down. It was no surprise to me. I knew what was happening.

"Di…… abetic…" was all that I was able to exhale in a whisper-soft breath as I reached my hand into my tux jacket to grab my insulin injector. Although I was an adult, and no longer needed any type of growth hormone injections, the aftereffects of those injections—and playing God with my body—had left me damaged. In order to grow, to thrive, I had used hormones and medications to trick my body for so many years. The problem was, my body adjusted, trading one problem for another.

Although we struggled to force my body to reach an adult height of five-foot-three, it came at a cost. I will forever be a Type 2 diabetic now, with troubled kidneys and a touchy liver that will forever need to walk a fine balance with my diet and depend on insulin to keep me alive. My thyroid went to shit, and I developed signs of early glaucoma including bursts of pressure in my eyes and random blood vessels blowing out. I now receive injections in my eyes every six weeks just to keep my eyesight. My blood pressure and cholesterol somehow stay in check, and my heart, for the most part, is behaving. Mentally, I continually battle between a mild depression and high anxiety, often being controlled by a whole drugstore of medications and a crew of therapists. I will never move north because my body couldn't handle the cold, as my joints suffer from severe arthritis because the low levels of hormones as a kid never allowed enough fluid to build up like it's supposed to in those areas. But, as I have learned in my battle to reach society's ideation of "normal," everything in this world is based on give and take. Would I do it all again? Was it all worth it? I don't even ask myself such idiotic questions.

I pulled the autoinjector out and wrestled with the cap. A look of relief flooded the poor old gal's face as soon as she realized what the situation had actually been. She grabbed the pen from me, flicking the cap off like a pro, quickly inspecting the window in the cartridge for bubbles, reached down swiftly to pull up my dress shirt and undershirt from my pants, and with zero hesitation, stabbed that injector into the side of my belly without even flinching, patiently waiting to hear the two clicks that meant a full dose of insulin had been released, then pulling the injector back out and recapping it.

"My husband is a diabetic too, kid. You'll be fine," she spoke, a warm smile sitting contently on her relieved face. She walked over towards the makeup chair, grabbing a crisp white washcloth from a drawer, quickly running it under cold water and wringing it the way my mama used to. Instinctively, I leaned forward in the chair, and she placed the damp cloth on the nape of my sweaty neck, giving me instant relief.

"Now, you just sit there a spell, and I will run and grab you some juice and snacks," she chirped, like a happy little mama bird heading out to retrieve supplies for her young. She was a nurturing soul, that one. Mama would have loved her.

"Thank you, ma'am," I almost whispered, my head in my hands now, not even looking back up at her. I felt myself coming around, the tunnel vision getting a little better, the heat in my trunk subsiding to a damp, clammy feeling. I hadn't even had time to think about what I was going to say on that stage, standing there, looking around at a room full of people who believed in me. Believed in what we were trying to do so much, that I was hoping, for their sakes and my own, that it wouldn't take much convincing to get them to open their pocketbooks and throw a few fat stacks of cash our way.

The sweet little old gal with the perfectly shined black

patent leather heels hadn't been gone but a few minutes when I heard the door open. But the voice that emanated from that direction hadn't been the one I was expecting. Not right then, I should say, as I had planned on meeting with him after the ceremony, as we had a little business to deal with.

"Hey, bud, you ain't lookin' so hot. You doin' alright there?" the voice wafted my way, being carried to me from another time, making my heart catch in my throat every time I heard it because it sounded so much like his quirky old man.

I lifted my head but stopped short of trying to get to my feet, as I still felt the effects of the tanking blood sugar levels and knew full well that I needed more time to feel fully functionable. "Dang boy, you are looking good! That baseball team of yours still working ya pretty hard or what?" I reached out my clammy hand for a shake, but of course, it was swatted away. Instead, two chiseled arms enveloped me, a hug amongst brothers, brothers who finally had their shit figured out.

He laughed, his salt and pepper whiskers tickling my cheek as he pulled away. "Naw man, this body used to be rock hard when I actually played. But owning a ball team? Now that's what led to this Buddha belly I'm starting to get," he said, slapping his small curve of a belly as he stood back up. "Seriously, though, you good?"

"Oh yeah, it's all good. Damn sugar levels is all. You know my shit. Another day in the life, I guess. You still out in Colorado?" I asked, feigning interest, and trying to change the subject.

"I go back and forth, staying out there as much as I can. But now that I went part owner in the Georgia ball franchise too, I am looking to lay down some roots there," he effortlessly offered, as if I wouldn't have any objections to what he just blurted out.

"Damn it! Georgia? Are you fuckin' crazy dude? That's too damn close. You are coming too close to the perimeter, man," I warned, still trying to keep my temper and heart rate in check. "For Christ sakes, seeing you here is bad enough. He's here, you know! Stopped to say hi and scared the shit outta me," I hissed. There was a stalled silence that filled the room, neither of us knowing where to take the tense conversation next.

"It's been years, dude. Years. I don't see how there's any way that Alvaro would figure out who I am, man. Most of those players are long gone. And we just took out one of their major players only weeks ago! You worry too damn much, bro. You worry enough for us both," he said. "But, damn it, you know I love ya for it."

There was no reasoning with him, I knew that. He was a full-grown adult with his own goals and dreams and his own way of doing shit. Always acting the part of the dutiful brother, I still worried. Alvaro and his crew operated on more of an eye-for-an-eye mentality, and I didn't want my eyes to be the ones he was gunning for. Although, maybe he was right. Maybe the well laid out charade that had been put into motion all those years ago would be enough to keep him safe. Maybe I was worried about nothing.

Although I knew that he loved me, a brotherly love that had been forged by the hand of another and essentially man-made, I still knew my place. My alliance would always stay intact. He had not only come to watch me accept the award, but also to collect. I reached into the breast pocket of my tuxedo jacket to grab the check that I had quickly filled out before leaving the house that afternoon, carefully checking the ledger and moving the money around as I had been trained to do, keeping all the checks and balances in place so that no accountant would be the wiser. "You shouldn't stay for the ceremony. You really should get out of here, just in case," I tried once more to argue with him, something I knew wouldn't work anyways as he had always been just as stubborn as his old man had been. I found it comical that they resembled each other so much. I had always thought that it was such a pity that they never got to see each other grow old, that time and circumstances from the shitty hands they'd been dealt forced them to separate and live their lives as strangers. There was no other option. His life had depended on it. In fact, I didn't even get to meet him until after his dad was gone, an orchestrated event that I wasn't in control of. One more thing I hadn't signed up for but yet, would still be the one held accountable for the rest of my life. And that was okay by me. I owed my dear friend at least that much.

"Man, I will sit in the back and leave as soon as you are done with your speech, okay? I'm here for ya, bro!" Smiling, he stepped forward to take the check from my hand as the little old gal made her way back into the room with my juice and a dessert plate of hand-selected snacks for me to indulge in before I had to pull my shit together to go indulge the crowd that had just taken their seats as the lights began to dim. It was almost showtime. I wanted to puke.

"Oh! You spooked me! Who have we here?" the little old gal questioned, setting the plate of treats down next to me on a small side table.

"This is…." I offered, stumped as to what my next choice of words should be.

Looking briefly down at the check that was written out with so many zeros to a name that still made me giggle to this day, I just relaxed and smiled. I'm not sure what his dad was thinking when he chose that name as a good alias. Who would have thought that a name like Joshua Muffenmen would be a good one to hide behind? (An homage paid to Scroggs as the underground crew of Jake's Way Home would whistle the first bars of the old nursery rhyme out into the darkness to each other in the woods as they were passing off a boy to safe passage.)

"I'm one of his brothers, ma'am. Good to meet ya!" he jumped in, saving me from looking like a fool or tipping her off that something wasn't sitting right here. We were like that now, he and I, always jumping in to save each other, just like his dad had saved me. He grabbed the check from my hand and sauntered out of the room, hollering over his shoulder as he left, "See ya out there, kid! You'll do good. Dad always said you would do good."

The sweet little old gal left the room after warning me that I had a fifteen-minute window until the ceremony began and then she would be back to get me about twenty minutes after that when it would be my turn to take the stage. Thankfully, I was feeling better. I went over to the sink to splash a little water on my face and pull myself together. Leaning forward over the black marble sink, I stared into the mirror, took a few deep breaths, and closed my eyes, splashing water on my cheeks and eyes before burying my face into the plush towel that created a familiar darkened effect, one not unlike the day I had the bag pulled over my head.

Chapter 15:
Do You Know Our Secrets?

After the canvas bag was harshly yanked over my head, I instinctively let go of the grip that I'd had on Scroggs' throat, and I could hear him begin to gasp for air. "Thank God!" I thought to myself, relieved that I hadn't killed the old man because I did truly love him, but also didn't want to believe that he did anything to hurt Mags.

There was no screaming. I believe that I had either gone into shock when that bag was put over my head, or maybe, I thought from somewhere deep in the darkened pit of my soul, the part that no one really likes to admit is there, I just wanted the ride to end. Maybe I had finally given up the fight. Maybe it really was a failure to thrive.

I didn't kick or struggle as the bag was held in place and the barrel of the gun rested contently in the side of my ribs. If Mags was gone, then I wanted to be gone, too. There was nothing to argue about. At seventeen, I thought of it as more of a mercy killing, if that was the way it was going to actually go down.

Breathing heavily in that canvas bag, the moisture from my hot, angry breath slowly dampened the bag around me and made my cheeks hot. I didn't even realize that I had begun to sob, the tears sliding off my cheeks and snot trickling out of my nose, tickling my upper lip. Footsteps were shuffling around, and then I felt slender, yet strong fingers rest on my shoulders, gently nudging me to walk. Not a word was spoken.

The side door to Scroggs' trailer, located beneath the overhang of the canopy where the car was sitting, creaked open. I instinctively knew to step up as I had done hundreds of times before. I knew his place like my own home. I trusted him. Or I thought I did. The hands guided me into the living room area where I was shoved down into the old recliner. Before the bag was taken off my head, though, Scroggs' voice spoke out to me, trying to rescue me from the dark space that I was falling into.

"Now boy, we are gonna take this damn thing off," he started, obviously still shaken and out of breath, his words broken by unsteady gasps for air as a tremble laced his throaty words. "I want you to stay quiet, okay? I need you to shut your face long enough so we can explain."

I made no movement and emanated no sound. I was still swirling in a sea of confusion, welcoming the thought of a swift death, while at the same time pissed because I had spent so much of my time and my family's money on trying to survive. To think that it was all for nothing, that it would end on the shag carpeting of this old man's trailer with my mama probably never knowing what happened to me, just like all the other kids around that damned town who lost their way and somehow or other, ended up here, in Scroggs' trailer before they disappeared. "Now, I don't need no more old biddies spreading gossip around town, boy, ya hear? If we take this bag off, not a damn peep! I ain't botherin' to tie your ass up 'cause I don't think you have the will to try and run."

Still, I said nothing. I sat there, bag still on my head, the acidic smell of my own breath filling my air space, contemplating the last few moments of life. Was it all worth it? Where does my soul go now? Is this really the end? Reluctantly, I finally decided to just give in to the darkness and go where I was destined to go. A new calm washed over my soul. I sat there, listening to my lungs inflate and deflate. Inflate and deflate. Inflate and deflate. Time just stopped.

I wasn't exactly surprised when the bag was lifted to see Pencil Man sitting in front of me on a stool, gun in hand, but not completely sure what it was that he was aiming at since he couldn't see much of anything anyways. For his part, Scroggs looked completely defeated, standing to the side of Pencil Man with his hands on his hips.

"How can you think so little of me, boy? I understand what it all looks like, but how can you believe that I could do awful things?"

Still, I said nothing. I just sat in the worn recliner, my soul broken and defeated, patiently waiting for an explanation, anything that would restore my faith in him, any proof that he wasn't the insane old man that the neighborhood liked to make him out to be. I had always thought that we were of the same cloth, two people who didn't fit the mold, always stood out no matter how hard we tried to fit in. I couldn't have been wrong about him because, in my mind, that would mean that I would have been wrong about myself for all those years as well. That I *was* a freak, I *was* weird, I *didn't* deserve friends and to have a good life. We had to be who I believed we were.

We *had* to be okay.

Pencil Man spoke up. "Awe hell, boy, Mags is just fine! Damn it... why did you have to lose your fool head like that out there and attack him like that? You really think he would lay a hand on that girl? You really think..."

I had had enough of staying silent. Mags was my Achilles tendon, and my wick was lit with a blinding fury at the mere mention of her name. "Her bloody fuckin' dress was in the trash! The car reeked of that spray shit that you two concoct to keep bugs away and to get blood out of your clothes after you've been fishin, and it's too goddamned clean!"

"Now, look..." Scroggs attempted to counter the evidence, but I kept going, gritting my teeth and trying to keep my voice low and calm, emitting a persona of a stronger soul than I actually was capable of ever being. My voice cracking and wavering, I went on. "Turk's wallet! Can you explain that shit to me? Why's it in the trash too, magically as soon as he has gone 'missing'? I mean, geez you two! What kind of fucking maniacs are you? I just saw them last night... I just danced with her. She can't be dead. She can't!" my pleading had quieted back down to a near whisper, my heart still shattered into pieces at the thought of my poor Mags lying in a shallow pit somewhere, her poor body bloody and naked, and for what?

"Boy, Magdeline is at my brother's house!" Pencil Man said again, more sternly than the first time. "I just saw her this morning!"

"What the hell? Why did you take her body back over there? Why would you do that? What the hell is going on?" I whimpered, beginning to panic again and suddenly realized that I had no idea what the hell these two old coots were up to. I didn't know what to believe. I was also fighting the primal urge to piss myself out of fear at that point, the calmness of an impending death now gone and a magnetic fear of the unknown instead squeezing my heart.

"We can't keep it from you anymore, boy. You have wandered into something so much deeper than you can ever imagine. We never meant for you to know, but you just got too damn close," Pencil Man explained, his hands now resting gently in his lap, the small gun laid down delicately on the green shagged carpeting at his feet.

Scroggs walked over towards one of his massive bookshelves and reached for the old photo that Mags and I had questioned when we were younger, the picture of the boy in the Twins baseball hat. We hadn't ever come right out and asked him about it, and he had never talked about anyone in his life other than his wife. "I'm afraid now, boy, that we have to tell you all of it just to keep you alive. Let's start with this. My son, Jake."

We sat in that trailer talking for hours, and while I don't remember every part of the conversation, I remember the main parts, the ones I had accidentally injected myself into, changing the path that my life was on without knowing it. I hugged them both before I walked away that afternoon, something that I rarely did with my own dad. But on that day, it felt right. They had unburdened their souls to me, trusted me, and brought me into their fray. We would be bonded from that point forward, and I would spend the rest of my life carrying their secrets and improving on their life's work, adding to what they were already able to accomplish. My fate was sealed that day, sitting in the old worn recliner in the living room of Scroggs' little trailer that smelled of old cigars and a lemony mix of witch hazel and herbs. A fate that included getting everything that I had ever wanted out of life.

I finished drying off my face and grabbed the notecards out of my tuxedo jacket pocket, determined to get it right, to ensure that I was thanking the people who needed to be thanked and concealing the whole truths behind veiled accomplishments that the Foundation had been able to achieve.

There was a light tap on the green room door before it opened, revealing the little older gal once again standing patiently like a mama bird coming to pluck her baby from its nest. "It's time. You're up next," she calmly cooed, walking over to me with a lint roller to give my tuxedo jacket one more quick primping.

I took the stage and was pleasantly surprised that the view from up there was slightly obstructed by the bright overhead house lights, limiting who I could see to the first few rows, which was perfect for me because those are the only rows that I wanted to see anyway. Those seats held the important people in my life.

"Thank you all for having me here tonight," I slowly began, trying to remain somewhat composed and focusing on those first few rows to calm myself down. "We all know that I am not the one who started our beloved Foundation, Jake's Way Home. That honor lies at the humble feet of a great man whom I loved like a second father, a man who spent the earlier part of his life teaching, then after the loss of his son, Jake, spent the rest of his life trying to ensure that the local children always had what they needed to survive, whether that meant helping with housing for the abused children who had run away, securing a bed in a treatment center for the kids who had become addicts, or securing attorneys for the juveniles who found themselves on the wrong side of the law and needed grace and a solid treatment plan in order to right their wrongs and become productive members of society."

This is the veiled truth that I offered the audience in my speech. What I didn't tell them was that Jake had gotten himself into an ass-load of trouble when he was a teen, a kid who had started out as a gifted baseball player but got wrapped up into drugs, then wrapped up into dealing, then shot a cartel member in supposed self-defense. Jake was the first to disappear with the help of a guy whom Scroggs had grown up with just like brothers, The Pencil Man. Pencil Man was, in fact, the brother of a very high-ranking boss in a local Italian "family," the D'Andreas. With their associates and friends, as well as a long list of people who owed them favors, they were able to give Jake a new identity and move him across the country, staging his disappearance as a believable death back home so no one would question where he had gone. Scroggs knew, however, that for the plan to work, to keep his son alive, he could never see him again, as it would be too risky and could expose the whole "family," possibly leading to retaliation and the loss of a huge dynasty of generational wealth.

What I left out of my speech that evening was that after surviving the heartache of losing his only son, Scroggs not only saw how easy it was to create new lives for these already troubled teens, but that really, the search for these kids would start out strong, only to fade away quickly or be overshadowed by the next big news story. Plus, if the kids who were disappearing were the outcasts of society anyway, nine times out of ten their families weren't out there looking too hard, and society would rather give up on them anyways. It became easy to see how fast they were able to make people disappear.

"But the kind soul that Mr. Scroggs was couldn't have done it on his own, of course. That is where all of you lovely people come in. By having the support of talented teachers, doctors, social workers, lawyers, shop owners and supportive people in our community, he was able to build these kids a safety net, a caring support group that reached out when they didn't have to in order to get these children the resources that they need, so they don't end up on the street, in the same position Jake had been in."

I didn't tell them that Jake was alive and well. That he had done okay for himself. More than okay, actually. When he was first handed off outside of Florida, he stayed for about a year with a business owner and his wife out in California where he simply played the part of their nephew, was enrolled in a prestigious boarding school, and headed off to college. The collegiate baseball team may have gotten a friendly "nudge" from a lucrative Italian third-party donor, but that was just so Jake could clean up and learn how to be a better ball player while in school. He graduated with a business degree and yet went on to play for a major league baseball team under a second assumed name. I never breathed a word of that name though, the one he used to play ball, as he was far too popular. If anyone had realized which one of the Minnesota Twins he actually was, it would only be a matter of time before people would start to scour old tapes of the games, easily identifying who was sitting in the players suites. It wouldn't take much to realize that there was a lot of "family" support and money being funneled in and out of the league, especially when he went on to become a silent owner for a few more ball teams, again, simply a front for racketeering more funds for the "family."

The truth was, while their hearts were initially in the right place, it was easy to see how the situation could also lead to a hell of a lucrative proposition. As Scroggs explained it to me, these kids from awful homes would come to him when they were a year or two away from turning eighteen, begging him for help in getting them out of abusive homes, away from a life on the streets, or to escape the gangs that wouldn't let them go. It was easy enough then to stage a simple abduction, only leaving enough clues for people to realize that the kids were gone and probably not coming back. Instead of just giving them new identities and hiding them away until they turned eighteen, they would be given an education, groomed in the business, and treated so well that they would adopt this new lifestyle and, in return, pay back the "family" with either a percentage of their businesses or through favors that could be called in at any time. Over the years, this network had managed to produce its own doctors, attorneys, sheriffs, businessmen, congressmen, actors, pilots, FBI agents, and morticians. It had also sprouted new business ventures such as scrap processing, operating cargo barges, opening schools, and funding new police headquarters. They were all heavily connected and well-protected. The income from this blueprint alone was astronomical.

"I met Mr. Scroggs when I was a young boy, I, a self-proclaimed outcast who was on a medical journey to find treatments that doctors hadn't even thought of yet. He seemed to hold all the secrets of the universe in his back pocket," I continued, giving the audience only enough information to quench their thirst while holding back the dark side, the parts they didn't want to know about, that were too dangerous for them to know about.

I glanced up briefly from my notecards to see my stunning wife, Mags, staring contently at me, her demeanor calm, the picture of class and high society, which always struck me as funny because she could be one hell of a tomboy when we were growing up.

I didn't tell them who she was. There were many in this particular circle who already knew, but we've always tried to keep her out of the spotlight. Her daddy was never good enough in the eyes of her granddad, Ernie D'Andrea. Even though her daddy was abusive towards her mama and even cheated on her, it still shook Mags pretty hard after he killed himself in the big ol' house that she grew up in, which was her granddad's place. The town was well aware that the D'Andreas had generational wealth and ran the successful fishing charter fleet in town. But most didn't know about their "family" dealings and from where their generational wealth stemmed. Nor were they wicked enough not to ask. I had no idea until that fateful afternoon in Scroggs' trailer when I was seventeen how to make sense of it. That was, until Pencil Man explained to me that his brother, Mag's granddad, was the head of a very high-powered Italian "family," and the exact nature as to why the family was so powerful. That was what I loved about Mags. You would never know she came from great wealth and extensive connections. She had a pure heart and never alluded to the power that she was connected to. She was a chameleon like that. It was easy for her to just blend in, unassuming and unnoticed.

That afternoon in the trailer, Mr. Scroggs and Pencil Man explained that there *had* been blood spilled that night. But not in the way I had assumed. The plan was that Mags would take the car home, but along the way, she ran into Turk, pulled over on the side of the road and stumbling around in the dark, badly beaten and bleeding all over. He told her that the cartel was pissed about the car and also thought he had stolen some money from them. He explained that the only reason his life had been spared at all was that they were respectful of who his mama was dating, someone who sat in a higher position than they did on the chain of command. Turk knew that as soon as they had the chance, though, they would kill him, so he wanted to disappear. Mags picked him up in the car and took him home.

They refused to tell us what they did with him or where he was taken. Sometimes in this business, the less you know, the safer you are, so Mags and I were okay with that simple explanation. Turk's car was left out by the Glades, his gold necklace and ring left in a pool of blood on the steamy asphalt that wound through the Glades, an ominous sign that, although he may have walked into the Glades after dark, he didn't make it back out. Pencil Man's car was extensively cleaned, and Mag's bloody dress and Turk's wallet were burned. No one really bothered to look for him anyways, just another troubled teen from a tough upbringing that the town wouldn't have to worry about anymore. I never actually heard where he had ended up, but figured it was someplace far enough away that no one would find him. I half expect him to show up at some point in my life, maybe in the back of a crowded room at an event like this. I have often wondered, would I notice him, the ghost that still haunts my memories? The terror that still taunts me, telling me that I'm not good enough? I'd like to think that we have both moved on, and that maybe a peace would be found on common ground as thriving adult men.

"Through his generosity," I continued, staring at Mags and our boys, "we were able to keep the Jake's Way Home Foundation rolling, and were able to expand into the medical realm. We are helping to fund cutting-edge treatment and advancements that are only possible because of the generosity of people like you, people who see that we are able to do so much more when we work together, changing people's lives…"

Seeing Jojo in the audience sitting with his wife, Monica, and their two boys, both of whom are accomplished high school athletes, my nerves settled, and my heart was full. I grinned and motioned for him to stand up. Jojo, leaning forward on one cane for balance, rose to his feet and waved as I told the story of his surfing accident and the experimental treatment that the Foundation was able to fund, focusing on a cleaner and more effective way to stimulate and regenerate nerves of the spine, allowing my sweet friend to walk again. For his part, dear Jojo waved, playing the role of a star that he has been playing his entire life.

I didn't tell them that Jojo's dad was not only a gifted NASA engineer, but that his family and the D'Andreas went back for years. I didn't tell them that his dad was best friends with Mags' mama back in the day and when they realized that Mags' "daddy" couldn't have babies, Jojo's dad was asked by Mags' mama to help make that happen for her. They never spoke of it, as Jojo's dad was already married to Mags' mama, his high school sweetheart. Hell, Mags didn't even know, and I wish I didn't. But one night when Jojo and Mags were fighting about something stupid, Ernie let it slip to me while we were hashing over the situation. The D'Andreas are forever indebted to Jojo's family for providing Mags, and work was done at the federal level to get clearance for Jo's legs. Family connections and alliances run deep.

I then went on to talk about my sons, Nicky and Vinny. I told the audience the story of how we used Foundation-funded technology to perform an in-utero treatment to eradicate the genes that plagued me for so long. This treatment had effectively allowed Vinny to have very little of the growth hormone deficiency that I'd had growing up, leaving him with a minimal medication regimen and the ability to live a relatively normal life, as the technology that we'd developed could identify the issues in his pituitary gland that caused the deficiency in-utero. Although he was still affected with growth hormone deficiency, his body wasn't as severely impacted overall, and his other systems remained unaffected. Thankfully, the number of surgeries that he has had to endure are far fewer than what I had gone through. The hope is that eventually the Foundation will keep funding the research to eradicate the deficiency all together, and we can move on to attacking something larger, like cancer research.

I left out the part that as much as I love the D'Andreas, my soul was in my throat the day the surgery was performed because I had Ernie whispering in my ear that if his granddaughter and the heir of the family didn't survive that surgery, neither would I.

While begging for further funds to feed the Foundation, I didn't tell the audience that half of all the money flows right back into the families' coffers, something that I have a tough time stomaching. After all, the original vision that Scroggs and Pencil Man had started was pure at its base, to take care of our own within the community and to give kids a shot at a decent life that they may not have had otherwise. I liked that idea, and wanted to give as many kids as I could the opportunity to thrive and just be a kid. I secretly have stashed away most of Scroggs' money that was left to me, staying true to exactly what he wanted me to do with it. As the Foundation continues to grow, however, and the D'Andreas continue to take larger and larger chunks of it, staying true to Scroggs' wishes has become more and more problematic.

Scroggs had always been a tech junkie, like myself. He lived a very modest lifestyle as the keeper of our little trailer court, so no one ever suspected how much money he actually had hidden away. After all, he came from nothing growing up and formed an alliance with his best friend, Pencil Man, in grade school. Because of that, he really didn't want for anything because whatever Pencil Man had was considered his as well. When Pencil Man lost his sight, he became more dependent upon Scroggs, and the D'Andreas were very grateful for Scroggs' unwavering friendship. This meant that they lavished gifts on him and by the time he hit high school, they offered to pay for his college, provided he attend the same one as Pencil Man. This way, he could assist his friend by staying in the dorm and helping to give him a normal college experience. So, Scroggs became a teacher. Knowing none of that though,

I was unprepared for the reading of his will.

We had previously discussed his son and how I was the sole person named in his will; however, I would be responsible for doling out finances to Jake on a monthly basis. Aside from the percentage of the accumulated wealth that that figure came to monthly, anything else that I decided to do with the money, I had the green light to do it. My thoughts at the time, before the will was read, was that I would hopefully be able to keep the Foundation afloat for a few more years, and maybe even branch into some form of donations to children's hospitals and research, if there was enough left over to do that.

At the reading of the will, I went alone, as was requested, and the will was read by an out-of-state lawyer whom Scroggs had been friends with and trusted. My dear quirky old friend's love of technology paid off, and in a big way, because in 1980 he'd invested heavily in a little tech stock called Apple.

Mr. Scroggs' wealth was beyond even what the D'Andreas held, but absolutely no one but me knows that. I keep on giving Jake his monthly dividends and slowly invest in my own favorite up-and-coming tech companies. Recently, I have teamed up with a new startup that focuses on manufacturing affordable prosthetics for people who have lost limbs as a way to stick it to the insurance companies who charge alarmingly high rates to their customers, yet don't set the approved allowances high enough to pay for a decent prosthetic. I have also purchased shares in a quickly growing cellular data company that is being backed by some big wigs in Hollywood who may or may not hold alliances to the D'Andreas.

Staring at my family, I see my brothers sitting at a table right behind Jojo. They have had a good life, I think. I have managed to put them both through school, and they are both successful now, although neither has gotten married yet, or has even come close to finding the right one.

Pops died of a heart attack when my youngest brother, Jax, was still in college. Mama passed away two years ago, oddly enough, of a heart attack as well. My brothers are both showing signs of heart issues in their young age, so I am racing the clock as far as investing in new treatments. A few months ago, I thought I was having a heart attack, but was later diagnosed with a panic disorder and had another handful of pills shoved down my throat. Sometimes I don't know which pills make us better and which ones make us worse, a lot like when Alice fell down that damn hole.

"Mr. Scroggs accepted this award over thirty years ago for his service to the community and his unrelenting bravery to face the tough streets and be willing to put himself in harm's way for the good of what he considered to be 'his children.' I, of course, do not see myself as being half the man that he was, but I am hoping that he, as well as my own parents, are proudly looking down on me and saying I have done a good job. Because really, that's all I want… for my boys to think of me after I'm gone and say, 'Good job, old man. We'll take it from here.'"

Although I was just about to sweat to death beneath those blazing spotlights, I was proud of myself for making it through the whole thing, hopefully sounding half-assed professional and educated and giving the crowd exactly what they were looking for without telling too much.

Taking a deep breath as I exited the stage, I was trying to

run down everything that I had just said, doublechecking that I hadn't let anything slip that I shouldn't have. This life was exhausting. I was still feeling pretty damn proud of myself, actually, when my brothers came walking up to me backstage just as I had taken off my jacket and grabbed a water.

"Good job, buddy!" Mac said.

"Mama and Pops would be so proud, dude. You killed it out there. You should hear people talking! I think they are really believing in your purpose and the Foundation's vision, and you are really gonna rake in some dough on this one," Jax said as the sweet older gal came up to congratulate me on a job well done, like any good mama bird would do.

"Really excellent speech you gave out there. Very informational and compelling!" She patted me on the shoulder before turning towards my brothers. "Well, hello, I don't believe we have met, and I know just about everyone here. I'm Aliana, the head of the Civil Courage Prize Award Coordination Committee."

"Hi!" Mac replied, eagerly extending his hand like a proper gentleman, just like Mama had taught him. "I'm Mac and this is Jax. We are Jett's younger brothers."

"Well, how nice that the whole family could make it! I know that Jett had said that your parents have both passed, but I was able to meet your other brother before the ceremony."

Everything that I had worried about, stressing over every word that I would say in my speech, every intricate lie that I had sewn together... none of that mattered. The years of planning and hiding, doing everything in my power to keep Jake safe, to keep the family safe from retaliation… when the universe wants something from you, she gets what she comes for no matter how you try to hide. My mouth felt dry, and my heart began to beat wildly in my chest with a nervous anticipation as to what was going to come next.

"Oh, no, you must be mistaken, we don't have another brother," Jax quizzically replied, waiting for my response, too. But I couldn't respond. I had nothing left to say because at that moment, I nervously glanced up from my water bottle only to see Alvaro standing behind my brothers, staring at me, and slowly shaking his head before cracking a devious smile like a cat who swallowed a canary before offering a hollow echo. "Hi Aunt Aliana! Are you giving these gentlemen a hard time?"

My world began to spin, and my heart threatened to stop beating altogether. The darkness once again came to me, like an old friend.

Epilogue:
Do You Know the
Ghosts in the Glades?

I never feared him. Never knew enough to understand that I was supposed to fear him, although maybe that was just the naivete of adolescence.

Jett was gorgeous. Jett was sweet with an unassuming quality about him. He was my safety net who became my home. I craved stability and seeing the way he treasured his mama growing up, I knew that was what I wanted, even as a kid.

The man I was supposed to think of as "dad" was an asshole. He'd beat my mama mercilessly in the middle of the night, then head out to the bars, returning days later, reeking of cheap perfume, not even having the decency to shower off the stench of the town whores before coming home. Granddad never liked him, that was always apparent. I think my mama felt like she was trapped in that marriage because she had fought so hard to be with him. When they were in high school, things weren't so bad, I guess. He wasn't hitting her back then at least. Mama had said that she was so swept away by his good looks, and he was so charming, that she didn't care if he was piss-poor. She would run away with him if she had to, believing there was a romantic quality in thinking that their lives could just be the two of them against the world. The thought of losing her made Granddad even more furious, so he figured that at the very least, they would live at his estate since my grandmom passed when Mama was in middle school.

Living under Granddad's roof didn't stop the abuse, the carousing, or the drinking. My so-called "daddy" just tried to avoid the old man. My poor mama simply tried to keep the peace. Talk about having no stability. Shit, when I was a preteen, a time when I should have been worried about getting zits and feeling the first flutters of my heartbeat when I realized boys weren't so bad after all, my granddad took me out to the hill one humid afternoon beneath the sweet Cypress and he and I had a little talk.

"Now, little squeak," (that's what Granddad called me from the time I could toddle around the worn decks of his charter boats) "you know that your granddad has a big boat business, ain't that right?"

"You bet Granddad, I sure do! I love those boats!" I can hear myself answering, innocence still clouding my young eyes as the world had not yet snarled her vamped teeth into my young flesh.

"Well, kid, it's like this… your granddaddy's business is much bigger than boats, my girl. Much bigger. And you know what?" he questioned, no different than if he were telling me a wonderful fairytale full of princesses and happy endings.

"What?" I answered, my toe now out of my flip flop, anxiously drawing circles in the clay-filled, dusty sand beneath my feet. My bare legs had a patchwork of bandages running up and down them from the bikes I rode, the trees I fell out of, and the dogs I ran with.

"Someday, little squeak, someday it will be you who will run the whole thing," he damn near whispered, his soft blue eyes wide with anticipation, knowing that I could be easily lulled into doing whatever he was about to ask me to do. "But to be able to run something so big, child, you have to be able to handle big things. I need you to be strong and brave, and above all else, always have your family, your blood, at heart."

"Sure, Granddad, I get it! But don't worry, Mama will help you with all that. She's strong and brave and…" I attempted to reason with him, suddenly realizing that my 11-year-old self may be made to bite off more than I was willing to chew. The stifling heat radiated up from the hot dirt floor and I could feel its warmth on the back of my banged up, yet strong calves.

"Oh, I know, little squeak, I know. And I love your mama so much. But she's not like us, Squeak. Just look at the way her husband treats her! That poor woman can't see her own strength when he is constantly wearing her down. Squeak, you know that ain't your daddy, right?"

Looking back now, I cannot fathom what had gotten into my granddad that day. I mean, how could you just blurt out something like that to a young kid without being able to gauge their reaction? He must have known already that I had figured it out. He had to have known that I never felt a connection to that man, that evil darkness who liked to call himself my daddy and make me sit on his lap when I was wearing a skirt and he had been drinking, holding me there a little too tight. That man was no one's daddy.

Granddad went on while we ate ice-cream down by the boats, exposing all of our family's lineage to me, leaving out only the small detail as to who my real daddy was, and I don't remember asking. Those answers came much later, one night after "Daddy" died, and Mama had had a couple of boilermakers. Granddad was right about her, though. She was the weaker individual. There are women in this world who need to be taken care of, and women who do the taking care of. Granddad pointed out to me pretty early on that I was of the latter.

By the time my twelfth year had rolled around, I was working the boats more and more with Granddad, trying to stay out of the house as much as I could, tired of watching that man beat on Mama, tired of watching her cry and huddle in the corner, sweeping up whatever thing he had thrown against the wall and shattered that time. He was smart enough to never act like that in front of Granddad, although I think it was a crucial misstep that he didn't see me as a threat.

I hadn't planned what I did. I suppose it truly was just the order of the universe. Mama had decided to run a fishin' charter after she had been arguing late into the night with him. I spent most of the night trying to squish my head between two goose down pillows so I didn't have to hear her cry, didn't have to hear the sound that emitted from the palm of his hand slapping her face. No child should have to hang onto those memories and mark them for safe keeping. Granddad was out playing cards with the uncles, so the house was empty. That meant this man could be as loud as he wanted, thrilling himself in the power of making her beg him to stop. I pissed the bed that night and then laid there in fear, chasing sleep in a pool of dampness, praying for a peace, a reprieve that would never come.

He was gone the next morning and Mama did what she could to cover her bruises. Granddad said nothing, just looked at her and shook his head when she said she needed to get out of the house and was going to run a charter that day. I was exhausted but threw on my suit, tossed on a tank top and shorts, and out the door we flew. I was actually excited that Mama would be with us for once. I had thought maybe Granddad had been wrong about her. Maybe this time she would be strong enough to walk away from him, or at least stand her ground and throw his ass out.

We had gotten down to the docks and Mama had just crawled on board when Granddad hollered over to me. "Squeaks, I forgot the damn second rigging for the nets. They are up on the porch. Could you run up and grab them for me?

Looking back, I wonder if he had known what I would be walking into… if it had been some part of his plan all along. I kind of believe, though, that it was just the universe setting her wheels in motion knowing that I was strong enough, knowing that I would have to eventually be my mama's backbone anyway.

Kicking off my flip flops, I ran up the hill back towards the house, the sharp blades of grass licking painfully at my toes. I landed on the top step of the porch and looked around. I didn't see where Granddad had left the rigging, so I swung the door open into the breezeway, where I saw an ominous pair of work boots sitting where they shouldn't have been, one knocked over sideways and the other filthy on the toe from spilled blood or beer. It could have been either. I heard the toilet flush, and shortly after the bathroom door flung open as the man who liked to call himself my daddy came sauntering out, clearly still drunk as a skunk and pitiful.

"What you staring at girl? Thought you was working the boats today?" his words spat like venom as he walked over to the fridge, grabbing yet another beer. He disgusted me. When I looked at him, all I could see was the man who beat my mama, the man who had disgraced that sweet woman and made her beg.

"Nothing, sir. I was just back up here looking for the netting stuff for the fishermen. Granddad forgot it, that's all…" I sheepishly whimpered, noticing that he was already so drunk that he was swaying and just about unable to stand. I stood trembling in the kitchen, knowing that freedom was just a few feet away. All I had to do was take off out that door. All I had to do was to walk away.

"Damn it, your granddaddy can wait! That ol' man thinks he can just snap his fingers and we jump. Well, I am tired of jumping for him, you hear me?" he shouted, the smell of beer wafting towards me from his hot breath as he walked over to the doorway and grabbed me by the hand, his gnarly fingers sticky and damp. "Where's your mama at anyway? I couldn't find her when I got home. Is she out whoring around? Is that it?" he shouted, standing directly in front of me, staring me in the eyes.

His pupils were huge and manic. Sweat was beading at his temples and crawling down his filthy face. Even from a few inches away, I could smell the perfume on his neck from whomever he'd assaulted after he'd left the house earlier that morning.

"She's running the charter this morning. And she ain't

a whore!" I screamed at him, my cheeks fiery hot and my legs trembling. My heart sunk as I feared where this may be going. While I was only twelve, and not yet sure about the intricate details of what went on between a man and a woman, I could recognize by the way he was swaying back and forth and rubbing the crotch of his pants that I was not going to like what was coming next.

"Don't be such a bitch. Don't be like her!" his vile lips spat back at me, quickly kicking out a chair from the little dining room table that sat in the corner of the kitchen over by the door. He spun me around, pulled my hair and sat down, yanking me down on top of his lap. He wouldn't look at me, though. Only my back, while the front of my trembling body faced the front door. Pulling my head backwards by my hair with one hand, his other filthy hand slowly slid up my thigh. "Look how pretty you have gotten! Look how grown up you are..." his words began to slur as vomit started to form in the back of my throat.

Terrified, I froze, no longer thrashing around, no longer trying to escape. I could feel him beginning to writhe around in his chair beneath me, not knowing what was happening or what was to follow. Then it happened. My poor, terrified twelve-year-old bladder couldn't handle the fear and it let go, pissing all over his lap.

Now enraged, he jumped out of the chair, throwing me to the floor, staggering as he went. "What the hell did you do that for, you asshole! What the hell is your problem? Damn it!" he shouted, reeling back, and kicking me once in the ribs as I lay on the floor in front of him before he began peeling off his peed-on clothes.

Panicked, I rolled over onto my belly and began to army crawl over towards the door. But he caught me by one leg and dragged me back towards the living room, the carpet catching my tank top as he pulled me, making it roll up over my nearly-there tiny boobs in my new swimsuit. He flipped me over, noticing what had happened and disgustingly hooted out, "Damn, little girl!

Look at those perfect little titties!" Before dropping down on top of me, straddling me in nothing but his ripped boxer shorts and the smell of the town whores emanating from his body. He was so drunk that he was sloppy. He had worn himself out just dragging me in there, so it wasn't much of a struggle for me to knee him once pretty good and roll him off of me. It wasn't a struggle at all, I discovered, because the damn fool had passed out before anything else could happen.

I do not know what took over my soul that day, who flipped the switch that turned my lights out. But it happened. I stood in that living room, shivering in fear in my pee-soaked clothes, staring at the asshole who called himself my daddy passed out on Granddad's living room floor. Methodically, I walked over to Granddad's gun case and spun open the latch, the code having always been my own birthday. My young fingers reached in to extract a heavy 9mm that already held a full clip. (That one was Granddad's favorite, and I was surprised to find it in there because he usually wore it on him when doing the fishing charters.)

I calmly walked over to where the monster was lying, and my only thought was, "I wish he wasn't passed out right now so he could see what was coming," right before I aimed the gun at his head and pulled the trigger.

The story in town was that he killed himself. After all, the story fit, and Granddad was above questioning for such things. It would be considered an insult. He and I never really spoke of it,

yet, somehow, I understood that I had done a good job, had protected my family and that he was proud.

I was already an outcast at school growing up because when your family had money like mine did, you were either used for whatever people could get from you or whispered about because the kids thought you were a stuck-up bitch. I had Jojo, of course, who had grown up with me like a cousin, so he knew what I was really all about. And then I was blessed with Jett. Sweet, unassuming, take me for what I am and not wanting to be noticed, Jett.

I was a little nervous, however, the summer that he came to town and started snooping around Scroggs' place, questioning the mystery behind the missing neighbor and casting accusations at my Uncle Luca and his buddy, Scroggs. I had worried that he was going to get too close to the truth, so I tried damn hard to throw him off, which thank God, worked, I guess. At least when we were younger, he had come to believe that boys like Bradley James just disappeared, eventually realizing that Scroggs and my uncle had helped them to disappear. That's what we willed him to believe, anyway.

Truth was, I was pretty good friends with Bradley James' sister, Gracie, who was in my grade. Her brother had always been kind of an ass, like most older brothers were, but my disdain for him came from a much-hollowed place in my soul. It was bad enough that Gracie came from a rough home, her mama working double shifts down at the hospital, so she wasn't around often enough to keep their daddy from hittin' on Bradley when he needed someone to take his life's frustrations out on. (Bradley had his own problems, and it wasn't until Gracie had come to school upset one too many times that she finally confided in me one day in the locker room what was going on.)

Her brother, her own damned flesh and blood, had started coming in her room at night while she was sleeping. It had become more and more common for him to wait until everyone was sleeping and quietly let himself into her bedroom. Sometimes she would wake up because she heard the floorboards creak. Other times, she wouldn't know he was there until he sat on the edge of her bed, slid his filthy hands under her pajama top or down her pants, and touched her while touching himself. Always, though, she pretended to stay sleeping out of fear, not wanting to look her own brother in the eye. Except one time.

The night before she confided in me, she had had enough, and bless her sweet young heart, her eyes shot open and with a raging fire in her belly she told him to get the hell off of her and out of her room. The payback was a pissed off and embarrassed older brother who grabbed her by the hair and tossed her to the floor, warning her that she would tell no one. To seal the warning, he then reared back and kicked her right in the stomach, knocking the wind out of her and clipping a rib or two with the second blow. That was all I needed to hear.

I think that when family and loyalty is woven so deeply within your soul, it's easy to disconnect from emotion and move into a survival mode of sorts, not of self-perseverance, but of family devotion and a lineage that goes back further than anyone can even remember. I also grew up watching my granddad's closest friends protect each other and stay silent for each other out of respect, that same type of loyalty that was afforded family members.

Maybe it was this. The way that I had grown up. The simple things that had always been ingrained in me, like respect and family and bravery. Things that helped shape me into a leader, a no-holds-barred princess who became her own knight in shining armor, pushing fear aside and slaying the monsters herself to keep her kingdom safe. Maybe it was because I had already slayed one monster in my life and, seeing how I was protected by the family and therefore having no repercussions for my actions, that I did what I did. Or maybe, just possibly, I was methodically hardwired to kill in order to protect.

Whatever the reason, Gracie and I came up with a plan to get rid of the asshole so she would no longer have to fear him. Knowing that he would come back for more, she snuck me in through her window and I hid beneath her bed. I cannot tell you how utterly puke-inducing it was when I had to lie there, allowing him to sneak in and sit next to her, allowing him to get to his most vulnerable point before I could strike. I lay beneath them as I felt the sagging springs squeak above me while he settled down next to her, barely breathing himself. It must have been the thrill of doing something truly awful, the thrill of getting caught that got him all revved up. Funny. That was what did it for me, too.

I didn't let him get too far. At most, I figured he may have grabbed her boob and unhooked his belt with his other hand. Shrouded by the dark, I crept out from the foot of the bed, peeking up to see his position. He was sitting next to her, just as I had thought, staring out the window next to her bed, his back towards me. She was doing one hell of a job pretending to be asleep, just like that pervert liked it. What I hadn't anticipated was the sound of him gently sobbing in the darkness as he was wrestling around with his hand in his pants.

Some monsters are born bad. Others are slowly inhabited by ghosts of the horrible things that have been done to them over time, gradually darkening their own souls until they can no longer see the light. He may at one time have been her brother. But on that evening, he was just another predator, another ghost in our Glades.

I took my chance when I saw it and pounced, just a young girl with a five-pound hand weight in her fist, landing my punch right in the back of his head. He collapsed on top of Gracie, and I

quickly grabbed the plastic dry-cleaning bag from where I had left it under the bed, forcing it over his head, unaware if he was already dead or not, but taking no chances in finding out.

It was honestly a decently efficient killing, looking back on it. I just sat there next to him on the bed, gripping that bag over his mouth and nose as the blood from the back of his head began to ooze within the bag and I was sure there would be no further signs of life. We sat like that in total silence for a few more minutes, the dead brother collapsed on top of Gracie, and me next to them on the bed. Knowing that no one was home, there would be no getting caught.

Although I had become desensitized to killing, she obviously was not and lay there crying. But not for long. In fact, when we were absolutely sure that he was dead, we rolled him off of her and she actually cracked a smile. I knew the feeling, that glorious weight that had been lifted from her too-young shoulders, knowing that somehow, her life would move on.

Although I had thought the killing through, disposing of his body I had not. I had no choice but to run over to Scroggs' place. He knew where his loyalties lie. We carried an old trunk over from his place in the middle of the night before Gracie's mama got home with her little brother or her daddy showed back up. We broke the window to Bradley's bedroom and put a little of his blood on the sill. Then, to confuse anyone who may come looking, we smeared a little blood on the front door too. We shoved the now heavy trunk onto a skateboard on the front porch and wheeled it back over to Scroggs' place, going up the small ramp on his porch that had been left there since his wife had gotten sick years earlier and been wheelchair-bound.

And then you know what we did? We let that trunk sit there on the porch while we went back in the darkness to change her bed sheets and get her some clothes. We left the trunk there while we melted marshmallows around the burn barrel in Scroggs' backyard, secretly smoldering the soiled sheets and bloody clothes that she had taken off, letting our gooey marshmallows drip all over the only evidence that was left of what we had done. We let the trunk sit while she called her mama at work to say she was going over to my house (her reason being that she was scared because she "thought she had heard noises in the house and her brother wasn't home yet").

We let that trunk sit there the next day while the police were called in, the family not too worried cause they thought he had gotten himself in trouble again and had just run off. In little towns like these, a problem becomes less of a problem if the problem becomes someone else's problem. That next evening, after the looky-loos had gone home and before the gossip began, Granddad came over to Scroggs' place to "go fishing," loading up their fishin' gear and a mysterious trunk. To the Glades they went. I never asked what or how. I just noticed a few days later that the trunk was back on Scroggs' porch, freshly cleaned, an aroma of witch hazel, alcohol and lemon hanging thick in the air.

That was the second time in my life that I had gutted the monster.

Then, Jett showed up, all sweet and innocent with too curious of a mind. When he started to sneak around Scroggs' place, I made sure to go with him each time, always offering up lame reasons for whatever he was trying to pin on him. I think that Jett wanted so badly to believe that an underdog, a perceived outcast like Scroggs could be vindicated, that he would believe just about anything I threw at him. My sweet, sweet, naïve Jett.

When Jett collided with my world, I had never met someone like him, someone with such a small sense of self-worth that was so easily drawn out when nurtured. It was through Jett that I learned I had another powerful side to myself, one that was just as good at nurturing and mothering as it was at defending. I watched him blossom from a meek twelve-year-old who spent his days trying to grow and yet be smaller, trying to rise above, yet not stand out, into a man who proudly acquired an empire and finally knows his place in this world, a doting husband and loving father, a man who does what he says and is fiercely loyal. I would have done anything for that man, if only he had stayed as innocent as he was back then.

Although he had been picked on for most of his childhood, by the time we made it to high school, he had finally gotten to a point where he could breathe. All the years of medical trials and painful treatments had paid off for him, at least in his sweet mind. He had grown to a height of five-foot-three, and on most days, got along well with just about everyone in school. Not that he cared. Not that the three of us—Jett, me, and Jojo—ever really gave a crap about what other people thought when we were together. We had become each other's family, and that was all we really needed.

Except for Turk. That asshat was still riding Jett's butt any chance he could get, which was mostly my fault because Turk had always had a thing for me. The thing that sucked was that when Turk was younger, we had actually been pretty good friends. He didn't turn into a prick until we hit junior high school, when his mama started hanging around with one of the heads of the largest Cuban crime families that Florida had ever seen. That not only made him an asshole, but it also made him dangerous, and an enemy of my family.

I had known of some of the key players in that family because they had been guests at Granddad's table from time to time. Although my family was high enough on the food chain to garner their respect, we also knew that they were equally dangerous and were a better ally than enemy.

I should have found a better way to handle it. If I had, maybe history wouldn't have haunted us and our lives would have played out the way I had always intended. Maybe we could have lived out our little fairytale.

But I was young and insulted. I was caught in a cycle of defense, and when I saw Jett hurt and his soul cracked wide open again that night when Turk damn near killed him after prom, knowing that I was the one Turk was really after and that he wouldn't stop until I was his, I knew there was no other way out.

I hadn't fully thought out my plan after prom. I just knew that I wanted to end the painful cycle that my poor Jett was being put through, and once again, the universe intervened. Jojo and I were taking Scroggs' car back to his house, and Jo's chair was in the trunk. We were still too revved up about the night and wanted to hash some sort of a plan to take Turk out of the game. We knew it had to be carefully orchestrated, planned out so precisely that his absence could never be tracked back to us. For the shits and giggles of it, we headed out towards the edge of the Glades, planning on sneaking around the barricades out towards Cape Canaveral on Playalinda Beach Road, which winds around for miles in pure darkness and the swamp comes alive with animals who've crawled onto the blacktop to warm themselves at night. Although the road legally closes at sundown each night, the locals know that no cops actually want to patrol out there. In fact, you don't really see anyone unless you try to get too close to Kennedy Space Center, which is heavily patrolled and locked down. The night shift out there took another, more traveled and well-lit road on their way out. With close to sixty thousand acres of darkness to explore, the possibilities of what could happen were wild and endless.

This was just a dumb pastime that a lot of local kids engaged in. We weren't stupid enough to get out of our cars, all of us knowing damn well that a gator is faster than a human on land and that the real threat would be getting trampled by a wild and pissed off hog or hunted by the Florida panther. No, the excitement for us was always to drive in just a little bit, flash the headlights around, and then get the hell back out of there. I had never thought of the Glades as anything but a wonderland of animals and an inky, yet thrilling darkness that sings the songs of hog toads, illuminated only by the glowing eyes of gators that cut through the darkness, dancing in the reflection from the glow of a flashlight or headlights. I hadn't known then just how lucrative the Glades were, and what a safe haven they would become.

Jojo and I had just made the turnoff from the main road and were heading into the wide opening that would soon narrow and lead towards the first set of barricades, when we saw an unexpected surprise that the Glades had put in our path.

In front of us, just off to the side of the road and hidden from the main road, my headlights landed on a familiar vehicle, one with a nasty scrape embedded in the driver's side.

I pulled up behind the car, watching for any movement. A hand stuck itself out the window and was waving in a frantic pattern.

"Shit! Stay here!" I told Jojo, not giving him time to argue with me. Scanning quickly around the culverts in the ditches, I ran the couple of feet to Turk's car in record time. As soon as I made it to the door, I could see that we weren't the only ones looking to make Turk pay for what he had done. His head rolled back on the headrest and his hand stopped waving as soon as he saw me.

"What the hell, Mags! Why are you out here?" he questioned, his lips swollen and bleeding from the beating he had been handed. "Do you see what they did to me? This was because of your boy, Mags! He did this! It's his fuckin' name on the toe-tag for this one, messin' up my car like that," the words escaped from his lips, but his eyes had swollen so fiercely that I was surprised he could even tell who the hell I was. Blood was beginning to clot on his scalp from where an unknown force had exacted its revenge.

Pissed, I threw my hands into the air and walked away as he screamed, "Don't fuckin' leave me out here, Mags. I'll die! Please!" a panicked voice of a child now wafted out of the broken car where a defiant asshole had just been.

I jumped in the car and sat there with my hands on the wheel, explaining the predicament to Jojo. I couldn't understand why someone from the Cuban crime family would do this to a kid whose "sort of" stepfather has such a high ranking within the organization. The next idea that hit me would be one that would work out much better than I could have ever hoped.

Jojo crawled into the back seat and hid on the floor. I took a deep breath, did the gator scan of the culverts again, and ran back over to his car. "Get out, I'll drive you home," I ordered, opening his driver's side door and not waiting for a response. He flung one leg out and tried to stand, and only then did I see just how badly he had been beaten. They must have pulled him from the car, kicked his ass, and thrown him back in. A new fear hit me as he stumbled around, his fractured and bleeding leg struggling to find balance beneath his already swaying body. Shit. Blood.

We had only a couple of seconds before that blood began to pool, enticing every carnivore within a two-mile radius to move in for a quick supper. Normally, this would have been an okay ending, thinking about him like this. But we couldn't leave him out here at the entrance like that. He would be found too quickly and there was a chance it would be by someone other than the gators. No, that wouldn't do… he had to become a ghost.

I tried not to gag as I threw his arm around my shoulders, acting as his support. We limped over to the car. "Nice, girl, nice," the asshole blurted when I realized that his hand was already balancing on my boob. Even seconds away from death, Turk was still a pig.

I glanced towards the back seat. I couldn't see Jojo from where I stood but was happy to know that he was secretly stashed away for my safekeeping. I opened the passenger side door, still frantically scanning the edges of the culverts for any signs of movement and hustled him into the seat. Then I hightailed my ass around to the driver's side again and jumped in, just as I heard ghostly splashing sounds from a few feet away, coming from the darkness that I didn't dare try to see into.

"Shit, that was close!" I screamed out, shaking as my trembling fingers turned the keys in the ignition. It wasn't only terrifying; it was exhilarating. I felt a deliciously wicked smile crawl across my lips as I stared ahead into the darkness, knowing what this asshole's fate would be.

"I can't turn around here. This car's too damn wide and the road is too narrow. I don't want to get stuck. I'm gonna drive out aways until I get to that first barricade at the old pay toll station where the cops sometimes sit. It's good and wide and I can turn around there," I spoke calmly, not really giving a shit if he bought the story that I was trying to feed him or not.

We crept slowly along in the car, our headlights cutting through the blinding darkness, each curve of the asphalt leading towards the possibility of another predator, or ghost blocking our way just ahead. We said nothing as we drove on. His body must have been in too much pain form the beating that he had taken. Or, he was humiliated and didn't have much to say. Maybe it was his embarrassment, his pride trying to save itself that caused him to make a decision that would alter all of our lives that evening.

As our wheels steadily rolled along, making our way to the wide-mouthed turnaround point, Turk leaned closer towards me and put his hand on my thigh. "You know, I have had a thing for you forever…" he warned. "Why don't we just put the car in park and I can show you what you've been missing." His putrid words crawled out of his face as his entire body shifted even closer towards me, his left hand now gracing unwelcomingly higher up on my inner thigh, his bloody mouth leaning in to lick at my neck. I wanted to puke. I became astutely aware that even now, when his life hung in my hands, he was still willing to risk it all just to mark his territory and come off as being the "big man," perceptively climbing a little higher on the rungs of the ladder that he had created for himself.

This monster who had been formed by a faulty society, forging his own way in this world by being a bully and creating fear everywhere that he went in order to garner a little respect… this asshole was still a kid too, still scared of things that went bump in the night. He knew that out there in the darkness, surrounded by Glades with only one way in or out, he had me caged. It's not like I could get out of the car and run, and he knew as well as I did that the chances of anyone passing by was slim to none since we were hours away from the early morning shift change at the Space Center.

My stomach churned at the thought of what was about to happen, or at least what he was hoping was about to happen. I was grateful that Jojo was in the back seat.

I threw the car in park and gave him one last chance to redeem himself. "Look, Turk," I began, shoving him away from me, "I don't like you like that! Just calm down and let me get us out of here."

"Girl, you don't know what you want! But that's okay, I'm just gonna show you…" he said before forcibly lunging towards me. Although he didn't have much strength left in him since being so savagely beaten, he was still a brute of a guy, way larger than me, and used one of his scarred hands to grab a handful of my hair at the nape of my neck, pinning my head back while shoving his other hand beneath my tattered gown, grasping at my underwear to pull them down.

"Stop it, Turk! Get the hell off me you asshole!" I screamed at the top of my lungs, trying to shove him off of me as my panicked body flailed about, catching his left eye with one of my perfectly manicured fingernails mid-jab, only infuriating him more.

"Ow! You bitch" he squealed. With one hand still perched between my legs, he reflexively let go of my hair with the other one to slap me across the side of the head with such force that my ears began to ring. As angry as I was, my guard was momentarily let down with the shock and pain of that slap, and he was able to overpower me, his entire upper body now weighing me down against the seat, one hand pulling my hair back so hard that I thought he was going to rip it out, while the other hand fumbled with the zipper on his own pants. "People like us belong together, Mags," he hissed into my ear, his breath tainted with the irony scent of blood. "You don't have to fight me so hard. I mean, hell… you've been spreading your legs for that little freak for months now, right? I'm just going after what's mine," he spewed at me as he released his grip on my hair just slightly while rising out of the seat to push the skirt of my dress up with his other hand before attempting to yank his pants down lower.

My heart was crumbling, and my ears were still ringing. I was able to turn my head just enough to see Jojo lunge from the back seat as the car became electrified. I don't remember hearing the gun go off. I don't remember if Jojo said anything at all. I just remembered Turk's scream, a painful, sorrowful bellow that emanated from his body, like a child who had just been hurt and was crying out in pain, begging to be nurtured.

Turk retreated away from me immediately, throwing himself against the passenger side door, gripping his thigh which was angrily spewing blood from the bullet wound. "Jesus Christ, you assholes! You shot me! What the hell did you go and do that for?" he bellowed in-between howls of searing pain.

I knew that this life's circumstances had damaged Turk beyond repair. He would remain a monster, terrorizing people and hurting them wherever he went for the rest of his life. I could have saved him that night, could have made the decision to take him to a hospital and get him help. But what good would that have done? He still would have gone after Jett… still would have kept trying to get to me. I had to protect not only the life that I wanted, but the one that I was born into as well.

I glanced around quickly at the culverts on the side of the road. I still wasn't able to hear anything as I carefully watched the darkness for signs of movement… a reflection of light off the eye of a gator smoothly gliding across water towards dinner, or the rustling of Palmetto bushes being parted by a stalking panther or bobcat on the prowl.

I made my move, throwing open the driver's side door and jumping out, the day's heat still emanating upwards from the asphalt. I ran around to the other side of the car, carefully keeping an eye on the culvert next to us. I pulled the door open and the wounded Turk rolled out backwards, his gold chain necklace catching on the latch of the doorframe and snapping in half. With his hands, he was trying to put pressure on the bullet wound in his thigh, the one that I guessed must have hit his femoral artery. Weak from blood loss, he murmured into the night, "What the fuck are you doin? You can't just leave me here!"

I said nothing in response as I quickly walked back around to the other side of the car to hop back inside. He didn't deserve a response. I said nothing to Jojo who was quietly sitting up now in the back seat, lovingly cleaning up my granddad's gun and stowing it back beneath the driver's seat where he'd found it. We put the car in drive, leaving Turk lying there in the dark as we headed further up the road to an area where we were able to turn around. It was there, beneath the dim lighting of the old toll station that I noticed Turk's wallet had slipped out in the scuttle and landed on the floor. His tux jacket was still folded and draped across the back of the passenger seat where he had placed it when I helped him into the car. As we continued to drive along, heading back in the direction from where we had just come, it struck me as odd that a person's life can be brought to an end so abruptly, and that, in some small aspect, your decisions help direct where your life will end.

Jojo and I still said nothing as we slowly drove by the spot where we had left him, begging to be saved, hearing water splashing about in the distance. The only evidence that the ghosts had left behind lay in the shimmer from our headlights as they hit on a broken gold chained necklace and a ring that lay in a tacky pool of blood on the side of the cooling asphalt.

The Glades looked back then, just as they are tonight, as Jett and I drift over them, mindlessly bobbing about on the surface, each of us having a different idea as to where this night is going to lead. If the Glades, and the ghosts that inhabit them, have taught us anything in this lifetime, it's that they are a great highway of sorts on which to do business. The typical person isn't leisurely floating around in the Glades, which means far fewer prying eyes or witnesses of whom to be careful. The same goes for law enforcement. For the most part, I think that they are of the mindset that if your dumb ass wants to venture out into the river of grass that houses both crocs and gators, then whatever happens to you out here has been brought on yourself. And if you don't make it out? Lesson learned.

For my family, the Glades have always brought a calming peace. I have grown up here, and the Glades are just an extension of my home. Through the years, these brackish waters have been very good to me, producing a lucrative charter boat business for my family, giving my uncle and Mr. Scroggs a viable highway of sorts to sneak kids away to find them better lives, including a way to get Jake out of town. Jake was quite a bit older than me, but we still grew up like cousins. I have been trying to protect him, to keep him and the family safe my whole adult life.

And now this.

Even now, these Glades are a secret highway that we use to privately exchange goods and services with investors for the Foundation when we are dealing with particular ghosts who like to remain on the fringes of the spotlight. The Glades have always been an impenetrable curtain that can magically make things disappear when they need to, holding the secrets that no one dares ask about.

"Babe, where were we supposed to be meeting them at? Did you say it was over by the old docks where Scroggs used to fish?" I asked my sweet husband, as the calming silence of the Glades buried my small voice into its nothingness.

"Yup, that's what they said, I think. We should be just about there," he said, his right hand on the steering wheel and his left hand reaching over to pat the top of my leg as I sat next to him on the captain's bench seat.

He was beautiful, my Jett. The years have been kind to him, leaving his hair thick and now salt-and-peppered with time, his skin tanned from the sun yet not too creased and worn. The small breeze that danced over the surface of the Glades bounced off his neck, splashing the intoxicating scent of his aftershave my way. Oh, how we have been so good together, built such a wonderful life for the boys together.

I looked straight ahead, holding up the spotlight as we glided along, watching for the signs of life we were hoping for. Although we had built an empire, it was funny how things, business dealings, were still done in such a primal way. In fact, this primal waterway system was how so much in my life had been achievable and my family's wealth accumulated, starting with my uncle and Scroggs when they would use these waters as a mechanism to traffic boys out of the area and place them on better paths in life. In the beginning, it was only for the soul-serving profit of feeling good, meeting out here in the middle of the night, just floating about with a stowaway kid hidden in a trunk or wrapped in a blanket, whistling into the darkness, then patiently waiting for the direction of the return call to know where they were meeting their saviors.

Then, they had figured out that an even better thing to do would be to not only help these kids escape their shitty homes, but to also give them purpose and value in this world, teaching them skills that could be utilized not only by them, but also the "family." The program continued like that for quite a while, landing the family contacts in very high places. After all, these boys had such gratitude for the lives they had been afforded, they wouldn't think twice about using their positions to help pay back the family who had put them there.

When Jett inherited Scroggs' Foundation, it had only come as a surprise to him, since the D'Andreas were already consulted on every move that Scroggs made, as he was such a close affiliate to the family. Scroggs himself in a way had been the original boy from where the whole program kind of began. He came from very modest means and had become very close to my uncle growing up. When my uncle lost his eyesight due to my granddad's miscalculations with a rival family and a debt that was owed, Scroggs stayed on, ever faithful, without once asking for anything for himself. This impressed the family, and from that time forward, Scroggs was afforded a life that was well beyond what he could have ever imagined, yet he chose to live very simply. Wealth and luxuries had never suited his tastes.

When he passed away and the bulk of his estate was left to my sweet Jett, part of that stipulation was that Jett would dole out a set amount of money each month to Scroggs' son, Jake, who had to remain in hiding for the rest of his life, not only to stay safe, but also to keep the "family" on the safe side with the Cuban crime family that Jake had pissed off all those years ago.

The sweet man that I now sit next to has no idea that I am well aware of the unfortunate dealings he has made with Jake, and the darkness that has now come for us all, whether that was intended or not. My sweet Jett had only ever wanted to build a better world for his boys, a world where they had a fighting chance to live normal lives. Jett wanted to build the fairytale, and in order to do that, the Foundation had to keep making money. Alongside heavily investing in medical experimentation, disease eradication, and DNA modification, he also now dabbled in gun running, black tar heroin smuggling, and even human trafficking, something that I have absolutely no tolerance for.

It's one thing to try and help a kid by "abducting" them from this life in order to get them to a better one. But when money starts being exchanged for human lives, there is no guarantee where those lives will end up, and I, as well as the family, want no part of that. We are Catholic after all, and although there are many things that we have done in this lifetime for which we've had to ask forgiveness, some cardinal sins bear no forgiveness.

I have my sons to worry about now, with Granddad and Mom both gone. Things now have taken place exactly how Granddad had always said they would. I am in control.

I have to be brave and strong. I have to do what's best for the family, including the best way that I know how to protect my boys.

This life, our existence, is based on a very cat and mouse game of give and take. Piss someone off, give them a little something to make it better. Get pissed off, ask for payment to ease the pain.

"It should be right up around this next bend, babe," Jett said, still never looking away from the water that lay out ahead. I turned to look at him, once again, my hand reaching under our seat for Granddad's old gun that I had stowed there. He had become careless. He had developed some type of God complex where he now felt untouchable, which put his sons directly in the line of fire for retaliation.

When Jett stumbled into my life, he came to me during a time when I had few friends and was struggling with my place in the world. First, we had become friends, then best friends, before we found love. He was quiet and unassuming, yet silently wished to be greater than. Greater than his parents had hoped he would be. Greater than the kid who was relentlessly picked on for his size growing up. Greater than the older brother who garnered no respect. Greater than the small kid who would get beaten down by the bully in the school parking lot.

We built a life, a family of our own, and he was proud. He loved me way before he found out who my family was, long before he should have known to fear us all. If only we could have stayed like that just a little longer. But now, my sweet Jett has become consumed with building an empire and investing in the next big thing, and Jake has turned into his sideways business partner. Money piled up on top of more money, and investors came knocking in all forms. The problem with sitting too high on a pedestal is that it leaves your life exposed, your family exposed, and your judgment momentarily blinded by the thought of equity and loyalty at your disposal.

I have laid awake many nights worrying about him, about us, and what our best course of action should be. I have boys to protect now and that trumps everything else in my world. Sadly, that also leaves my sweet Jett out of the fray, a painful memory of a life we used to have that somehow has become buried and swept away. Jett's quest for more, to be greater than, when what we have is already more than enough, has now put the family in danger.

It has become hard to swallow as a lump forms in my throat, and dare I say regret and pity have also taken hold in my heart. Tears begin to crawl down my cheeks in the darkness, yet I make no sound. Jett has given me the best life, a life that I could never have built on my own.

Closing my eyes, I let out the signal, the whistle of the first few bars of the old children's nursery rhyme, "Muffin Man," just as my uncle and Scroggs had done time and time again, then silently pausing to wait for the callback to know which direction we should head… to know that they are out there, the ghosts that slide effortlessly through the waters, dangerously traveling with cargo or taking orders for jobs of which no one speaks, or will ever whisper about again.

In these few seconds as my fingers wrap assuredly around Granddad's old gun beneath the seat, I focus solely on being quick and swift, giving my sweet Jett a reprieve from this world, and humanely, making sure he never feels it or sees it coming. I think only about my boys.

Memories flicker rapidly in my brain, flipping over and over like the boys' old baby books stored away in our basement. Nicky as a toddler sleeping on the captain's bench of one of Granddad's boats, Vinny in preschool standing on the end of a dock fishing with Jett and the uncles, Christmas Eve when they were in preschool, snuggled up on the couch in front of the fire listening to Jett tell stories of Christmases when he was young. Their beautiful little faces haunt me and tease me at the same time, tempting me to just put the damn gun back down. I know, however, in my heart that there is no other way out.

Just as I am about to bring the gun to chest level and aim it at my beloved, a whistle emanates from somewhere in the distance, a low sweet song much like the one I'd heard so many times as a child out here in these waters with Granddad.

"Mags?" Jett shocked me, breaking the silence and my resolve, my fingers now trembling on the trigger of the gun that is still wedged beneath my seat.

"Jett?" I questioned, nothing left to say.

"Remember when we read *Macbeth*?"

"Of course! Of course, I do, Jett! We never wanted to be great." I sobbed, heaving now, letting my fingers fall from the trigger, my head down, unable to look at his sweet face and not wanting him to see weakness in my falling tears.

His response was swift and cut right to the point. "It was to be you and me against the world, what has been done, can't be undone" was the last thing I heard before he pulled the old canvas bag over my head, whistling in response to the ghosts in the distance.

I never feared him. I never knew enough to understand that I was supposed to fear him.

THE END

Acknowledgements

Thank you to my editor Melanie Berbrier, for her wickedly sharp eye, imagination, and support. She turns a manuscript from great to hauntingly spectacular.

About The Author

Staci is a married mom and newly minted grandmother who, after years of working as a dental assistant, ordained pastor, and public health worker, decided to rekindle her passion in life and start living again, kicking off her second half as a thriller/suspense author. She has been nominated as a finalist in the Killer Nashville Claymore Awards as well as the Hawthorne Awards, London's Page Turner Awards, Literary Global Awards, Screencraft Awards and the Hollywood Book Festival. Her books have won the Five-star Gold and Four-star Silver awards from Literary Titan and placed in the BookFest Awards as well. She is also a Maxy Award winner.

Connect with Staci on social media.
Instagram: @author.staci.andrea
Twitter: @StaciAuthor
Facebook: Staci.Andrea
TikTok: @staciandreaauthor
Website: https://staciandrea.com

"A suspenseful read. Readers will never guess the big reveal at the end!" - *Author Melanie Berbrier*

"An unparalleled mystery genre masterpiece!" - *Thomas Anderson, Editor in Chief of Literary Titan.*

Beneath Her Lies is a beautifully twisted thriller that weaves together the dark past of a 32-year-old recovered drug addict, Ruby, with the delicate new life that she is trying to obtain.

It has been said that you can't go home again. You can't go home to the past, to where your favorite childhood memories lie. You can't go back to where you once felt the most content and safe.

Ruby has run away from safety for her entire adult life, while running right towards danger. A true wild child, she found a false comfort in the arms of a man who drug her into his own personal hell. It would take years for Ruby to claw her way back out and be strong enough to crawl back home.

But what was home? Was it truly the place that her contorted heart remembered it to be? After the death of her Granddad, she was lulled back under the pretense of sorting out his affairs, only to be blindsided when she arrived, finding herself in a web of lies and deceit, while still trying to cling to her newly found, and carefully rebuilt sober life.

The twisted web becomes all-consuming, as Ruby is still struggling to find solid footing with her own past.

She may be able to outrun her own shadows, but can she keep her family secrets buried?

BENEATH HER LIES

STACI ANDREA

KINGSLEY
PUBLISHERS

Prologue

Gripping the edges of the white marble sink of the bathroom in the farmhouse, I could only faintly hear her fists pounding against the wood, her voice echoing incoherently on the other side of the old, worn, walnut farmhouse door with the chipping paint that divided us.

An exasperating scream emanated from the most painful depths of my disillusioned soul, and no matter how hard I tried to drown it out, the absolutely stagnant and vilifying remnants of our past had caught up to me and attacked me with such force that they were blocking out all of my typically even-keeled sensibilities.

My ears could only hear the harsh electrical buzzing sound from the overhead fluorescent bulb, magnified enough to fill my head and block the voice of my own sister from the opposite side of the old door. The bright bulb flickered, trying to keep the room lit while doing its best to keep the shadows at bay.

"God damn it, Ruby! Would you let me in? Please!" I faintly heard her voice echo away before being drowned out once again by the loud overhead buzz. I had become numb, entering a state of shock, I suppose, as I stood there in Granddad Bub's old farmhouse bathroom, gawking at myself in the bronze-framed mirror. It still had the little blue rosebud-embroidered sticker that was trapped in the corner which Gramma Pearl had put there after Sunday school one day when we were kids.

Emblazoned across the front of the little blue rose on the mirror was a single word, a solitary sentiment that Gramma had believed in with such force that she had permanently affixed it to the mirror. Every time we stayed at their place, we were reminded of this single word's importance as we brushed our teeth or combed our hair. We would look at the sticker of that little blue rose, willing its way to grow from a crack in the dry earth and take in the full meaning of the word. Life.

Still gripping the sides of the white marble sink with my swollen and trembling fingers, I let my gaze crawl up from the little rose only to be met with a frightened reflection of myself. There was now a glaze over my eyes that hadn't been there just a week ago, before our world had begun to unravel. Now, I stared back at my puffy face and the look of defeat that tormented it.

Staring blankly into the glass with a cold chill attacking my spine, clinging to the sides of that old sink with swollen fingers, it was all I could do to will myself to breathe, force a suffocating gulp of stagnant air into my stunned chest. Steadying myself against the sink with trembling legs, I tried to calm my breathing, now terrified that I was going to hyperventilate and pass out, all the while trying to remain as silent as humanly possible so not worry my sister any more than I already had.

"I'm almost done, Banks, hold on!" I tried to shout out, but the words had become half lodged in my throat as I choked back the hot tears that were blinding me. Of course, she would have known something wasn't right. We were sisters, for God's sake! We peed with the door wide open and had in-depth conversations while climbing naked out of the tub. For me to barricade myself in there was an oddity, a foreign concept for two girls who had grown up as "thick as thieves" as Granddad Bub would have said.

Granddad Bub. Damn, I missed that man. There was so much he should have said, so much we didn't know. Staring into the mirror's reflection in an almost zombie-like state, I focused on one thing, one talisman that anchored me to him, to the past, to all of our undoing.

Hanging from a silver chain around my neck was the silver pendant with the Lord's hands folded in prayer. On the reverse side was the wording of the serenity prayer, "God, grant me the serenity to accept the things I cannot change, the courage to change the things I can, and the wisdom to know the difference."

Granddad had worn that old thing around his neck for as long as I could remember. He never was an outwardly spiritual man, but he loved my gramma who spent her Sundays being the devout and proper Lutheran she had been raised to be. That old farmer had dutifully tagged along, carrying her cookies or bars in for Sunday school, or helping to wash dishes after Wednesday coffee service. I had never really questioned that pendant. I only knew it had been a part of him, so when he passed, I claimed it as mine so he could be a part of me too.

Most people associate that particular prayer with recovery, whether from alcohol or drugs, maybe even a gambling addiction… addictions that I myself had battled to overcome. But not him. These things were not afflictions of my granddad. This was not his attachment to the pendant.

With a weighted apprehension, I let go of the side of the sink and brought my fingers toward my neck, curling them tightly around the pendant and giving it a swift tug, snapping the chain from behind my neck.

Banks had given up, if only briefly, as I could no longer hear her on the opposite side of the bathroom door. With the pendant in the palm of my hand, the chain delicately hanging limp beneath it, I turned my back towards the sink and slowly lowered myself to the floor, careful not to make any noise that would trigger Banks. Keeping a death grip on the pendant, I cautiously reached out with trembling fingers to retrieve the source of my fury, my exhaustion, my confusion, and pain.

Lying there, on the gleaming black and white tiled floor was Gramma's journal, the soft green floral cover worn and peeling at the edges from years of anxious torment and repentance, right where I had dropped it in shock. My gramma wasn't one to write or to journal. She wasn't one to tell stories. This wasn't a part of a series of diaries about her life, or even an ode to a life well lived.

This was more along the lines of a confession of sorts, a place where she could unburden her conflicted soul onto paper and ask for forgiveness, even if it was in secret, from a God that she whole-heartedly believed would be able to save her.

This had been her soul work, her book of redemption, originally never to have been seen by anyone, I had assumed, other than her and the big man upstairs himself. Trouble is, I found it by her design, whether or not I had asked for this assignment.

Deciding that I needed to make a noise or do something to throw my sister off, I tried to flush the toilet. But my body was weak and I had a hard time willing my arms to work.

Damned sugar must be low again, I thought to myself, mentally noting how many times I had been brought to my knees recently by this disease, briefly chastising myself once again for the debaucherous way that I had treated my body over the past ten or so years.

I calmed myself enough now that the screaming in my head and buzzing in my ears stopped. I could hear Banks rattling around out in the kitchen now. I flipped the back of the tattered journal open, taking in one last gaze at the picture that had been taped there.

Here she was, this mystery woman, with her long brown hair pinned neatly back with a barrette, grinning at the camera. And there, hanging ever so sinfully around her neck, was Granddad's pendant.

I hurriedly slipped the pendant and chain between the pages and closed the old journal, having just finished reading the myriad of secrets that she had held. Hopping up too quickly, I lifted the old beige wicker hamper lid that sat in the bathroom's corner next to the toilet beneath the macrame plant hanger. Shuffling around some sheets that were still in there, I had intended to bury the book of sins deep beneath, in order to buy some time to figure out what the hell I was going to do about it, if anything at all. But I just couldn't let the damned thing go. I couldn't put it down, couldn't rattle the stunned thoughts that had now been unleashed upon my brain in a wild, furious state. The world had begun to spin, and the tiny little farmhouse bathroom that held the secrets of my youth was now a blur.

Standing once again, I spun back around to face the mirror, purposely ignoring my reflection as I sat the journal down next to the sink and tried to turn the water on to wash my hands. My hands no longer wanted to cooperate and had begun to tremble. I didn't want to see what my eyes held, whether it be panic, pain or just indifference.

I could hear Banks in the kitchen getting dinner ready, waiting for me at the same little Formica table where we had sat with them for all those years, eating off the same green herringbone patterned plates, listening to the same gentle country breeze that would roll in off the fields and dance its way in through the open kitchen windows. Everything would be the same as it had always been. Except now, I held the dark secrets of the ghosts at our table.

"Hey Ruby, come on! Why are you being so secretive? It was a long freaking drive, Rube's, I'm exhausted and I'm starving. Can we just eat please?" a frustrated and cranky Banks hollered from what I was guessing was behind the refrigerator door, a cold beer in one hand and a bowl of Granddad Bub's radishes in the other, cold from the fridge where they rest in their little silver mixing bowl of water.

Blinking widely into the mirror, I quickly assessed the damage, flinging a drawer open and retrieving a half-used tube of lip balm. After slapping on a quick coating of that minty goodness, I ran my fingers through my hair and grabbed a tissue from the doll's head that had lovingly adorned the back of the toilet since the 70s, blotting my eyes.

"Well, this is about as good as it's gonna get," I mumbled

to myself beneath my breath, still unsure as to what I was going to do next. How do I tell Banks? I grabbed the sides of the marble sink one more time and bowed my head, trying to find answers that weren't coming, trying to find my way out of this. As I tried to muster the courage to go out and face my sister, I calmly raised my head, opened my eyes, and once again was met by Gramma's little blue rosebud. Life.

Chapter 1: Serenity

Where Ruby Began

It is said that the best stories are the ones that resonate within your heart and set fire to your soul, the ones that have been truly and unapologetically lived. I guess then that it would only make sense that my story, our story really, would be the one that is bubbling beneath my skin, keeping me awake at night and begging me to barf its contents onto my keyboard, relenting dark corners of my past and the multiple heartaches that have held me down for so many years. I exhausted my soul by trying to protect them all, trying to keep the darkness from coming to light.

It was my therapist's idea, really, to shamelessly walk down this trail of unearthing the past, unlocking the dark chasms of my soul in order to unleash the fury that burns within. Addy (that's my therapist, by the way) has been a veritable force to be reckoned with as far as my mental well-being has been concerned. She has pushed me to dig deeper so I can sort out what the hell it is that has been holding me down for so many years—try to figure out why I constantly sabotage my own happiness.

I only began to seek help from Addy last year, after my marriage had officially crumbled and the pain of two miscarriages haunted not only my sleeping hours but had also menacingly begun to stalk my waking hours as well. I couldn't sleep well and came close to losing my job as an accountant too, all because I was constantly preoccupied with a darker thought, a deeper issue that hung in a stale cloud over my life for years now.

Addy was actually my neighbor at the new condo I had moved into after the chaotic divorce. (I hadn't wanted the house in the divorce, as it held absolutely nothing but painful reminders of the failure I thought I'd been at being both a wife and mother. Plus, the drug dealers that my ex-husband had been in business with often used it as a hangout. I was just trying to put as much distance between all of us as possible).

My new condo was the sweetest little thing! It was only two bedrooms, one of which I had turned into a den with a sleek black leather futon shoved against one wall, just in case I ever actually had an overnight guest.

The sun that came in through the spare room on a sunny afternoon enticed me to relax at my writing desk and piddle away the day by journaling some of my life's tragedies at my keyboard, grateful for the outlet to unleash the burdens for which I'd been holding myself responsible.

I had even begun to write a couple of manuscripts, one of which was based on the dark life that my ex-husband and I had sadly fallen into over the course of our marriage. The other manuscript that had been graciously devouring my time… well, that one was a little darker, if anyone could believe that. The thing about that particular story was that it was rooted in my family history, a secret history that I had just unearthed.

My sweet little condo also had a quaint faux marble counter-top island, equipped with a couple of little wooden bar stools that, more often than not, only the butts of my cats ever graced. Gonzo and Kermit were two stray kitties I took in not long after my divorce.

The condo, while seemingly a safe and quiet place to restart my life, had an air of incompleteness to it when I first moved in, a sense of emptiness that crept through the shadows and echoed off the walls. It was an absolute no-brainer of a decision then, when one day I saw two mangy, scrawny-looking kittens snuggled up against the dirty old dumpster in the back of our parking lot.

I was sure that some asshat had dumped them back there, leaving them to fend for themselves in an unknown world with no means to take care of themselves beyond their fading will to survive. I had just gotten home with some groceries after a soul-sucking day at work and had planned to have a quiet evening at home alone with a bottle of red, when I pulled into the lot and saw two tiny, scraggly kittens struggling by the edge of the dumpster.

Gonzo bee-lined for me as soon as he saw me get out of the car, his mangy orange fur sticky with some sort of goo that had run down the side of the dumpster. He had no fear of life, just a goofy gallop in the way that he ran, an uncanny quirkiness to him that instantly made me want to love and protect him forever.

As Gonzo ran towards me, throwing all cares into the wind, I noticed Kermit, the shivering, gray little ball of fluff he had been, steadfastly standing his own, hissing wildly at the air, hovered against the edge of the dumpster's feet as he watched his brother effortlessly and boldly run out into the unknown. Kermit was the one that I had to win over, the one that I ended up having to prove myself to in order to gain his trust.

While Gonzo had jumped immediately into one of my grocery bags, making it known that I was now *his* human, little Kermit stayed put, intensely watching what his brother was doing, no doubt nervous that he was going to be forgotten about once again and left behind. For him, it took a slower approach from me with a gracious amount of canned chicken to get him to relax and let me into his world.

It worked out though, Gonzo, Kermit and me, happily learning to build a little life within these condo walls, thankful for each other, thankful to be able to just lay in the sun together, napping on a sunny afternoon. I had needed their companionship, and they had needed to be cared for. Those two fur babies were actually how I first bumped into Addy.

I had taken the garbage out and was about to send it down the chute in the hallway when I saw an orange flash out of the corner of my eye go bounding down the hall. That dang Gonzo must have snuck out while I had been dragging out the garbage. I dropped the trash into the chute and took off down the hallway myself, almost bumping right into Addy as I went barreling around the corner towards the front of the building. There she stood, looking stunned and holding a pitiful-looking Gonzo in her arms.

Addy had introduced herself and invited me over to lunch the next day, which is when I found out that she was single as well, spending most of her time tending to her business that she was building, a mental health organization that housed many therapists focusing on multiple different specialties. Being a therapist really was Addy's life's work, and it was easy to pick up on her love of the profession as we spoke over lunch that afternoon.

Over the following few months, Addy and I would talk more, have lunch, go to local farmers' markets and flea markets, just enjoying the single life. My little condo slowly had begun to build a life of its own, an alternative history for me, although the life of my past seemed to seep out in the most unexpected of ways.

One afternoon, I had been trying to organize my bookshelf wall that Addy had helped me build, prioritizing my first edition copies of some of my favorite books that I had picked up at flea markets, while trying to weed out books that no longer held any significance to me and were simply taking up space.

I had come to a time in my life when I knew I needed to do a lot of unpacking, a lot of making room for the things that really mattered which meant getting rid of the things that merely took up space. Addy had been helping me reorganize my books, showcasing the oldest, most collectible ones, when a tattered and thinner book fell from one of the shelves and landed at my feet.

As I spun around to pick it up, my eyes fixed upon the tattered and faded dark green cover with the dog-eared corners, the green and blue floral print showing its age. Slithering out from between the pages was just an echo of a sparkle, a dull silver chain that had appeared to be holding a place for someone.

Before my fingers could grace the worn cover of the book that held so many tales of insanity and torment, Addy gracefully picked it back up, flipping through it quickly and unearthing the pendant that had been gently tucked within.

"Well, this is just lovely!" she gasped as she dangled the pendant midair from her fingers, the light hitting it in such a way that the silver stunned my eyes momentarily. Gonzo jumped from his shelf, now playfully batting at the pendant that hung from Addy's fingers as she continued to glance through the worn pages that held the handwriting of my gramma. That was it. I was gone.

The last thing that I can remember from that afternoon, the last thing that was seared into my exhausted brain was the vision of Addy perusing that old journal, the pendant delicately hanging from her fingers as if taunting me to say something, taunting me to tell her the story that I had managed to keep buried for the last few months.

I woke up with a cold, damp washrag draped over my eyes and forehead, Gonzo sitting on my chest purring contently and the rugged tile of the condo floor mercilessly digging into my back beneath me. Moaning, I raised my hand to move the washrag from my eyes.

"Just slow down, Ruby, slow down and take it easy," Addy's voice hummed soothingly, as it had always been trained to do in times of despair and uncertainty. "You really passed out that time. What's going on with you? You have been doing this a lot lately."

"This time," she had said. In the few months that I had known the poor girl, I had already bitten the dust, briefly fainting and slipping away into a forgiving unconscious state a couple of times while in her presence. Once, it was when we were at a flea market and my ex-husband let out a laugh from across the aisle, seemingly enjoying his day with his presumably new girlfriend. Well, at least I had tried to convince myself that the man was him, and it took a lot of convincing from Addy to dissuade me otherwise. He will always haunt me. It didn't matter if it was in reality or at night in my sleep.

Another time had been when my sister, Banks, had come to visit and was showing me a family tree she had been working on. The past, it seems, had not been kind to me. The past is what I try to put out of my mind.

It made sense then, on that beautiful sunny day in my little condo while working on putting my life back together, organizing a few of my favorite things, building a comfort zone around me like a safety cocoon, that the little book with the tattered green cover would bring it all careening down around me, forcing my mind to freeze, wanting so badly to hold on to the present, to the things that I actually had control over.

"Are you sure you're OK, Ruby? You hit that tile pretty good," Addy whispered in astonishment, a look of confusion crawling across her furrowed brow. Beyond her, though, to the right of her head upon the bookshelf, I could see it. The little dark green tattered journal now rested upon my beloved collection of Edgar Allan Poe, the tarnished silver chain draping lazily over the worn and fraying spine, teasing my mind.

Forcing myself to inhale a painfully thick gulp of stale air, my voice echoed shakily around the condo walls. "I'm OK, Addy. I'm OK. It's just that…" my voice trailed off, my mind reeling back to when I first laid eyes on that damned journal, my heart now ramping up again to a painfully deep palpitation, making me feel nauseous all over again.

"Ruby, you have to slow down that breathing. I think

you are going to make yourself hyperventilate," she said in a calm demeanor, her breath now warm against my cheek. I tried to focus on the present, the feeling of her breath, the sound of her voice. I tried to hang on to this life, the way the condo felt in the afternoon sun, the vibrations from Gonzo lazily purring on my chest. I glanced around again, noticing Kermit, now perched on the Lazyboy within eyeshot of where we were sitting, staring at me, judging me with such disdain. He still didn't fully trust me. Hell, at that point, I guess I didn't fully trust myself.

I slowly nudged Gonzo off my chest and pulled myself up to a sitting position, drawing my knees up and hugging them to my chest. It was the first time in many years that I just let myself feel. To feel numb for so long had certainly done its damage. I had a crumbled marriage to prove that to be true. Sitting in the afternoon sun in my warm and lovely little condo, I felt so small. The emptiness of my life had somehow enveloped and tried to suffocate me once again.

It was a burden that I had chosen to carry, a life of secrets that I, somehow, had become the keeper of, protecting all of those whom the secrets could crush. I hadn't realized, though, that by holding on to those secrets, to the atrocities of my family's past, while also balancing my own sins, I was slowly smothering my soul, fighting monsters in the night. I'd spent so much time blocking it all out that I had inadvertently left little room for any sliver of happiness to worm its way in.

Being the older sister had always been like that, though. Being the first grandchild had always been a chore. Being the responsible first daughter, first granddaughter, big sister, oldest cousin… the list goes on endlessly. The insurmountable pile of expectations that are hoisted upon your shoulders solely due to birth order is crushing. It had always been expected of me to be the responsible one, the one with the level head, the giving one. I had always been expected to share everything with the younger ones, look after them, to lead the way.

At family gatherings, cherished holidays, and family reunions, it was I who looked after the younger ones, kept them busy, kept them safe. I was the one to blaze the trails first, ensuring safe passage for all of those who would follow after me. They watched what I did, learned what to do and what not to do, who allowed them to get away with things, and who put their foot down.

I had always been expected to be giving, yet not too trusting. Brave, yet also understanding that I was better than no one else. Expected to share everything that I was given, yet give away to the younger ones who wanted more. By design, birth order appoints a person's standing in a family, and in mine, I would forever be the one left holding all the cards, the watchdog herding the lambs into the pens, protecting all of them from the wolves.

I can only assume that my upbringing, my birth order, is what led me to slowly drive myself insane, literally giving myself ulcers as I lie in bed at night trying to figure out what is best for them, what I can do to protect and help them all, while worrying about trying to stay one step ahead of my own past, trying to keep both worlds from colliding.

When you are raised in a very close-knit family, somewhere along the line, everyone's burdens become your own. Being the oldest of the offspring, you are clued in to more, involved in a little more of the family conversations. You are entrusted with secrets and put in charge of wills and lofty decisions that need to be made. You are expected to be at the bedsides in the end, acting with compassion and behaving as if you are a pillar of strength, when in reality, you are slowly crumbling on the inside, your soul quietly sobbing as you watch the strong protectors of your family, the ones you looked up to, age and wither away. Time is a bitch like that.

Perhaps all of it, the love, the disdain, the pain and honor that comes with family, is what had driven me to this place of self-destruction, the utter undoing of my own life. For so long, I had tried to keep the family secrets, my secrets hidden, tried to protect them, to keep them all safe, while struggling down my own little path of destruction.

In doing so, there was no room left for me, for my life, the things that made me whole. I was at a crossroads now, trying to find a way to make all the darkness work in my favor instead of killing me by way of heart palpitations and ulcers, manic episodes, and depression. It didn't help that I was also a diabetic who had a hell of a time keeping my glucose under control. There had to be a way out of this.

I could no longer be the strong pillar; my body had had enough. I needed an out, a way to get these fears out of my heart and to find a certain peace again in my day-to-day life. I wanted to be able to look at my family again without feeling deceptive, without trying to cover the lies. I had to be able to look my little sister in the eye.

That was where the plan was formed, right there on my cold tile floor of the entryway of my sunny little condo next to my beloved bookshelf one warm afternoon. Sitting with my back against the bookshelf and knees pulled tightly to my chest, I began to tell Addy the story that had haunted me for the past few months. She sat intently on the floor across from me, her eyes wide and nonthreatening, stroking Gonzo's unruly orange hair while Kermit looked down on us from his chair, full of distrust.

When I had finished with my tale, sharing with Addy the things that haunted my heart and rolled around in my head day in and day out, she sat in silence for a moment, contemplating all the secrets I had now unburdened myself from, secrets I had now laid down at her feet.

I wanted her to tell me what I needed to do, tell me how to get my life back together. I needed someone to be a pillar for *me*, to be *my* light in the darkness. I was exhausted from being the caregiver for so many years; I needed someone to take charge, be honest, and tell *me* what to do for a change.

She put Gonzo down and arose, reaching for the tattered, green, dog-eared book on the bookshelf. Quizzically, she began thumbing through the pages, stopping when she reached the center of the book, running her index finger over the folded hands of the Lord that was emblazoned on the front of the pendant, then flipping it over with her thumb, she eyed the imprinted lettering that was written on the back.

"God grant me the serenity to accept the things I cannot change, the courage to change the things I can, and the wisdom to know the difference," she half whispered, staring at Bub's old pendant. "Are you hearing what I am saying, Ruby?"

Although I had held a great belief in something for many years, I had always wrestled with the intricate ins and outs of organized religion. I liked to question things, and I liked to be given straightforward answers in a world that didn't always allow that. I had my own beliefs, my own relationship with God. The world isn't always as it seems, and sometimes I had a tough time figuring out where that left me standing spiritually.

Make no mistake. I had been driven to my knees many times in prayer, begged God through tears to help me while silently screaming in a shower had in-depth conversations with the big man upstairs in my car, mindlessly driving back and forth to work. I just didn't know what type of relationship that was anymore. When someone has danced on the darkest side of life for so long, how much forgiveness can they possibly expect to receive?

"Ruby, are you hearing me?" Addy repeated herself as I realized I was zoning out, chasing some old memories down dark hallways again. I cleared my throat and kind of grunted "Huh," in response.

"Look Ruby, take it for what it is at face value. There are things in this life that have happened that you have no control over. You can't change that, and you can't change the outcome of those events. You need to find a way to gain peace with this! You have to be able to accept the past, find the best way to deal with it, let it go, and move on." She spoke gently in ears that were finally ready to listen.

I needed to unburden my soul, make peace within my heart. What I needed to do was get all of this damage out of my body. Maybe if something good can come of what I'd been through, it wouldn't have all been in vain.

Addy had suggested journaling as a means to unburden my heart and release that pain and fear. What I had heard, though, in my one-time writer's heart, was to begin writing again. If I could tell two tales, my own as well as my family's, maybe some good could be squeezed out of all the hell that we had walked through. Maybe I would be spared after all.

With a deep sigh, I stood and reached for my granddad's old pendant. Maybe Addy was right. Maybe it was time to finally deal with what had haunted me for the past five years of my marriage, combined with the stunning family darkness that had recently come to light, robbing me of my sleep and threatening my sanity. I reached for the tattered old book, running my fingers gingerly over the cover. My gramma wrote these words. This was the journal that she used to unburden her own soul all of those years ago.

With my gramma's old journal in one hand and the tarnished pendant that Granddad Bub had worn in the other, a decision was made that afternoon that would alter the trajectory of my life. If spilling her guts on paper in that old dog-eared journal covered in blue roses had somehow brought my gramma peace, or at least an assumed forgiveness, then maybe that was the road I should be traveling as well.

That afternoon, in the lazy evening sun out on my porch, sipping a glass of wine with my lifeline, Addy, as both Kermit and Gonzo sprawled out in the warm beams upon the deck, a plan was formed that would be the beginning of a new life, a new me. I had decided that, I too, needed to get what I knew out of my head, to unburden myself from the guilt of harboring secrets of which I could not change the outcome.

I needed something good, something fruitful, to come out of all the suffocating darkness. In order to do that, to get my story out into the world, I would have to go back, allowing myself to be ripped wide open once again to the raw emotion and torment that comes from family with a darkened past, hoping that all the greatness that my past had also held would be enough to sustain me, enough to anchor me on this journey. Addy assured me that she would walk that road of redemption with me, assured me that I wouldn't have to face it alone.

This was the starting point, the point at which I decided to take my life back and once again step up to the plate as the big sister, the oldest cousin, the first daughter, the first granddaughter and the keeper of family secrets. I was once again determined that I was going to pave the way, allowing all of those who followed to have an easier past. So I began to write, letting my mind take me home again. Apprehensively, I went back…

Chapter 2: Saving Oz

Ruby's First Day Back Home

I stood out there behind the barn beneath the old walnut tree, just staring out into the field in a childlike wonderment. My eyes danced from car hood to truck box, methodically surveying the rust and trying to fast forward through any memories the old junkers tried to bait me with. This was his, this graveyard of metal memories, the rusted-out skeletons of the cars and trucks of Granddad's past.

He had only been gone a few weeks now, and the ghostly memory of his hilarious and gentle spirit still danced within my heart, carrying with it a childhood full of memories that I now found myself a little too scared to relent to—for the pain was still too fresh and I had a job to do. There was no time to be weak.

I exhaustively fought with time that lazy summer afternoon in the bright Wisconsin sun. I paused, leaning against the side of the old brick hog house behind the barn, letting the warm breeze dance across my face and gently lift my hair. There was and never would be again a place that held so many of my childhood memories, a place of peace and contentment and warmth.

Looking back now, I realized that on that warm summer day as I was preparing to sort through some of his most treasured belongings, I had also been preparing myself to let go, something that would end up being much harder for me to do than I had ever dreamt it to be.

Something small and soft brushed across my ankle as I paused there, and I could feel the vibration of his purr emanating from his warm body as he rubbed against my bare shin. It was Oswald. Ozzy for short. That old guy had been around for quite a few years and was only one of Granddad's small herd of barn cats and kittens he had amassed over the years since his days of farming had come to an end.

The funny thing about it was that, as a farmer, cats had always been a nuisance to him. Sure, the grandkids would always drag them home, and my Gramma Pearl had found no greater joy than rescuing the lost or broken little furry souls. But to an old farmer, they were just more mouths to feed, more chores that needed to be taken care of.

It wasn't until he retired about ten or so years ago that Granddad Bub took a deeper liking to the little fur-balls. I suppose as a farmer with no livestock, no animals to tend to, he had felt out of his element. He needed something to be held responsible for. His life demanded structure, which had become even more of a prevalent part of his daily activities after Alzheimer's started to doggedly gnaw away at his once brilliant mind.

He started tending to the various cats and kittens like they were his livelihood, as if they were his purpose, his newly found job that would give him something to be held accountable for, a reason to get up in the morning.

He had researched the best variety of milk-replacers to use and studied which brand of kitten food was best. Every day, he would begin his mornings still on a farmer's clock, up before the sunrise, to sit at the small white Formica kitchen table in the brown Naugahyde chairs with silver castors that had been a mainstay of my childhood. While Gramma slept in just a little later, he would quietly flip on the old AM radio that had always perched high above the fridge, listening to the local farm report, rolling his eyes at the current cattle index or the crop yields.

Granddad Bub would start every morning off with a bowl of wheat or bran flakes at that little kitchen table, with only the slightest sprinkle of sugar thrown on top to curb his sugar craving. Then every day like clockwork, he would set out to tend to his farm. It no longer mattered that his livestock had been replaced with cats and that his fields were no longer his to tend to, as he had rented those out now to the young family across the field who had taken over their family's farm when their grandfather died.

It didn't matter that instead of spending his time tinkering on old tractors to get a little more life out of them, he now just hosed them off and polished them down every now and then. His greater pleasure of tinkering on old cars had taken form not long after he retired, when he finally had the time to slow down.

After a monotonous, yet practical and scheduled breakfast, Bub would then change out of his "house" work boots and into his "outside" work boots so not to make a mess of Gramma's house. (He even did this after she passed, about six months before he left this earth). It was routine. It was what he knew. It was comfortable.

He would then grab his gallon pail and slowly clomp down the steps in the entryway, flicking on the overhead bulb, heading down to the packed dirt floor basement where his cats' and kittens' milk-replacer and food were kept in sealed plastic drums. They had always sat next to the washer and dryer, which had been placed upon old wood pallets in order to escape the spring stream that would trickle down the old walls and threaten to electrocute anyone brave enough to do the laundry during that time.

He would then fill his pail with the mixture of crunchy goodness and milk replacement powder, adding a little water from the wash sink that was positioned off the same line of pipe that fed water to the shower. The old shower head had poked out from the middle of the room with nothing but a shower curtain strung around it, suspended by wire and clothespins with the floor drain beneath. Taking a shower down there was always an adventure. My eyes would casually track the overhead pipes that were mere inches from my head for the spiders or centipedes that called that little basement home. The fear of electrocution was always real as well, as I laugh now thinking about what we must have looked like as kids standing down there under that old shower head, buck naked except for the over-sized rubber flip-flops that Gramma kept at the foot of the stairs for this sole purpose.

I had watched Bub's routine hundreds of times over the years while he was farming, and then after he had retired. The man never wavered in his routine. There seemed to be something poetic about it, but maybe it was just a safety net.

After getting the pail full of cat breakfast, he would stop once more at the top landing of the entryway, reaching into the wooden bin that he kept out there lined with a plastic bag. Inside of that bin usually was day-old or a couple days-old bread loaves that he would pick up for cheap during his weekly trips into town to the local bakery. This was a delicacy to the cats and the grandkids as well, because when Bub was going into town for day-old loaves, that also meant a box of maple-coated long Johns would be making their way home right alongside him, a special treat and welcome reprieve from the ceremonial bowl of cereal at the little white Formica kitchen table.

As a kid spending the night at the farm, or a teen hanging out at the house over the summer, there was one thing that stood out is this scene that to this day still lulls me to bed at night. After Bub would get the cat food and scraps ready every morning, he would head out the back door, quickly followed by the sharp "slapping" sound of the door against the frame as it slammed shut. If you weren't awake yet, you would be then, like an unwelcome wake-up call to start your day.

I would crawl across the bed in one of the upstairs bedrooms of the farmhouse (it used to be my mom's room, actually)… and stick my head up into the window frame to watch him, my granddad, start his day dutifully serving the animals that had been entrusted to him.

It's who he was. Who he had always been. A man who was strict yet loving. Set in his ways and taking care of what needed to be done. His hands were never idle. He liked to keep his brilliant mind busy, even before the Alzheimer's began to rob him of the secrets and dreams he had kept.

We would sit there on the bed, watching as the backside of his shadowy silhouette crept across the "big yard." Not to be confused with the yard up by the house where Gramma used to grow her flower gardens, the "big yard" was an open area where we would play ball as kids, the outer edges of which would line up with the barn, machine shed, and the lean-to shed that housed tractors, his little wood shop and, of course, the hog house. We would watch as he made his way towards the old hog-house, the pails of food gingerly bobbing along at his sides.

Before he would make it to the old brick hog house, a couple of his feline friends would usually be creeping out of the hole in the lower left corner of the old wooden door, excitedly winding around his feet as he tried to take a step. If the windows were open and the wind hit just right, you could hear his halfhearted, angry voice holler out, "Oh, jeepers cripes, you dumb things! Get!"

He may have acted like he didn't care about them. He may have tried to put on a stern face. But we all knew that those cats had kept him going, had kept him tied to the farming life, the only life he had ever known.

I hadn't realized that time had caught up to me as I leaned over to lift Ozzy, the old furball who was still relentlessly rubbing against my leg, purring loudly. The easily flowing memories had welled up in my eyes and I had gotten lost for just a moment, stuck somewhere between the sweetness and innocence of childhood and the staunch reminder of what life takes from you as an adult.

Looking down at Oz in my arms, I kicked off my flip-flops and sunk down into the overgrown grass that Bub would be so disappointed in. I sat stroking his fur, my back leaning into the chipped red brick, my eyes fixed on the field that lay out ahead of me, dotted at the edges with old oak and walnut trees where a precisely curated graveyard of the past now sat.

"I miss him too, Oz," I said in a broken sigh. I knew that the neighboring farmer, the one who now rents the surrounding farmland, had crated all the cats and taken them down to his farm to live out their days in his family's barn. But it wasn't the same and Oz knew he didn't belong there. He had spent his whole life gracing the front porch of our old farmhouse, enticing Granddad to love on him. Many summer afternoons were spent by the both of them, sprawled out in old lawn chairs, listening to a ball game on the radio while shucking corn or snapping peas for Gramma. Oz knew of no other life.

Thinking about it now, I don't really know what Oz's beginnings were. He wasn't born on the farm. I knew that much. I do remember Bub being excited about one of the mama cats taking Oz on as her own. Bub was sure Oz would make it, even though it was a harsh winter when he showed up.

"Now, what are we gonna do?" I whispered to the chunky gray ball of fluff nestled snugly on my lap. How old was he at this point? I had no clue. Old. That was all I knew. Oz and I sat like that for a few more minutes in the afternoon sun, shaded by the big walnut tree that loomed above the barn and hog house. As Oz sat purring, just happy to have human contact again, I stared helplessly out towards the old rusty vehicle graveyard, overwhelmed by what lay out there.

He had been so precise, so methodical in how he arranged them over the years, grouping them by make and leaving a space between each so that he could tinker on them at will. That was the problem.

As the thief that was Alzheimer's slowly invaded his mind, he had begun to obsess with mechanical things in his later years, obsessively wanting to know how things worked, taking them apart and putting them back together again. As time rolled on though, and his brain became more jumbled, it became more of an exercise to just take things apart, never remembering how to put them back together again.

So there I was. The only grandkid that had any interest in those old cars or trucks. The only one who had ever spent any time out there puttering on them at all. My mom and uncle had begun cleaning this place up, as my family had planned on renting out the house and barn, scrapping and salvaging what they could as they went through the process of purging a lifelong treasure-trove of stuff. Good stuff. Stuff that you couldn't find anymore. And some stuff that had only sentimental value to just a few of us.

My mom and uncle had talked about just hauling all of these old rusty piles of bones on out of there, but I had convinced them to give me just a few days to let me see if there was anything laying out there that I could save, anything that I might be able to piece back together again, something that I could find worthy of redemption and breathe life back into again. Mom had figured since I was spending a few days out at the farm here and there over a couple of months, maybe I could also take a look around at what was left in the house to see if there was anything worth saving.

That was me, had always been me really, the keeper of memories, the hoarder of mementos. It wasn't too surprising that the family had thought of me when they were trying to pick and choose what talisman from the past gets to be tied to us a little longer and which baubles we toss, forever being a lost piece of a life well lived.

I think it's called personification, when you look at objects and give them human attributes, feelings, attach them to memories that then sit on a shelf. That was me, being too weakhearted to toss anything out that may have once held such a prominent space in someone's heart. I admit, it's my downfall. I like to blame it on moving around so much when I was little. You wouldn't think a tight-knit little family like ours that had sprung from a solid farm family would travel like gypsies, but boy did we see the world, or at least it had felt that way as a kid, even if it was only a few states down south.

I was too little to remember much of why we moved the first time from this tiny little town, Trego, located just off of the Namekagon River. I have been told over the years that the first move was based on opportunity. Stocks had fallen and crops weren't bringing in what they had been. After Mom and Dad got married, Dad worked both at the farm helping out as well as doing accounting work for a car dealership in town. I guess he had a buddy who took a job on a construction crew heading out to Georgia, so he figured he could make more out on the road, trying to help save the farm.

That's what we did. I was too young to remember the move, but I can remember many of the moves after that initial one. The construction company that dad worked for took jobs all across the south, so really, the longest we ever stayed in one spot was about six months or so.

The towns tended to blur together, one apartment

looking a lot like the next. I suppose that's why I cling to things now, after living like nomads for so long, leaving everything behind that wouldn't fit in the U-Haul as we ran from place to place.

I can remember beloved bikes, dolls, kitchen playsets, all being lovingly donated to neighbors or watching people pick through the piles of our things that we had left on the curb as we pulled away. I had learned to travel with very little, but I also found that a few things being lovingly wrapped, packed, and unpacked, being moved from place to place, were all that I needed to identify a place as home.

A few things from my childhood still have managed to stick with me and adorn my shelves to this day. Mom had a garage sale when she and my dad retired, and sheer panic ran through brain and my heart semi-froze as I watched a handful of beloved treasures be marked for a dollar or two and thrown out on the lawn on tables for people to paw through.

Among the items that I have saved—hoarded as my little sister Banks says, are an old hand-carved wooden ox that has a girl riding on top holding a basket; a ceramic statue of a little old man playing a violin as his dog watched on; a Home Interiors figurine of yellow birds that Mom used to set her rings on when it graced the ever-changing dressers; and a small plastic nesting-barrel set that I think they used to call Kitty in the Middle, although the kitty in the middle had been broken off long ago. Growing up, I knew that wherever we were, as long as these things graced the shelves, we were home.

And here I stood, once again getting ready to salvage something, some piece of my past to pacify my soul, to help me feel grounded and feel that I was home. This was a bigger project, though, and one that I welcomed. I had grown to love working on cars when I was out here at the farm with Granddad Bub, even if I didn't know what I was doing.

Maybe what I was hoping for, as I intended to walk around, checking out the car graveyard, was that one of the rusted-out skeletons would speak to me, would let me know that they were the piece that I was missing in my little menagerie of life that I had lovingly resurrected from the curb.

What I was really hoping for was that I would feel him out there, in that field beneath the walnut trees, in that old boneyard of faded metal. I wanted him to know that I cared; I was still here, and I was still trying to do what was best, as I always had, trying to preserve the feeling of a close little family that I remember from childhood for just a little longer. I had set my own problems, my own torment, my own life aside to carry out these responsibilities, much like I always had.

Gently, I lifted good old Ozzy off my lap and sat him down in the overgrown grass next to me. I stood and slid my flip-flops back on with the flick of my toes. Looking down at my naked toes, I had to laugh at myself. I had been in the city for too long. What the hell had I been thinking? I couldn't go tromping through those overgrown weeds and shards of rusty metal in flip-flops. I knew Granddad had boots in the house, but I didn't want to walk back through the big yard to get them.

Glancing around at the buildings that had always stood silently by in every childhood memory that I treasured of the farm, I decided to check out his little woodworking shop, thinking he may have some muck-boots stored in there. Without even needing to ask, old Oz was more than happy to accompany me over to the shed.

I reached above the old door frame, dusting my fingers across the edge, searching for the key that should have been there. But there was nothing. I pressed my face against the glass panels and peered inside his little shop. It was a hard scene to absorb because his tools now laid forlornly in his workspace. His ruler and pencil looked as though he had just finished tracing out his latest pattern, and then had laid them down.

On one side of the room, I could see his pieces of planed walnut, neatly stacked, and across from that on the other side of his desk sat a little safe.

"That's right! The safe!" I shouted to Oz, excited to remember a tiny something that would make this journey just a little bit easier.

Bub always kept his titles to the auto boneyard in that old safe, content with it being out there in his wood shop because, like he always said, "If someone wanted to go through the hassle of trying to steal one of those old relics, my hats off to 'em."

Hell, he had still been living in an era somewhere in his mind that you needn't lock your doors and you just expected that people would do the right thing. Keeping that in mind, I lowered my hand and gave the doorknob a good tug. Sure as shit, it opened right up. Of course he hadn't locked it.

Entering his wood shop was a surreal experience. I could hear echoes of the past catching up to me. I could see him sitting with my cousin over at the side bench, working on repairing one of Gramma's bird feeders.

I could hear the glass baby food jars rattle from where they sat in their shelves as he would sit for hours sorting his latest auction finds of boxes of odds and ends of nails and screws. Hell, if I tried hard enough, I could just about smell his Old Spice aftershave.

I stood on the threshold of that rickety old doorway, glancing around, looking for some shoes as Oz hopped from counter to counter until he became infatuated with one of the cabinets. He froze, patiently looking at the cabinet, then back at me with a look on his face that made me feel like an idiot.

I walked over and opened the cabinet he was so intent on staring at. Sure enough, Granddad had a jar of cat treats standing there, high on a shelf, between his tractor manuals and some other paperwork.

"OK Ozzy, I got it..." I appeased the little old cat, reaching for the treat jar. As I lifted it from its shelf space, some paperwork fell out and scattered about on the floor. Oz didn't care. He was just happy that for a tiny millisecond in time, things were as they should be, as they had always been, even if the people in his story had changed.

I dropped a couple of treats onto the counter and put the jar back up on the shelf in the cupboard. I began to reach down to pick up the disheveled paperwork, and as I did, I could see the toe of a muck-boot sticking out from beneath the workbench. Grinning, I hurried to grab the old muck boots and patiently walked back towards the door, waiting only long enough for Ozzy to finish his treats and meander back outside.

I waited until I walked over to the edge of the big yard to kick off my flip-flops, because the last thing I needed was a rusty old nail or shard of glass or metal to slow me down now. Kicking off the flip-flops and sinking my feet into the damp, cold, two-sizes-too-big old boots, all felt right with the world. I was excited to head out to the field and check out those cars. Maybe with a little luck, one of them would speak to me and my decision wouldn't be quite so hard to make.

I glanced at my watch as I stood at the edge of the overgrown field, the wind whipping my hair into my eyes. I had a couple hours of daylight left to be digging around out there. I could taste the grit billowing through the air off the gravel road and honestly, nothing had ever tasted so good in my whole adult life.

As I went to step towards the field, I turned, seeing little old Oz stop at the edge, now resting peacefully in the sun. "Don't worry, little old man. I got this. I'll be OK on my own. You just wait for me here, OK?" I called to him, almost expecting an answer.

With a mouth full of gravel dust and excitement and wonder pulsing through my veins, I pointed one toe of my two-sizes-too-big muck boot towards the field of rusty metal bones, and off I went. It was time to get this done. It was time to figure out who I was saving.

9 781776 483778